AUG - 4 1998

Be Not Far From Me

Be Not Far From Me

THE OLDEST LOVE STORY

LEGENDS FROM THE BIBLE

retold by ERIC A. KIMMEL

illustrated by DAVID DIAZ

Simon & Schuster Books for Young Readers

SIMON & SCHUSTER BOOKS FOR YOUNG READERS
An imprint of Simon & Schuster Children's Publishing Division
1230 Avenue of the Americas, New York, New York 10020 Text
copyright © 1998 by Eric A. Kimmel. Illustrations copyright
© 1998 by David Diaz. The maps on pages 252-255 are illustrated by Edward Miller and are copyright © 1998 by Simon &
Schuster Books for Young Readers. All rights reserved including the right of reproduction in whole or in part in any form.
SIMON & SCHUSTER BOOKS FOR YOUNG READERS is a trademark
of Simon & Schuster. Book design by Paul Zakris. The text
for this book is set in 12-point Elysium Book. The illustrations
are rendered in mixed media. Printed and bound in the United
States of America.
First Edition
10 9 8 7 6 5 4 3 2 1

LIBRARY OF CONGRESS CATALOGING-IN-PUBLICATION DATA

Kimmel, Eric A.
    Be not far from me : the oldest love story : legends from the
Bible / retold by Eric A. Kimmel ; illustrated by David Diaz. —
1st ed.
        p. cm.
    Includes bibliographical references.
    Summary: A collection of stories drawn from the Bible and
the Midrash telling of twenty heroes and heroines including
Abraham, Moses, Samson, Deborah, Elijah, and six other
prophets.
    ISBN 0-689-81088-1 (hardcover)
    1. Bible. O.T.—Biography—Juvenile literature. 2. Bible sto-
ries, English—O.T. [1. Bible stories.] I. Diaz, David, ill. II. Title.
BS551.2.K47 1998
221.9'505—dc21
97-24543

For Sharon Friedman
A valiant woman, where can she be found?
She is worth more than pearls or rubies. (PROVERBS 31:10)
—E. A. K.

For Stanley
—D. D.

Contents

This thou hast seen, O Lord:
keep not silence:
O Lord, be not far from me.

PSALM 35:22

PROLOGUE:

In the Beginning

This is a love story. It began four thousand years ago and continues today. It is about God, the Creator of the universe, and a people, Israel, through whom God made Himself known to all the nations of the earth.

Ever since human history began, people have worshiped forces they saw as greater than themselves. They prayed to the sun, the moon, the lightning, and the wind, all of whom they believed to be gods. The gods they imagined were beautiful human beings. People worshiped them with poems, songs, and elaborate ceremonies. They created stories about them that are still told today.

These gods represented forces of nature, and nature is cruel. The strong devour the weak. The old, sick, or injured quickly perish. Only a tiny portion of young live long enough to become adults. Right and wrong do not exist. The only law is to survive.

People loved the nature gods they worshiped, but did these natural forces really love them? How could they? Can a farmer love every stalk of grain in his field? Can a shepherd love every lamb in his flock? People are born; they live and die, and others take their place. It is nature's way.

But there is a force above and beyond nature. That force is God Who created the universe out of nothing and set it in motion. Unlike nature, endlessly repeating itself for millions of years, God brought the world into being for a reason. He is aware of the existence of the smallest creature. He cares about the poor and the helpless. Time has a beginning and an end. History has a purpose.

What is that purpose? God wants human beings to love each other as much as He loves them. He taught them the difference between good and evil and granted them the power to choose good. Through His prophets, He gave humankind a vision of a time when violence and injustice would cease, and all creatures of the earth would live together in harmony.

Before any of this could happen, the people of the world first had to know about God. Yet for thousands of years they were not even aware He existed. God waited. Then one day a man came seeking Him.

This story begins with that man. His name was Abraham.

Abraham
AND HIS
Children

The Story of Abraham

Long ago, when the world was new, people worshiped many things. They worshiped rocks, trees, and animals. They worshiped the sun and the moon, and the stars in the sky. They made idols—statues of wood, clay, and stone—and bowed down to them. They did not worship the One God Who made the universe. They did not know about Him.

The Boy Who Went Looking for God

At this time a boy lived in the city of Ur. His name was Abram. Abram was not like other people of his time. He wondered about things. He asked questions.

"Where does the sun go at night?" he asked his brothers.

"It goes into a cave beyond the horizon. There it sleeps until morning," they told him.

"Why does the moon get smaller and smaller, until at last it disappears?" he asked his mother. She answered, "A great dragon bites off a piece of the moon every night. When he eats it all, he spits it out again. Then there is a new moon."

"Why do people worship statues and call them God?" he asked his father, Terah.

His father scolded him. "Why do you ask so many questions? Why can't you accept things as they are?"

Abram stopped asking questions. But he could not stop wondering.

On Abram's street there lived an old man who did not bow to idols. Abram decided to ask him about God. One as old as he would surely know the answer.

Abram asked his neighbor, "You do not worship the idols. Whom do you worship? Which god is the true God?"

The old man took Abram aside and whispered to him, "I worship the Sun. The Sun gives warmth and light. He is the true God."

"I will worship the Sun, too," Abram said.

Abram went to the fields outside the city. The bright sun shined overhead. Abram offered prayers to the sun. "You are the true God," Abram said.

But a cloud came up and covered the sun. *The Cloud is mightier than the sun,* Abram thought. *The Cloud must be God. I will worship him.*

Abram offered prayers to the cloud. But then the wind came up and blew the cloud away. *The Wind must be God. I will offer my prayers to the Wind.*

Abram started praying all over again. But then the wind died down. Abram stopped praying. He didn't know to whom to pray. He sat for the rest of the day, wondering. The sun went down. Darkness fell. The full moon rose above the towers of Ur.

"The Moon must be God. I will worship the Moon," Abram said.

Night after night, he offered prayers to the moon. But every night the moon grew smaller and smaller, until nothing remained.

"The sun is not god. The cloud is not god. The wind is not god. And the moon is not god, either. Where is the true God, the One Who made all these things?"

Then Abram heard a still, small voice speaking within his heart. "I am God, King of the Universe. I made heaven and earth, and all living things."

"If you are the True God, why do people worship the sun and the moon? Why do they bow down to idols?"

"It is because they do not know Who I am," the voice answered.

"How will they come to know you?" Abram said.

The voice answered, "You will teach them."

Abram listened to the voice within his heart. As his understanding grew, he had less and less patience with those who worshiped idols.

Abram and the Idols

Abram's father, Terah, was an idol maker. He carved idols out of wood and stone. He molded them out of clay. He made big idols and little idols, old idols and young idols, idols in the shape of men, women, and animals.

Abram had once enjoyed helping his father. It thrilled him to see the figures emerge from wood and stone. He loved molding the wet clay into different shapes. Now his joy fled. His skill left his hands. He dropped the clay figures as he took them from the kiln. His chisel slipped as he carved wood or stone, cutting off a figure's nose and ruining a week's work. Exasperated by Abram's clumsiness, Terah banished him from the workroom. Abram spent his days in the shop, selling idols to the people who came by.

One day Terah said to his son, "I must go to the palace to talk to King Nimrod about the new idols he ordered. Mind the shop while I am gone. Try not to be clumsy. I can't afford to lose any more idols."

Abram promised to do his best.

Soon after Terah left, an old man entered the shop. "I want to buy an idol," he said to Abram.

"What kind do you want?" Abram asked.

"A smart one," the old man answered. "I am faced with difficult problems that I don't know how to solve. I need help. I need an idol filled with wisdom."

"Do you see any here that look wise?" Abram asked.

The old man pointed to an idol on the top shelf. "That one. His long beard makes him look very wise. He'll have the wisdom I need."

Abram took the idol down from the shelf and set it on the counter. "How old are you?" Abram asked his customer.

The old man replied, "I am eighty-seven years old."

"Would you ask a week-old baby for advice?"

"Certainly not!" the old man said.

"Well, that idol may have a beard, but he is only a week old," Abram told him. "I made that idol. Before I molded him, he was only a lump of clay. How can a week-old lump of clay know anything?"

The old man left the shop, sputtering with anger. Abram put the idol back on the shelf.

Soon afterward, a woman came in. Her face was red. She looked frightened.

"Quick!" she cried to Abram. "I need idols, big, strong ones. Thieves broke into my house. They took everything, even my idols. I am afraid to go home without new idols to protect me."

Abram laughed. "You say the thieves stole your idols. If the idols could not protect themselves, how can they possibly protect you?"

The woman stormed off without answering. Abram looked around at the idols in the shop, from the little ones on the shelves to the big one sitting beside the door.

"What stupid things you are! You have eyes, but you cannot see. You have lips, but you cannot speak. You have ears, but you cannot hear. Everyone who believes in you will become like you." The more Abram thought about the idols, the angrier he became. It was wrong for people to worship idols. It was even more wrong for his father to make them.

Abram could not contain his anger. He took his father's hammer and went around the shop, smashing the idols to bits. He smashed the big ones and the little ones, the wooden ones, the stone ones, and the clay ones. He smashed them all, except the big idol sitting beside the door. Abram put the hammer in the big idol's hand. Then he went down the street to the baker's shop, where he bought a large basket filled with bread and cakes. He placed the basket on the idol's lap and sat down to wait for his father's return.

"My shop! My idols!" Terah cried when he saw the wreckage. He turned to Abram. "Tell me what happened."

"Oh, Father! I am so glad you are home. It was terrible!" Abram said.

"Did robbers attack you? Speak!"

"It was worse than that, Father. When the time came for the noonday meal, I asked the idols what they wanted to eat. They told me to get something from the baker's shop. I brought back a basket of bread and cakes. The moment I came through the door, all the idols began pushing and shouting. They snatched the basket from my hands and started fighting over it. The big idol who sits by the door lost his temper. He grabbed your hammer and smashed the other idols to bits. Then he took the whole basket of bread and cakes for himself. There it is on his lap!"

Terah stared at the idol by the door. Sure enough, it sat with the basket of cakes on its lap and the hammer clutched in its hand. Terah turned to Abram.

"Have you lost your wits? Since when do idols eat? Since when do they quarrel? I made these idols out of wood, clay, and stone. They cannot move unless I move them."

"Then why worship them?" Abram asked. "Why make them, Father, so that they can be worshiped?"

Fear replaced anger in Terah's face. "You must not speak this way, Abram. All who refuse to worship the gods of the city are severely punished."

"I cannot help myself, Father," Abram said. "I know there is only One God, the God Who made all Creation. He alone will I worship."

Abram and Nimrod

Nimrod, the king of Ur, heard about Abram's refusal to worship idols. His soldiers arrested Abram and brought him to the palace.

Nimrod asked the boy, "Do you know that the penalty for refusing to worship idols is death?"

"I know," Abram replied.

"Then why won't you worship them?"

"Because I do not believe in them."

"I will tell you a secret," Nimrod whispered. "I do not believe in them, either. I will tell you who is God. I am—Nimrod, the Mighty King! You can bow down to me instead."

"No," said Abram. "You are not God. You do not cause the sun to rise and the moon to set. You do not sustain the universe or give life to all creatures. The One Who does these things—He Alone is God!"

"Then you must die!" The king ordered his servants to build a furnace of clay bricks. When it was done, they dragged Abram inside and stacked bundles of wood around him.

Abram's mother and father begged him to change his mind. "It is not too late! Bow down to the idols and save your life!"

"Worship me, and I will spare you," Nimrod said.

Abram spoke in a clear voice as the flames rose around him. "I will not bow to idols. I will not bow to the king. I only worship the True God, Who made heaven and earth."

The furnace burned for seven days and seven nights. The smoke from its chimney blackened the sky over Ur. The furnace had to cool for forty days before Nimrod could approach it.

He expected to find bones and ashes. Instead, he saw Abram sitting in the middle of a perfumed garden. The logs for the fire had sprouted roots and buds. They had grown into trees, bearing ripe fruit. Abram plucked a pomegranate and offered it to the king.

"How is it you are still alive? You must be a great wizard," Nimrod gasped.

"I am no wizard," Abram said. "It was God Who protected me. He sent angels to shield me from the fire with their wings. He caused the dry wood to grow and blossom, so I could eat of its fruit."

The people of Ur asked Abram to teach them about the God he worshiped. This angered Nimrod. He said to Abram, "I will spare your life, but you must leave the city at once. Those who wish to follow your God must go with you."

Abram, his family, and all who wished to follow him prepared to leave Ur. On the night before their departure, Abram prayed to God for guidance. God answered, saying, "Go from your country, from your birthplace, from your father's house, unto a land that I will show you. There I will make you the father of a great nation."

Abram Becomes Abraham

God kept his promise to Abram. He brought him to Canaan, a land so rich and fertile that people described it as "overflowing with milk and honey." Abram prospered. His herds and flocks multiplied. His followers increased.

Abram grew powerful in the land of Canaan. Kings sought his friendship. He became one of the greatest men of his time. God had truly blessed him.

However, God did not grant Abram one important blessing. Abram did not have children.

Sarai, Abram's wife, spoke to him about this problem. "You and I are old. Who will lead our followers after we die? Without children to succeed us, the message about God that you and I have worked to spread will be forgotten."

"Be patient," Abram told Sarai. "God will provide an answer."

"God also gives us wisdom to solve our own problems," Sarai said. "I am an old woman. My childbearing days are over. You must take another woman as your wife so that she can bear children for you."

Abram refused. He wanted no other wife than Sarai. She had been his only wife since the day they were married. This was unusual, for during Abram's time it was common for men to have many wives.

Sarai persisted. "God must have a reason for making me unable to bear children. Perhaps your descendants will come from a woman other than me. If that is God's wish, we must accept it. Take my Egyptian handmaid Hagar as your second wife. She is modest and God-fearing. I will love any child she bears as if it were my own."

Abram gave in to Sarai. He took Hagar as his second wife. In time she gave birth to a son whom she named *Ishmael*, meaning, *God Heard My Prayer*.

God spoke to Abram after Ishmael's birth. "You will be the forefather of many nations," God said. "From now on, you will no longer be called *Abram*, but *Abraham*, meaning *Father of Multitudes*. I will give the whole land of Canaan to your descendants. They will possess it forever, and I will be their God. As for Sarai, your wife, I will change her name, too. She will be called *Sarah—Princess*—for she is a princess among women. I will give her a son of her own who will be called *Isaac*. My promise to you will be fulfilled through him and his children."

Abraham laughed with joy to hear that he and Sarah would have a child of their own at last. But then he thought, *What of my son Ishmael? Do these words mean that God will not bless him, or that he will die?*

God reassured Abraham. "Have no fear for your son Ishmael. I will bless him, too, and will make him the father of a mighty nation. But Isaac, who will be born next year, will receive My special blessing."

Abraham did not tell Sarah about this conversation with God. However, soon afterward, three travelers appeared at the entrance to Abraham's tent. Abraham invited them to rest in a cool, shady spot beneath a great tree. Sarah prepared a fine meal. Abraham brought the food to his guests.

"Where is Sarah, your wife?" one of the travelers asked.

"She is in the tent," Abraham told him.

The man replied, "When I return next year, Sarah will have a son."

Sarah, who overheard these words, laughed silently to herself in disbelief. *What is this fellow talking about? I am nearly a hundred years old. Abraham is even older than I am.*

The traveler asked Abraham, "Why is Sarah laughing? Is anything beyond God's power? I say to you again: At this time next year, Sarah will have a son."

Sarah came out of the tent. "I did not laugh," she told the stranger, a little frightened. Her laughter had been within her own mind. No ordinary person could have heard it.

"No, you laughed," the stranger insisted.

The three travelers rested with Abraham and Sarah for a short time. Then they arose and continued their journey toward the city of Sodom. Abraham went with them to point out the way.

Sodom and Gomorrah

When Abraham returned, God spoke to him. "I will not conceal what I am about to do. I am going to destroy the cities of Sodom and Gomorrah. The sins of their people are great. Their wickedness cries out for punishment."

Abraham understood why God wanted to destroy the cities. The people of Sodom and Gomorrah enjoyed doing evil. In Sodom, the strong preyed on the weak; the rich preyed on the poor; and everyone preyed on strangers. Justice was bought and sold. Every judge in Sodom sat behind a large scale. People entering the courtroom had to weigh their bribes. Whoever paid the biggest bribe won the judgment.

Showing kindness to others was against the law in Sodom. Anyone giving charity was put to death. A little girl once took pity on a starving stranger. She gave him a piece of bread when her parents weren't looking. But a neighbor noticed. The judges of Sodom arrested the little girl and condemned her to die in the cruelest manner. She was smeared with honey and left tied to a stake in the blazing sun. Bees, wasps, and ants, attracted by the sweet honey, swarmed over her body. After three days, she died.

The people of Sodom and Gomorrah laughed at her sufferings. But God heard her cries. He had given the two cities more than enough time to change their ways. Now He decided to bring their wickedness to an end.

Although Abraham knew God's decision was just, he could not bear to see anyone suffer. Perhaps if God gave them another chance, the people of Sodom and Gomorrah might change.

"Surely not everyone in the city is wicked," Abraham said to God. "There must be a few good people. Will you destroy the good with the wicked?"

God replied, "If I can find fifty good people, I will spare the cities."

Abraham pleaded with God again. "Do not be angry with me for speaking, but what if there are only forty-five good people? Will you spare the cities for their sake?"

God answered, "I will spare them."

"But what if there are only forty. Or thirty. Or twenty. Or even ten. Will you spare the cities for the sake of ten good people?"

God said to Abraham, "If I can find ten truly good people living in Sodom and

Gomorrah, I will spare the cities for their sake." Then God turned away and spoke to Abraham no more.

Abraham sat down at the entrance to his tent, his head bent with sorrow. He had done all he could, yet he knew it would not be enough. He grieved for the people of Sodom and Gomorrah, and feared for his nephew Lot, who lived there with his family.

Lot had resided in Sodom for many years. The people of Sodom disliked foreigners, but they allowed Lot to live in their midst. His skill in trade enriched the city. Lot was not a bad man, but neither was he a good one. In order to live in Sodom, he learned to shut his eyes to the cruelty and injustice he saw every day.

Lot was sitting by the city gate when he saw two figures approaching. Although they were dressed as men, he recognized them as angels. Lot had seen angels many times when he lived with his uncle Abraham. Lot feared what might happen if the two remained in the street, so he invited them to his house.

News of the strangers spread through Sodom. A mob gathered on Lot's doorstep. "Give us the men you are harboring in your house!" the people of Sodom shouted.

Lot went outside to plead with the mob. "These visitors are my guests. Do not harm them. I have two daughters, both young and beautiful. Take them instead. You can do as you please with them. Only spare my guests!"

"Who are you to command us? Don't talk to us about your daughters! We want those men! Send them out! If you delay, we will do ten times worse to you!"

The men of Sodom seized Lot and began pounding on the door, trying to break it down. Suddenly, the door flew open. There stood the angels in all their shining glory. They pulled Lot from the hands of the mob and brought him inside. Brandishing fiery swords, they struck the crowd in the street with blindness. The people of Sodom stumbled here and there, crashing into each other in terror and confusion.

The angels said to Lot, "Take your family and leave the city at once. God has promised to destroy Sodom and Gomorrah. All who remain within their walls will perish."

But Lot hesitated. He could not believe that two cities as great as Sodom and Gomorrah could ever be destroyed. The angels seized Lot, his wife, and their two daughters and pulled them through the streets, never stopping until they reached a ridge far beyond the city walls. "Run for your lives," the angels told them. "Do not look back, or you will be swept away."

Lot and his family fled to the hills while the angels turned around to face Sodom and Gomorrah. As they raised their arms high, the windows of heaven opened. Rain began to fall—a deadly torrent of fire and brimstone, consuming the wicked cities and all their inhabitants. A column of smoke rose from the place where Sodom and Gomorrah once stood. It was thick and black, like smoke from a furnace. Abraham saw the smoke from a distance. He threw himself on the ground and wept, for he knew that among the tens of thousands who dwelled there, God had not been able to find ten good people to save the cities from destruction.

Lot and his family survived. God protected them for Abraham's sake. However, Lot's wife disobeyed the angels' instructions. She turned around to watch the destruction raining down upon the two cities. All at once, she turned into a pillar of salt.

That salt pillar still stands on the shores of the barren waste known as the Dead Sea, in whose lifeless depths lie the ruins of the two wicked cities, Sodom and Gomorrah.

Ishmael and Hagar

Abraham's sorrow did not last long. Soon he rejoiced, for Sarah gave birth to a son. She and Abraham named him *Isaac,* meaning *Laughter.* For Sarah said, "God has made me laugh with joy. Whoever hears this news will laugh with me. Who but God could have done this?" Now Abraham had two sons to carry on his work.

However, as the boys grew older, signs of trouble began to appear. Hagar, Ishmael's mother, became arrogant. Since her son was the oldest, she felt she should be first among the women of the household. She spoke disrespectfully to Sarah. When Sarah asked her to apologize, Hagar answered with angry words. Sarah went at once to Abraham.

"You must get rid of this Egyptian woman and her son. Drive them out. They are both a danger to Isaac."

"How can I do that?" Abraham protested. "Ishmael is my son. Hagar is his mother. I love them both. How can I send them away?"

"You do not see what I see. They turn one face to you and another to me." Sarah went on to describe Hagar's rudeness and arrogance. She told Abraham how Hagar had resumed worshiping the gods of Egypt. Worse, she encouraged Ishmael to worship them, too. Ishmael was a wild boy, a deadly shot with the bow and arrow, and skilled in the use of other weapons as well.

"I fear for Isaac," Sarah told Abraham. "If you do not send Hagar and Ishmael away, they will corrupt our son. Or worse, kill him."

Abraham did not know what to do. How could he bring himself to banish Ishmael, his beloved and oldest son? On the other hand, could he ignore Sarah's warning? Sarah was not cruel or jealous. She would never suggest something so drastic unless she felt Isaac was in real danger.

Abraham asked God for guidance. God spoke to him, saying, "Do not be concerned about Hagar or Ishmael. Do what Sarah tells you. Listen to her, since Isaac's descendants will be your own. As for Ishmael, I will watch over him for your sake. He, too, will become the founder of a mighty nation, for he is your flesh and blood."

Abraham arose the next morning. With a heavy heart, he gave Hagar a goatskin water bag and several loaves of bread. He told her that she and Ishmael could no longer be part of his household. He was sending her and her son away. Hagar pleaded with Abraham to change his mind. How could she and Ishmael survive in a barren desert?

Abraham reassured Hagar that God would look after them. He described the track that would lead her to the wells at Beer-sheba. He made sure they had plenty of food and water for the journey. It broke Abraham's heart to send his wife and son away, perhaps never to see them again. However, God had told him what to do. He could only obey.

Hagar and Ishmael set out across the desert. As soon as they were out of sight of Abraham's camp, Hagar prayed to the gods of Egypt, the gods she had worshiped as a child. "Isis, protect me! Amun-Ra, shield me from danger!"

As soon as Hagar spoke these words, all the food and water that Abraham had given her vanished. Hagar was ashamed to return to Abraham's camp to ask for more. Instead, she started out across the desert.

The merciless sun beat down. Ishmael cried for water, but Hagar had none to give him. She turned from the path to look for a well and became hopelessly lost.

Hagar and Ishmael wandered for hours, until the boy collapsed from weariness and thirst.

Hagar could not bear to watch her son suffer. She laid him beneath some willow bushes, then walked away. She sat down on a stone, weeping and praying to God for help.

"Hagar, why are you weeping?" Hagar raised her eyes to see an angel standing before her. "Do not be afraid. God hears Ishmael's voice, crying in distress. Get up. Go to your son. Lift him from the dust, for God is going to save him and make him a great nation."

Hagar looked around and saw a well. She filled her empty goatskin with water and brought it to Ishmael. He drank, and was saved.

God watched over Ishmael. He lived in the desert and became a famous archer. When he grew old enough to marry, Hagar found him a wife in Egypt. Although Ishmael's children worshiped idols, God did not forget His promise to Abraham. Ishmael had many descendants. He became the forefather of the Arab people.

The Binding of Isaac

Soon after these events, God put Abraham's faith to a greater test. He called to him: "Abraham!"

Abraham answered. "I am here."

God said, "Take your son . . ."

"I have two sons."

"Your only son."

"Each one is the only son of his mother. Ishmael is the only son of Hagar. Isaac is the only son of Sarah."

"The one whom you love," said God.

"I love them both," said Abraham.

Finally God said, "Isaac. That is the one I mean."

"What shall I do with Isaac?" Abraham asked.

God spoke the most terrible words a father can hear. "Take him to the land of Moriah. Offer him up as a sacrifice to Me on a mountain that I will show you."

Human sacrifice was common in those days. The people of Canaan sacrificed children to the gods they worshiped, Baal and Molech. They proved their devotion by burning their sons and daughters on the gods' fiery altars.

Abraham denounced this savage custom. He taught his followers that God did not require the blood of innocent children. With a sinking heart, he heard God demand that very sacrifice from him. He had already sent one son away in obedience to God's commandment. Now God was asking him to offer up his remaining son as a sacrifice.

Abraham did not question God's word. He believed in God with perfect faith. He trusted that whatever God demanded from him was for the best. He would fulfill God's wishes, despite his own anguish.

Abraham rose early the next morning. He cut the wood for the sacrifice and loaded it on his donkey. With two servants and his son Isaac, he started for the land of Moriah.

They traveled for three days. On the morning of the third day, Abraham raised his eyes and saw a mountain in the distance. This was the place to which God had sent him.

"Wait here with the donkey," Abraham told his servants. "Isaac and I will go up on that mountain. We will offer our sacrifice and return."

Abraham loaded the wood onto Isaac's back. He took a flint knife and a smoking brand to kindle the fire. Then he and Isaac started up the mountain.

As they walked, Isaac spoke. "Father . . ."

"Here I am, Son," Abraham immediately replied.

Isaac asked, "I see the fire and the wood, but where is the lamb for the sacrifice?"

Abraham answered, "God will provide the sacrifice, my son."

Isaac was not deceived. He knew about the customs of the people of Canaan. He realized that if God did not provide a lamb, he would be the sacrifice. Isaac was young and strong. He could have run away. He could have resisted. Abraham was an old man. He never could have subdued his son if Isaac had decided to fight. But Isaac's faith was as strong as Abraham's. He submitted to God's will, as his father had done. Father and son walked on together.

At last they reached the top of the mountain. Abraham built an altar out of rough stones. He arranged the wood. Then he tied Isaac's hands and feet and placed him upon the altar.

Abraham took the knife in his hand. Tears streamed down his face as he placed the sharp blade against his son's throat. The angels in heaven wept, too. They cried to God, "Are You going to allow Abraham to sacrifice his son? If he does, what will become of the promise You made to him? Ishmael's children are idol-worshipers. How can Abraham become a 'father of multitudes' if his only son who prays to You loses his life? Look! The knife is already at Isaac's throat! How much longer will You wait?"

The angels' tears rained down from heaven. They fell into Isaac's eyes, making them dim, so from that day on Isaac saw only shadows and not the full shape of things.

At the last moment, a voice rang out from heaven. "Abraham! Abraham!"

Abraham turned his head. "Here I am!"

"Do not raise your hand against your son or harm him in any way. I know now that you are completely devoted to God. You have not withheld anything from Me—not even your son."

Abraham lowered the knife. He looked around and saw a ram whose horns were caught in a bramble bush. Abraham lifted Isaac down from the altar and sacrificed the ram in his place.

The heavenly voice called to Abraham a second time. "Because you did as I asked and did not withhold your son, I will bless you and multiply your descendants, so that they will be as numerous as the stars in the sky and the sands on the seashore. They will overcome their enemies. My blessing shall go out from them unto all the nations of the earth. They shall be blessed because of you."

Abraham called the spot where he bound his son *Adoni Yireh,* which means *The Place Where God Reveals Himself.* This site was earlier known as *Shalem,* meaning *Peace.* The two words *Yireh* and *Shalem* together form the word *Jerusalem.*

This is why the city of Jerusalem has a special holiness. It stands on the place where Abraham proved his devotion to God.

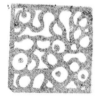

The Story of Isaac

Sorrow awaited Abraham and Isaac when they returned from the land of Moriah. Sarah was dead. She knew that God had asked Abraham to sacrifice her only son. Like her husband, she accepted God's will without question. When Abraham sent back one of his servants to tell her that Isaac was alive, that a ram had been sacrificed in his place, Sarah's heart burst with joy, and she died.

Abraham looked for a place to bury Sarah. He bought the cave of Machpelah from a man named Ephron the Hittite, paying him one hundred silver shekels. Isaac and Abraham buried Sarah in the cave. They carved two tombs from the living rock. One became Sarah's final resting place. The second, close beside it, was for Abraham. Abraham was full of years. He knew it would not be long before he joined his beloved wife and friend.

A Bride for Isaac

The time had come to choose a wife for Isaac. The kings of Canaan were eager to have him marry one of their daughters, but Abraham was wary. The daughters of Canaan all worshiped idols. Abraham did not want Isaac's children growing up to worship false gods, as had happened with Ishmael. He decided to seek Isaac's bride among his own family.

Abraham's brother Nahor lived far away in the city of Haran. Abraham was too old to make the journey, so he summoned his faithful servant Eliezer. "Go to Haran," Abraham told him. "See if there is a suitable wife for Isaac among the daughters of my nephew Bethuel." Abraham gave Eliezer rich gifts of gold and jewels for the bride, but he cautioned him not to show them at first. Nor was he to

reveal whom he was or who had sent him. Abraham suspected that Bethuel's daughters would try their best to please Eliezer if they knew he had come to choose a bride for Isaac. But how would they treat a dusty stranger? That was the real test.

Eliezer took ten of Abraham's camels and loaded them with gifts. He selected ten of Abraham's servants to accompany him. The journey to Haran usually took sixteen days. God sent angels with fiery swords to guard Eliezer's caravan, and a pillar of fire to guide it across the desert. The fire lit up the darkness, so that Eliezer was able to travel as easily by night as he did by day. Furthermore, God lengthened his camels' stride. When morning came, Eliezer was surprised to see the walls of Haran in the distance. He had completed the entire journey in one day and one night.

Eliezer stopped beside a well, just outside the city gates. He thought to himself, *I will rest here until the young women of the city come to draw water from the well. If one offers to draw water for me, my servants, and my camels, I will know that she is the one whom God has picked to be Isaac's bride.*

Eliezer watched and waited. One by one, young women of Haran came out. They chattered and gossiped as they filled their jars with water. No one paid any attention to Eliezer or his camels. Eliezer began to wonder if Abraham had made a mistake. He would not choose any of them to be a bride for Isaac.

Just then another young woman arrived at the well. She was so beautiful that Eliezer could not help noticing her. *She reminds me of Sarah,* he thought. Sarah was still extremely beautiful even when she was over a hundred years old. That was because her beauty came from inside. *I will see if this girl behaves like Sarah. She may be the one,* Eliezer said to himself.

The young woman put down her jar and began drawing water from the well. A little boy limped by. "What is the matter with your foot?" she asked him.

"I stepped on a thorn. It hurts!" The boy began crying.

"I will help you." The young woman sat the boy on her lap. She pulled the thorn from his foot. Then she washed the wound and tied it with her own kerchief. "I will carry you home," she said. "We don't want that wound to get dirty." The young woman lifted the boy onto her back and carried him into the city.

When she returned, she saw a blind woman waiting by the well. "Can I help you?"

"Yes," the blind woman answered. "Please be so kind as to show me the way into the city. I cannot find the gate. Last night I was forced to sleep in the fields."

"Tell me where you live. I will take you there." She took the blind woman by the hand and led her home.

The young woman came back again a while later. "Please forgive me. I did not mean to ignore you," she said to Eliezer. "I could see that you were thirsty, but the little boy and the blind woman needed my help right away. If you like, I will be happy to draw water for you now."

"Thank you," Eliezer said. "You are a very kind person."

"I only try to do what pleases God," she answered.

"What god do you worship?"

"I worship the God of my uncle Abraham."

Eliezer pretended not to know who Abraham was. "What god is that? Where is his image? Where can I find his temple?"

"He has no image. The whole world is His temple," the young woman answered. "My friends think my family is peculiar because we do not worship idols. I don't care what they think. They are foolish to bow down to statues of wood and stone. I worship the One True God, Who created heaven and earth." Suddenly she blushed. "How thoughtless of me! Here I am, prattling on and on about myself, forgetting how thirsty you must be. Allow me to draw water for you and your servants. I will draw water for your camels, too."

This is the sign I was waiting for, Eliezer thought to himself as he drank from the jar the young woman brought him. "Tell me your name."

"I am Rebecca, the daughter of Bethuel, the son of Nahor . . . "

". . . the brother of Abraham. And I am Eliezer, Abraham's servant. May I lodge in your father's house tonight? I must discuss something important with him." Eliezer gave Rebecca a jeweled nose ring and two gold bracelets. Rebecca accepted them graciously.

"My lord is too generous. Allow me to go ahead to tell my father you have come. I will return to lead you to his house."

Rebecca's father, Bethuel, her mother, Milcah, and her brother Laban were astonished by the ten camel loads of rich gifts that Eliezer brought. They eagerly agreed to a wedding between their daughter and Isaac. When Rebecca set out for her new home, she looked like a princess decked out in all her finery. Eliezer and his servants wore their finest clothes. A troop of angels flew overhead to guard

THE STORY OF ISAAC

against danger, while the pillar of fire guided the caravan across the desert.

Early the next morning Isaac awoke to the sound of camel bells. He looked out of his tent to see who was coming. He cried aloud when he saw Rebecca, for though his sight was dim, her beauty was such that it dazzled his eyes.

Abraham and his followers celebrated the wedding of Rebecca and Isaac with great joy. Sarah's empty place in the family was filled once more. Isaac thanked God for sending such a gracious, kind woman to be his wife. Rebecca thanked God for giving her such a gentle and righteous husband.

Abraham thanked God, too. He knew his life was almost at an end, but he was not sad. Instead he rejoiced, for he knew that Isaac and Rebecca would carry on his work for the next generation.

Abraham died when he was 175 years old. His two sons, Isaac and Ishmael, buried him in the cave of Machpelah, next to his beloved wife, Sarah. The cave is still there. The city of Hebron has grown around it. Abraham and Sarah and their children and grandchildren rest there to this day.

Jacob and Esau

God granted Abraham one last blessing before his death. He allowed him to live long enough to know his grandchildren and take part in their upbringing. Rebecca gave birth to twins. Her two sons wrestled in her womb as they were being born, as if each was struggling to be the first to emerge. The first to come forth was red and hairy, with skin like a rough cloak. Rebecca and Isaac called him *Esau*, which means *Thick-Haired.* The second came out immediately after, grasping tightly to his brother's heel. Rebecca and Isaac named him *Jacob*, meaning *Taking by the Heel.*

As the two boys grew and became young men, it was hard to believe they were brothers. Esau resembled his uncle Ishmael. A huge, burly man covered all over with thick red hair like a wild beast, Esau loved to hunt. He roamed the fields for days at a time, looking for animals to kill. Occasionally he killed men, too, if they got in his way. Esau respected only one person: his father, Isaac. He treated everyone else in a coarse, rude manner.

Jacob was Rebecca's favorite child. While Esau was rough and crude, Jacob was soft and gentle. He spent most of his time helping his mother with her daily chores. Rebecca favored Jacob, while Isaac favored Esau. The jealousy between the brothers was bound to increase.

One day, while hunting in the fields, Esau came upon an old man wearing a beautiful robe. He was none other than King Nimrod, who once put Abraham in the fiery furnace.

"I want that robe. Sell it to me," demanded Esau. When Nimrod refused, Esau killed him and took the robe for himself. Nimrod's servants pursued Esau. He struck down two of them, but was forced to drop the robe to get away. By the time Esau arrived home, he was exhausted, out of breath, covered with dirt and blood.

As Esau stumbled into camp, he saw his brother, Jacob, cooking a meal over a fire. "That smells good. What is it?" Esau asked.

"Lentils," Jacob told him.

Esau reached for a spoon. "I'm hungry. Give me some."

"Not so fast," said Jacob. "When did you ever give anything away? If you want lentils, pay for them. You always make me pay for anything I get from you."

"All right. What do you want?" said Esau.

"Sell me your birthright, the blessing of the eldest son, that was given by God to our grandfather Abraham, and from Abraham to our father, Isaac."

"Agreed," said Esau. "What good is the birthright? It's just some mumbled words. A blessing isn't going to fill my stomach. Take the blessing and give me some lentils. I'm hungry!"

Jacob handed a dish of lentils to his brother. Esau gobbled them down like a beast feeding at a trough.

Soon afterward Rebecca overheard Isaac say to Esau, "I am old in years. Soon I may die. It is time to give you your birthright, the blessing of the firstborn. Go into the field and bring back some venison for me to eat. Then I will bless you."

Esau took his bow and arrows and left to find some game. Rebecca waited until he was gone. Then she slaughtered two goats and prepared a tasty stew, cooked the way Isaac liked it. She handed the dish to Jacob. "Bring this food to your father. After he eats, he will give you the blessing."

Jacob protested. "Father's eyes are dim, but he can surely tell the difference between my brother and me. Esau is covered with hair like a goat. My skin is smooth. If Father feels my face or hands, he will discover I am deceiving him. I will receive his curse, not his blessing."

"Do not worry. I am prepared for that," said Rebecca. She took the skins of the freshly killed goats and spread them over Jacob's neck and arms. "Now bring the meal to your father."

Isaac looked up as Jacob entered his tent.

"Who are you, my child?" he asked.

Jacob trembled. "I am Esau, your firstborn," he stammered. "Come, eat of this good venison I bring you, so that you may bless me."

Isaac beckoned Jacob to come closer. As Jacob approached, Isaac reached out to feel his arms. "The voice is the voice of Jacob," he said with surprise, "but the hands are the hands of Esau." He told Jacob to kneel at his feet. Then he kissed him and gave him this blessing:

May God grant you the dew of heaven
And the richness of earth
And abundant grain and wine.
Nations will serve you. Kings will bow to you.
You will be lifted up above your kinfolk.
Your mother's children will humble themselves before you.
Cursed are those who curse you,
But those who bless you will be blessed.

Jacob had hardly left Isaac's tent when his brother, Esau, appeared, carrying a pot of rich venison stew. "Come, Father. Eat of this good venison I have brought you. Then you will bless me."

Isaac began to tremble. "Who are you?" he asked.

Esau answered, "Do you not recognize me? I am Esau, your firstborn son."

"Then who was that who just brought me venison? I ate it and blessed him. He has received the blessing of the firstborn."

Esau let out a cry of grief and rage. "My brother Jacob has robbed me of my birthright! Truly he is called *Jacob*, for he has taken me by the heels and stolen what was rightfully mine. Am I to go away empty-handed? Have you not another blessing left, Father, to give me?"

Isaac told Esau to kneel. Then he blessed him with these words:

You will wander in fields of plenty.
The earth will feed you, and the rain will water you.
You will live by the sword and serve your brother.
But not forever. One day you will break loose.
You will shake his yoke from your shoulders.

The blessing suited Esau. He was already a nomad who lived by the sword. Nonetheless, Esau swore vengeance. He would not harm Jacob as long as Isaac lived. But once his father died, he would kill him.

The Story of Jacob

Rebecca knew what lay in Esau's heart. She warned Jacob: "Esau is planning to kill you. Run to my brother Laban in Haran. Stay with him until your brother's wrath cools. Esau is quick to anger, but he is also quick to forget. I could not bear to live if he were to kill you. You would be dead, and Esau would be driven from our camp forever. Why should I lose both my sons in a single day?"

Jacob needed an excuse to explain his sudden departure. Rebecca went to Isaac and told him, "Behold, both our sons are old enough to be married. Where shall we find suitable brides for them? It would break my heart to see either of them, especially Jacob, marry one of the daughters of Canaan."

"We will do as my father did," said Isaac. "I will send Jacob to Haran to choose one of your brother Laban's daughters as his bride. Esau will go to his uncle Ishmael."

Isaac's plan was exactly what Rebecca wished. Jacob left for Haran, while his brother, Esau, traveled in the opposite direction to Ishmael's camp, where he married Mahalath, Ishmael's oldest daughter. Together they had many children. Esau remained with Ishmael in the desert. In time he became the ruler of Edom, a great nation.

Jacob's Dream

Jacob followed the camel tracks that led to Padan-Aram. One night he camped on a mountaintop in an empty place. The only sign that people had ever come this way was a pile of rough stones. Jacob took one of the stones and placed it under his head as a pillow. He closed his eyes and went to sleep.

That night Jacob had a dream. He dreamed he saw a ladder reaching all the

way to heaven. Scores of angels climbed up and down, ascending and descending. God stood beside Jacob and spoke to him:

> *I am God. Your grandfather Abraham worshiped Me, as does your father Isaac. I give this land where you now lie, as far as you can see, to you and your descendants. Your children will be as numerous as the dust of the earth. They will spread in all directions; to the east and west, to the north and south. Through you all the families of the earth will be blessed. I will always be with you. I will preserve and protect you, and bring you back to this land. Never will I abandon you until all my promises are fulfilled.*

Jacob awoke from his dream, trembling with awe, for he had spoken with God face-to-face. "Holiness fills this spot!" he exclaimed. "God dwells here! Here the gate of heaven rests on the earth!"

The mountain where Jacob spent the night was Mount Moriah, where Abraham had brought Isaac for his binding. Abraham had raised that pile of stones as an altar. The rock where Jacob laid his head was the same one that supported Isaac when he lifted his eyes toward heaven and saw the angels.

As soon as the sun rose, Jacob took the stone from beneath his head and set it up as a pillar. He poured oil over it as a consecration. At the same time he gave the place a new name. He called it *Bethel*, which means *The Place Where God Dwells*. Jacob swore a vow before God: "If You will be with me and feed me, protect me and clothe me, so that I may one day return to my father's house in peace, then You will be my God. I will dedicate my life to You and You Alone. This stone, this pillar which I have erected, will be Your place of worship. Whatsoever You choose to give me, I will return the tenth portion to You."

Jacob at the Well

Jacob continued his journey until he came to the land of Padan-Aram. He saw the walls of a great city before him. *This must be Haran,* he thought to himself. As he came near, he noticed a large well. A huge flat stone covered its mouth. Three flocks of sheep along with their shepherds stood beside the well. Jacob asked why they were waiting.

"We are waiting for our friends to get here," the shepherds replied. "It takes forty men to move the stone from the well."

As they were speaking, Laban's daughter Rachel arrived at the well with her sheep. She was so beautiful that Jacob stopped talking to the shepherds. He turned to gaze at her.

"I will water your sheep," he said. Then, all by himself, he lifted the huge stone, set it aside, and drew bucket after bucket from the well until all Rachel's sheep had drunk their fill. Jacob was able to do this because his strength was that of fifty men. It was only when compared to his brother, Esau, an enormous, mighty man, that Jacob appeared weak and mild.

Jacob kissed Rachel's hand. "Tell me your name," he pleaded.

"I am Rachel, Laban's daughter," she told him.

"And I am Jacob, your cousin! Rebecca, my mother, is your father's sister."

Rachel ran to tell her father the news. Laban came hurrying to meet Jacob. He embraced him several times, around the waist, arms, and shoulders.

There was more to Laban's embrace than love of family. Rebecca and Laban were as different as Jacob and Esau. Where Rebecca was kind and generous, Laban was selfish and greedy. He remembered the rich gifts that Eliezer brought to Bethuel's house when he came seeking a bride for Isaac. Laban thought, *Eliezer was only Abraham's servant, yet he came with ten camels loaded with treasure. Jacob is Isaac's son. He must be bringing a hundred camels.* That was why Laban ran so fast to meet Jacob. Far from having a hundred camels, Jacob did not even appear to own a donkey. This surprised Laban. But then he thought, *Jacob has disguised himself as an ordinary traveler as protection from robbers. He must have diamonds and other precious gems hidden away in his clothes.* As Laban embraced Jacob, he felt his waist, arms, and shoulders, looking for hidden jewels. To his disgust, he found nothing. Laban would have preferred to turn Jacob away. It was not his custom to offer shelter to poor travelers. However, it was his duty as a kinsman to welcome Jacob. So he did.

"Greetings, dear nephew! You must stay at my house. After all, are you not my sister's son? You are flesh of my flesh and bone of my bone."

Jacob stayed with Laban for one month. He cared for Laban's flocks and fields as if they were his own, as well as doing whatever work was required.

Rachel and Leah

At the end of the month, Laban said to Jacob, "My neighbors are saying that I am taking advantage of you. Perhaps they are right. Even though you are my nephew, it is still not proper that you work for nothing. Tell me what you want for wages."

Jacob knew exactly what he wanted. "I will work for you for seven years, for no wages at all, if at the end of that time you allow me to marry Rachel."

"Agreed!" said Laban. "If you work for me for seven years, I will give you Rachel to be your wife."

However, by this time Jacob knew his uncle well enough not to trust him. There were several ways for Laban to avoid keeping his promise. He might offer Jacob another girl named Rachel. He might change Rachel's name, calling her *Leah* and her older sister *Rachel*. In seven years he might have another daughter and name her Rachel. That is why Jacob said to Laban, "Which Rachel?"

"My daughter Rachel."

"Which daughter?"

"My second daughter. Leah's younger sister."

"Say it again, Uncle," said Jacob. "At the end of seven years, I promise to give you my second oldest daughter Rachel to be your wife."

Laban repeated these words, and Jacob was satisfied.

Rachel was astonishingly beautiful, and so was her sister, Leah. Both possessed the beauty of Sarah and Rebecca, whose loveliness shined from the goodness of their souls. Leah was especially devoted to God. When Laban tried to force her to marry a prince of Haran, Leah said she would rather die than marry an idol-worshiper. For a time Laban wanted to marry her to Esau. Leah wept so hard at the thought of marrying such a rough, violent person that she damaged her eyes. God took pity on her. He caused Esau to marry one of Ishmael's daughters. Though Leah remained nearsighted, God made her eyes so beautiful, they out-shined those of Rachel. Leah loved Jacob, and would have liked to marry him, but she was not jealous of her sister. She was happy that Rachel had found such a kind man, devoted to God, to marry.

Jacob served Laban for seven years. Yet so great was his love for Rachel that they seemed like seven days.

As Jacob's time of service was approaching its end, Laban spoke to his neigh-bors, the princes of Haran. "Our city has prospered during the past seven years.

Our wealth has grown; our flocks and herds have increased. Do you know why this happened? It is because of my nephew Jacob. God favors him. He has the blessing of his father, Isaac, the same one that was given to Isaac by my uncle Abraham. Good fortune will always follow Jacob wherever he goes. But now, my friends, the seven years he promised to work for me are over. I must give him Rachel, my daughter, as his wife. Once they are married, Jacob will surely return to his home in Canaan, taking his good fortune with him. What will happen to us then? Our fields will dry up. Our flocks will be barren. The blessing that Jacob brought to us will depart."

"No! No!" Laban's neighbors cried.

One of the princes of Haran dropped a bag of silver coins at Laban's feet. "Find some way to keep Jacob here and I will give you a hundred silver shekels!"

"I will, too!"

"And I!"

"And I!"

The princes of Haran swarmed over each other, thrusting money into Laban's hands, belt, and purse. Laban chuckled to himself. He already had a plan to keep Jacob in Haran for another seven years.

On the day of the wedding, Laban dressed his daughter Leah in Rachel's finest clothes and covered her face with a heavy veil. Rachel said nothing, for she did not want to humiliate her sister. Leah said nothing, for she loved Jacob and wished to marry him. Laban's servants said nothing, for they were afraid of their master.

Only Rachel's handmaid Bilhah and Leah's handmaid Zilpah made any attempt to warn Jacob. They despised Laban for his treachery and feared God more than they feared him. The handmaids could not speak to Jacob directly; Laban was watching too closely. However, when Jacob asked them to dance for the company in honor of his bride, they took their tambourines and began to sing, *"Halia! Halia!"* What they were really saying was: *"Ha Leah!* This is Leah!" But the effort failed. Jacob's heart was too full of joy to allow any thought of suspicion.

After the wedding ceremony, Jacob lifted his bride's veil. To his shock, he found himself facing Leah, not Rachel! He turned to Laban in anger. "I served you faithfully for seven years! You promised me Rachel! Why did you deceive me?"

Laban looked as astonished as Jacob. "Surely you are aware of the customs of

Haran! The younger sister is never given away in marriage before the elder. Come now, Jacob, do not be angry. I will fulfill my vow. After Leah's wedding celebration is over, you may marry Rachel. It is good for sisters to live together as wives and companions. I will not ask much for giving you both my daughters; only that you serve me for another seven years."

So great was Jacob's love for Rachel that he agreed to serve Laban for seven more years. This time Laban kept his word. After a week passed, he gave Rachel to Jacob as his wife.

Jacob's and Rachel's hearts overflowed with joy. Only Leah was sad. While Jacob always treated her with respect and affection, she knew he would never love her as much as he loved her sister. God took pity on Leah. If she could not have Jacob's love, she would have his children. Within a year Leah gave birth to a son. She named him Reuben. The next year she had another son, whom she called Simeon. The year after that she had another son, too. She called him Levi. Leah had one more son. She named him Judah.

Meanwhile, Rachel had no children. Her sister Leah had given Jacob four sons, while she had none. "Why can't I have children?" she asked Jacob.

"God decides who can have children and who cannot," Jacob told her.

Rachel said, "If God does not wish me to have children, take my handmaid Bilhah as your wife. She can have children in my place."

So Jacob took Bilhah as his wife to please Rachel. She bore him two sons. They named the first Dan and the second Naphtali.

Leah also wished to bear more children for Jacob. She offered him her handmaid Zilpah. Zilpah bore two sons for Jacob: Gad and Asher. Then God favored Leah again. She bore two more sons, Issachar and Zebulun, and a daughter, whom she named Dinah.

At last God blessed Rachel with a child of her own. She called him Joseph.

Jacob Returns to Canaan

Jacob's years of service were nearing an end. Laban had grown very rich during this time. Feeling generous, he told Jacob, "I know you will return home soon. Name your wages for the years you served me, and I will pay them."

Jacob told Laban, "Let us divide your flock. You will take all the dark and spotted sheep and goats. I will take all the white ones. When I am ready to return to

Canaan, I will let you look over my flock. All the white animals will be yours. The dark and spotted ones will be mine. I will take them as my wages."

Laban chuckled with glee. Jacob was asking to be cheated. After separating the flocks, Laban sent all the darker animals away, a three-day journey, to make sure they would have no contact with Jacob's flock.

But Jacob knew more about raising sheep than Laban. He knew the animals had already mated. He also knew that when a dark or spotted sheep or goat mated with a white one, the offspring were likely to be spotted. That is what happened. When the animals in Jacob's flock gave birth several months later, the majority of lambs and kids were spotted. Jacob raised them carefully. When they were grown, he mingled them with the rest of the flock. Within a few generations, nearly all of Jacob's animals were dark or spotted. Jacob set the few white ones aside and did not allow them to breed.

Jacob's flocks multiplied year by year, while Laban's dwindled. Nearly every animal in Jacob's care was dark or spotted, for God's blessing rested with Jacob, not Laban. And Jacob was a much better shepherd.

As Jacob's wealth increased, Laban grew jealous. Whenever they met, he spoke coldly to Jacob, staring at him with envy. Jacob realized it was time to go. He waited until Laban went off to shear his sheep. Then he gathered his wives and children, his servants, his flocks and herds, and all that belonged to him and started for the land of Canaan. Before they left, Rachel stole Laban's *teraphim*, the small household idols that he worshiped.

When Laban heard that Jacob had fled, he hurried home to ask his idols what to do. To his horror, he found the idol shelf empty. The teraphim were gone. Laban thought, *If Jacob has stolen my idols, he has the power to do me great harm. I must get my idols back. Then I can attack Jacob.*

Laban gathered his neighbors and servants and galloped off in pursuit of Jacob. They caught up with him seven days later near the slopes of Mount Gilead, in the hill country east of the Jordan River. That night God came to Laban in a dream. "Beware!" God said. "Do not think of harming Jacob! Do not try to entice him with sweet words or frighten him with threats!"

When Laban met Jacob the next morning, he spoke plainly. "Why did you run away? You carried my daughters and grandchildren off like a bandit. You did not give me a chance to say good-bye to them. Furthermore, you even stole my teraphim. Is this how you repay my hospitality for taking you in and sheltering you all these years? I could harm you if I wish, but the God you worship spoke to me last night. He warned me not to threaten you. I understand why you wish to return to your own land, but why did you steal my gods?"

"I know nothing about your gods," Jacob answered. "I do not worship them. I do not believe in them. Why would I steal them? Search my caravan. If you find your idols, you may have them back. I will put to death the person who stole them."

Jacob would not have spoken these words had he known that Laban's idols were hidden in the saddlebags of Rachel's camel. Laban searched throughout Jacob's caravan. He looked everywhere, without success. At last he came to Rachel. "Get down, daughter. I must look in your saddlebags."

"Let me stay where I am, Father," Rachel pleaded. "My belly hurts. It is hard for me to climb up and down from this camel. You know I haven't taken your gods. Why would I do that? I know how important they are to you."

Laban passed Rachel by. He finished his search, unsuccessfully. "You see," Jacob said to him. "I don't have your idols. You had no reason to pursue me. I served you well and faithfully for many years. I always kept my word. I never complained, even though you tried to cheat me many times. If your idols have mysteriously vanished, it is God's judgment upon you. You must accept it."

Laban shrugged sheepishly. "Let us not quarrel. Can you not see we are one? Your wives are my daughters. Your children are my grandchildren. Let us make a pact of peace. Let it be a witness of friendship between us forever."

Jacob did not argue with Laban, although he knew what his friendship was worth. Together they raised a heap of stones. There they swore an oath by the gods of their fathers to be friends forever.

Laban spent the night in Jacob's camp. In the morning, he departed. Jacob continued on his journey. As he rode out ahead of the caravan, he saw angels coming to meet him. *Surely this is God's camp,* he said to himself. And he called the place *Mahanaim*, which means *Two Camps*.

Jacob Wrestles with a Stranger

Jacob's caravan entered the hill country of Seir, near the plain of Edom, where his brother Esau lived. Jacob was worried. He feared that Esau might not have forgotten or forgiven how he stole his birthright. Esau was a mighty man, the ruler of a nation of savage nomads. If Esau attacked his caravan, Jacob could not hope to defend it.

Jacob sent a message to his brother. It said, "Your servant Jacob is on his way home. I have lived with Laban until now. I am returning with my flocks and herds, my family and my servants. If we find favor in your sight, permit us to cross your lands in peace."

The messengers came back to tell Jacob that Esau was coming to meet him, accompanied by an escort of four hundred armed men. The news frightened Jacob. If Esau meant no harm, why was he bringing an army with him?

Jacob prepared for trouble. He divided his caravan in half. If Esau attacked one group, the other might still escape. He sent his choicest animals—sheep and goats, cows and camels, donkeys and horses—as a gift to his brother. Jacob prayed to God to protect him. He asked God to remember his promise, to deliver him from Esau.

After dark, the camp settled down to an uneasy sleep. Jacob awoke in the middle of the night. He roused his wives and children, and all the people and animals who remained with him, and led them across a nearby stream. Once they were settled on the opposite bank, he returned to the camp alone.

Jacob sat in the darkness, thinking about the next day, when he would come face-to-face with Esau. Suddenly, he sensed that he was not alone. He looked up and saw a stranger standing before him.

Something about the stranger's face frightened Jacob. He did not look like a being from this world. "Who are you? Why have you come to me?" Jacob asked. When the stranger did not reply, Jacob reached out to touch him. The stranger grasped Jacob's arm. The two began to wrestle. Jacob and the stranger wrestled all night, but neither could prevail against the other.

At last dawn came. Seeing that he could not overcome Jacob, the stranger reached out and touched him in the hollow of his thigh, where his leg joined his hip. Jacob's leg buckled beneath him, but he did not let go.

"Release me, for day is dawning. I must return to my place," the stranger said.

Jacob answered, "I will not let you go until you bless me." For by now he knew his opponent was no human being.

"Tell me your name."

"My name is Jacob."

The stranger said, "Your name will be Jacob no more. From now on you will be called *Israel*, for you have *Wrestled with God* and with men, and prevailed."

Then Jacob asked him, "Tell me your name."

The stranger answered, "Why do you ask, since you already know?" Then he blessed him and disappeared.

For the rest of his life, Jacob walked with a limp because of the injury to his thigh. He called that place *Peniel*, which means *The Face of God.* For he said, *I Have Seen God's Face and Lived.*

Jacob Meets Esau

Jacob raised his eyes and saw a cloud of dust approaching. It was a vast army led by an enormous man in armor mounted on a tall camel—Esau!

Jacob crossed the stream to join his family. He gathered his wives and children in a circle. He put Bilhah and Zilpah and their children in the outer ring; Leah and her children behind them; and Rachel and her son Joseph in the center.

Esau jumped down from his camel. He stood facing Jacob with his huge arms crossed over his breastplate. A bronze helmet hid his face.

Jacob came forward. With every few steps he threw himself on the ground and bowed to Esau, seven times in all. Esau did not wait for Jacob to come near. He threw off his helmet and ran forward to embrace his brother. Esau lifted Jacob up, covering his face and neck with kisses. The two brothers held each other and wept.

"Who are these people?" Esau asked.

"They are my wives and children," Jacob said. Jacob's family came near and bowed before Esau.

"What was that great crowd of people and animals I met along the way?"

"That was my gift to you, in hope I might find favor in your sight," Jacob told him.

Esau laughed. "You do not have to give me gifts, brother. I have more than enough for my needs."

"Please take it," Jacob insisted. "Let it be a sign to all that there is peace between us."

Esau harkened to Jacob's words and accepted the gift to show his forgiveness. The quarrel between the two brothers was over. Esau invited Jacob and his family to visit him at his home in Seir. Jacob politely declined, being eager to continue his journey. "In that case," said Esau, "I will leave you some of my armed men to guide you through my country."

Then Esau said good-bye to Jacob and returned to his place in Seir. Jacob continued on until he arrived at the city of Shechem, which is in the land of Canaan. There he bought a piece of land as a place for his family to dwell. Now that Jacob's long, dangerous journey was over, he erected an altar to God, thanking Him for protecting him from peril and for bringing him safely home.

The Death of Rachel

When Jacob arrived in Canaan, he heard the tragic news that his mother, Rebecca, had died while he was in Haran. He set out at once to visit his father, Isaac, in Mamre, which is near the city of Hebron. Rachel was about to have another child. Along the way, in a place called Ephrath, she gave birth to a son and died. She spoke her last words, naming her son *Ben Oni, Son of My Sorrow.* Jacob did not like that unfortunate name. He called the child *Benjamin,* meaning *Son of My Right Hand.*

Benjamin was the last of Jacob's twelve sons. After burying Rachel, Jacob and his family moved on to Mamre. Isaac rejoiced to see Jacob once more, for he knew he had little time to live. Jacob remained with Isaac during his last days. Isaac died when he was 180 years old. His two sons, Jacob and Esau, buried him in the cave of Machpelah, beside his wife Rebecca and his parents, Abraham and Sarah. There he lies to this day.

The Story of Joseph

God kept his promise to Jacob, as He did with Abraham and Isaac. Jacob prospered in the land of Canaan. His herds and flocks increased. His family enjoyed the fruits of their labor. His older sons grew into mighty men, feared and respected by all.

Joseph was Jacob's favorite child. Whenever Jacob looked at him, he saw again the image of his beloved wife Rachel. Jacob could not help favoring Joseph over his other children. His other sons became jealous. Once they had loved their younger brother; now they hated him.

The Cloak of Many Colors

Jacob gave Joseph a beautiful cloak woven with stripes of many colors. None of Jacob's other sons possessed anything like it. Their jealousy turned to rage. Everything Joseph did or said filled them with anger.

One day while they were out in the fields herding sheep, Joseph said to his brothers, "Listen to this dream I had. We were all together, here in this field, binding sheaves of wheat. My sheaf stood up. Your sheaves came and bowed down to it. What do you suppose that means?"

"Do you really think we are going to bow down to you one day?" his brothers snarled.

Joseph continued. "I had another dream. The sun, the moon, and eleven stars came and bowed before me."

This was too much! Joseph's brothers complained to their father. Jacob spoke sternly to Joseph. "Why do you speak this way? Do you expect our

whole family to humble themselves before you?"

Joseph could not answer. He did not mean to be arrogant. But he could not deny his dreams.

As time went on, Jacob sent his older sons to pasture his flocks in the fields surrounding the city of Shechem. No word came back from them for several weeks. Jacob worried that his sons might have encountered trouble. He sent Joseph to learn if all was well.

Joseph caught up with his brothers at a place called Dothan. They saw him coming from a distance, wearing his cloak of many colors.

"Here comes the dreamer!" they sneered. "Let us kill him and throw his body into one of the pits around here. We will tell Father that a wild animal attacked him."

Reuben, the oldest brother, could not allow this. "Let us not be guilty of murder," he pleaded. "I beg you, do not take Joseph's life. I know a better way. Throw him into this pit if you want to teach him a lesson. But do not kill him."

Reuben persuaded his brothers to spare Joseph, at least for a while. When the boy came near, they pulled off his cloak of many colors and threw him into a deep pit. That night, after the others went to sleep, Reuben planned to rescue his younger brother and lead him to safety.

But before that could happen, a caravan of traders came along. Judah, the third oldest, said, "What good would it do us to kill Joseph and hide his body? Let us sell him to these traders instead. Then we will have the profit and not be responsible for whatever happens to him. For in truth, we can always say we did him no harm."

The brothers pulled Joseph from the pit and sold him to the traders for twenty shekels of silver, a considerable sum. They dipped the cloak of many colors in the blood of a fresh-killed goat.

When Jacob saw the bloody garment, he tore his clothes and wept. "Woe! Woe! This is Joseph's cloak!" he cried. "Some wild beast has torn him to pieces!"

Jacob mourned for his beloved son Joseph, and could not be comforted.

Joseph in Egypt

The traders traveled to Egypt, where they sold Joseph as a slave. He entered the house of Potiphar, a prominent Egyptian who served as treasurer to Pharaoh, the king of Egypt. Joseph impressed Potiphar with his intelligence and ability. Potiphar appointed him overseer of his house.

But misfortune stalked Joseph. Potiphar's wife, Zuleika, fell in love with him. Joseph refused to betray his master. When he spurned her advances, she complained to her husband, accusing their new slave of molesting her. Potiphar had no choice but to throw Joseph into prison.

Throughout these trials, Joseph kept his faith in God. Even in the bowels of the prison, he never lost hope that God would set him free.

Joseph remained in prison for several years. One day the door opened. The warden of the prison entered, followed by two prominent Egyptians, both in chains. One was Pharaoh's baker; the other was his butler. The two men were extremely downcast. The warden asked Joseph to care for them.

"Why were you thrown in prison?" Joseph asked them.

The butler sighed. "I was first among Pharaoh's servants. It was my duty to bring him his cup of wine. One day, through no fault of mine, a fly flew into the cup and drowned. When Pharaoh saw a fly floating in his wine, he flew into a rage. He threw the wine in my face and ordered his soldiers to take me to prison. That is what brought me here."

The baker told a similar story. "It was my duty to bake Pharaoh's bread. One day, without my knowledge, a mouse fell into the dough. When Pharaoh broke open his loaf and found a mouse inside, his anger knew no bounds. I was locked in chains and thrown in prison. That is why I am here."

Joseph pitied the two men and did what he could to raise their spirits. He told them about the God he worshiped and all He had done for his father and forefathers. He urged them to have hope, to pray to the God of Abraham, Isaac, and Jacob for deliverance. But the Egyptians continued worshiping the gods of Egypt.

A year passed. One day the butler came to Joseph with a troubled look on his face. "What is the matter?" Joseph asked.

"Last night I had a strange dream," the butler told him.

"Tell me what you dreamed. Perhaps I can interpret it for you."

The butler laughed. "Are you a magician? Who are you to interpret dreams?"

Joseph replied, "Dreams come from God. God also gives the wisdom to interpret them. If it is God's will, I can help you."

"Very well," the Egyptian said. "I will tell you my dream. Perhaps you can tell me what it means. In my dream, I found myself standing in a vineyard. A grapevine stood before me. It had three branches tied to a trellis. As I watched, the vine sprouted. It brought forth buds and leaves. The buds turned into clusters that ripened into grapes. I took the grapes and squeezed their juice into Pharaoh's cup. I brought the cup to Pharaoh. He took it from my hand."

"This is the meaning of your dream," said Joseph. "In three days Pharaoh will set you free and make you his butler again. Your crime will be forgotten. When you are restored to office, remember me."

Now the baker came forward. He said to Joseph, "I, too, had a dream. I was walking to Pharaoh's palace with three baskets of pastries on my head. Birds flew down from the sky and ate all the pastries in the topmost basket."

Joseph said to him, "In three days, Pharaoh will condemn you to death. Your body will be hanged on the gallows. The birds will strip the flesh from your bones."

Three days later Pharaoh celebrated his birthday. At the feast, he remembered his butler and baker. Pharaoh ordered that the butler be released from prison, but he condemned the baker to death. The baker's body was hung from a tree. The vultures of Egypt devoured his flesh.

As for the butler, he was washed, shaved, given new clothes, and restored to his former office. But in spite of his promise, he forgot about Joseph, and said nothing to Pharaoh about him.

Joseph lingered in prison. Despite this disappointment, he never lost faith in God.

One night, two years after these events, Pharaoh had a strange dream. He saw seven plump, fat cows come out of the Nile River. Behind them came seven lean, starving cows. The seven lean cows ate up the seven fat ones.

Pharaoh awoke, puzzled by his dream. He fell asleep again. This time he dreamed of seven ripe ears of grain growing on a single stalk. Seven thin, parched ears grew beside them. As Pharaoh watched, the seven parched ears consumed the seven ripe ears.

What did these peculiar dreams mean? In the morning, Pharaoh summoned all the magicians and astrologers in Egypt. None could explain his dreams for him. Then Pharaoh's butler spoke. "Your Majesty," he began, "while I was in prison I met a Hebrew slave who had the power to interpret dreams. The slave's name was Joseph."

"Bring him to me!"

The prison warden brought Joseph before Pharaoh. Joseph listened as

Pharaoh described his two dreams of the cows and the ears of grain. "What do they mean?" Pharaoh asked.

"Here is the meaning of your dreams," said Joseph. "Egypt will be blessed with seven years of plenty. These will be followed by seven years of famine so bitter that all the abundance of the seven good years will be consumed and forgotten."

"What must be done so that the people of Egypt do not starve?"

Joseph answered without hesitation. "Let Pharaoh appoint one man to be steward over all of Egypt. Let him collect one-fifth of everything grown during the seven years of plenty, to be stored in cities throughout the land. If this happens, there will be food for all the people of Egypt during the time of famine."

Pharaoh approved Joseph's plan. He appointed Joseph to be steward over his entire kingdom. For the next seven years, Joseph collected one-fifth of all the crops grown in Egypt and stored them in granaries. When the famine came, he opened the granaries and distributed grain to the Egyptians. Famine held the entire world in its grip for seven years. But there was food in Egypt.

The famine was especially harsh in the land of Canaan. Crops withered in the fields. Wells dried up. More and more animals died each day. Jacob said to his sons, "I hear there is grain in Egypt. Go there and buy some for us, lest we perish."

Jacob sent his ten sons to Egypt. However, he would not allow Benjamin to go with them. "He is Rachel's only living son," he told the others. "If something happened to him, as happened to Joseph, I could not bear it."

The brothers went down to Egypt. They were taken before Joseph, Pharaoh's steward. Joseph recognized them at once, but his brothers did not recognize him. Many years had passed since they had last seen him. Joseph now looked and spoke like an Egyptian.

"Why have you come?" he asked them.

"My lord," they answered, "we are twelve brothers, sons of a man named Jacob. We have come to Egypt to buy grain."

"You are lying," Joseph said. "I do not see twelve here. I only see ten. You are spies."

"No, my lord," the brothers insisted. "What we say is true. We are not spies. One of our brothers is dead. The other, the youngest, is with our father in Canaan."

Joseph pretended not to believe them. He threw his brothers in prison. After three days, he released them, saying, "If what you say is true, return to Canaan and bring back your youngest brother. I will keep one of you as hostage."

Reuben, the oldest, turned to his brothers and spoke to them in the Hebrew language, which he did not think Joseph would understand. "This is our punishment for what we did to our poor brother Joseph." The others sadly agreed. Joseph could not bear to hear anymore. He left the room. When he was alone, he wept.

After composing himself, Joseph came back. He ordered that Simeon be kept as a hostage. The others were to be allowed to buy grain and return home. Soldiers tied Simeon's hands with ropes and led him away. Joseph's brothers were taken to the nearest granary. Their sacks were filled with grain. They were given more grain to feed their donkeys on the journey home. Unknown to the brothers, Joseph also ordered that their money be returned. The Egyptians secretly placed their gold and silver shekels back in the grain sacks before sewing them shut.

On the way back to Canaan, the brothers stopped to feed their donkeys. Their gold and silver—all the money they brought with them to Egypt—lay on top of the grain in each sack. The brothers could not understand what was happening. First Simeon taken hostage, now this? *What is God doing to us?* they wondered.

When they returned home, the brothers told Jacob all that happened to them in Egypt. "Pharaoh's steward, the lord of the land, spoke harshly to us. He accused us of being spies. We had to leave Simeon with him as hostage before he would permit us to buy grain. He will not release Simeon unless we go back, bringing our brother Benjamin." They opened the sacks of grain and showed Jacob the money sewn in each sack.

Jacob threw himself on the ground, holding his head in both hands. "First Joseph is gone, now Simeon. And you tell me you want to take Benjamin, too! Cursed I am, that such misery is my lot."

Reuben spoke gently to his father. "Allow us to take Benjamin to Egypt. I swear to you, no harm will befall him."

Jacob thrust Reuben away. "No! Benjamin will not go! He is the only one left of Rachel's children. If anything happened to him, I would die!"

The famine continued. Soon all the grain that the brothers brought back from Egypt was consumed. They had no choice but to return again. This time, Jacob relented and allowed Benjamin to go with them. For without more grain from Egypt, the whole family would starve. Jacob gave his sons a rich present of gold and spices to give to Pharaoh's steward. He also told them to give back the money that had turned up in their sacks, in case it had been placed there by mistake. Then he kissed Benjamin and gave him into God's keeping, wondering if he would see him or any of his sons again.

The brothers went down to Egypt. They came before Joseph and gave him Jacob's gifts. They also returned the gold and silver, saying, "We found this money in our sacks after we came the first time."

"God must have given it to you, for I know nothing about it. I already had your money," Joseph told them. He ordered Simeon released. While waiting for the guards to free him, he chatted with the brothers. "How is your father? Is he still alive?" Suddenly, Benjamin stepped forward. "Is he your youngest brother?" Joseph asked. When told that he was, Joseph murmured, "God be gracious to you." Overcome with longing for his home and family, Joseph rushed from the room and wept.

After washing his face and hands, Joseph returned and ordered a banquet be prepared. All the brothers were given generous portions, but Benjamin received five times as much.

When the brothers went to the granary, Joseph gave the same orders as before. Their sacks were to be filled with as much grain as they could hold and the money they paid was to be returned. This time Joseph also ordered that his silver drinking bowl be hidden in Benjamin's sack.

The brothers set out for Canaan at dawn. They had not gone far when a troop of Joseph's bodyguards caught up with them. "Is this how you repay my master's kindness? By stealing his silver drinking bowl!" their captain asked.

"We stole nothing!" the brothers protested. "If we had come as thieves, would we have returned the money we found in our sacks the first time? Search our belongings. If you can find your master's drinking bowl, you may put to death whoever stole it. The rest of us will become your slaves."

"No," the captain said. "Whoever has stolen the bowl will become a slave. The rest of you will go free."

The brothers unloaded their donkeys. The Egyptians searched the grain sacks one by one. They found the silver bowl in Benjamin's sack.

Stunned, the brothers wept and tore their clothes. How could they return to Canaan without Benjamin? Their father would die when he learned his youngest son was lost. Together with the Egyptians, the brothers returned to the city.

There they came before Joseph. Judah threw himself on the ground. Looking up at Joseph, he pleaded, "My lord, our father is an old man. Our little brother Benjamin is the child of his old age. Our father dearly loved his mother; he is the only one of her sons still with us. His brother is dead. If our father loses this child, he will surely die of grief. I beg you, my lord, let the boy return home with his brothers. Let his punishment fall on my head. I will remain behind as your slave. Do as you wish with me."

Judah was no longer the harsh, violent man he had once been. Years ago, he had sold his brother Joseph into slavery. Now he offered to become a slave himself for the sake of his brother Benjamin.

Joseph could control himself no longer. He ordered all the Egyptians to leave the room. When he was alone with his brothers, he threw his arms wide, crying, "I am Joseph, your brother, whom you sold into slavery in Egypt. Do not be frightened or ashamed. It was not you but God who sent me here, to preserve life in the land during the time of famine. Go back to Canaan. Tell our father that God has made me a powerful man in Egypt. Come to me without delay. Bring your families, your flocks and herds, all your possessions. I will settle you in the land of Goshen. I will provide everything you need."

Jacob, his family, and all his household left Canaan and went down into Egypt. They settled in the land of Goshen, which is in the northern part of the country, between the cities of Rameses and Pithom. Jacob's children multiplied and prospered. God blessed their flocks and herds with abundance, and they continued to worship Him. Jacob's family remained a distinct people among the Egyptians. The Egyptians called them *Hebrews,* after their forefather Abraham, who had come *Across the River* from Ur. They also called them *Israelites* or *Children of Israel,* after their father Jacob, whom God had named *Israel* the night they wrestled together at Peniel.

Before he died, Jacob asked his sons to gather before him, along with Manasseh and Ephraim, the sons of Joseph. He gave them his blessing, each in turn.

Afterward, Jacob said, "My life is nearly over. Bury me in the land of Canaan, in the cave of Machpelah that my grandfather Abraham bought for our family to use as a burial place." Jacob lay back on his bed after saying these words and spoke no more. Soon he breathed his last, and was gathered to his ancestors.

Jacob's sons followed their father's bidding. They carried him to Canaan and buried him in the cave of Machpelah, between his father, Isaac, and his mother, Rebecca. Then Joseph and his brothers returned to Egypt.

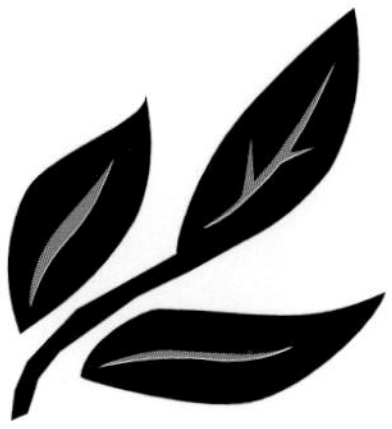

Out OF Egypt

The Story of Moses

Generations passed. The Egyptians forgot about Joseph and how he had saved their nation from famine. A new Pharaoh came to the throne. He noticed how numerous the Hebrews in Goshen had become and thought, *Who is this people that dwells among us? We must do something to reduce their numbers, or in time of war they may join our enemies and fight against us.*

Pharaoh sent taskmasters and overseers to the land of Goshen to enslave the Hebrews. The Egyptians put them in chains. They beat them with whips and set them to work at all sorts of heavy labor in the cities and in the fields. The children of Israel groaned in misery, and their cries went up to heaven.

The Birth of Moses

In spite of all the sufferings Pharaoh inflicted on the Israelites, their numbers increased. Pharaoh thought of a secret plan to stop them from multiplying. He summoned two Hebrew midwives named Shifrah and Puah. Pharaoh said to them, "Whenever you help a Hebrew woman give birth, take note of the newborn's sex. Let it live if it is a girl, but if it is a boy, kill it. Tell the mother it died naturally." Shifrah and Puah would have nothing to do with Pharaoh's plan. They delivered children as before, letting all live. When Pharaoh asked why the number of Israelites was not decreasing, they told him, "The Hebrew women are not Egyptians. They deliver their children very quickly. By the time the midwife arrives, the child is already born and nursing."

Pharaoh decided to punish the midwives for their defiance. He sent soldiers to kill them. But God protected the two women by making them invisible. The

Egyptians searched everywhere, but could not find them.

After this failure, Pharaoh changed his mind. He no longer attempted to kill the male children in secret. He commanded that in the future, whenever a Hebrew woman gave birth, the girl infants were to be saved, but the boys were to be thrown in the Nile River.

This decree caused great anguish among the Hebrews, who had to watch helplessly while Egyptian soldiers drowned their children or fed them to the crocodiles in the river. However, one woman was determined to protect her child. Her name was Jochebed.

She and her husband, Amram, had been married for several years. Like all Hebrews in Egypt, they suffered under Pharaoh's cruel decrees. Their first child, *Miriam*, was a girl. Her name means *Bitterness*, because she was born after the Egyptians enslaved the Hebrews and began to embitter their lives.

Though still a child herself, Miriam possessed wisdom beyond her years. Jochebed, a midwife, taught Miriam her skill. Miriam delivered Jochebed's second child, a boy named *Aaron*, meaning *Born in Sorrow*. Jochebed gave him that name because he was born after Pharaoh ordered the midwives to begin killing Hebrew children.

Together, Jochebed and Miriam saved many boys from death by delivering them in secret. Indeed, they were the two midwives whom Pharaoh tried to enlist in his secret plan. Shifrah and Puah were their Egyptian names. *Shifrah* means *Comforter; Puah* means *Helper*. Miriam, who was still a small child, helped her mother comfort the Hebrew women who were about to give birth.

In spite of the courage shown by his wife and daughter, Amram began to lose hope. He thought, *What is the use of having children? The boys are killed as soon as they are born. The girls grow up to be slaves.* He resolved to end this tragic cycle by divorcing Jochebed. Although he loved her dearly, he did not want to bring any more children into the world.

Miriam came home one day to find her mother weeping. She asked the reason. Jochebed told her, "Your father divorced me. He wishes to live apart. He does not want us to have any more children."

Miriam confronted her father. "You are more cruel than Pharaoh. He only wishes to get rid of the boys. You would eliminate the girls as well." Amram protested, but Miriam brushed his arguments aside. "Pharaoh deprives his victims of life in this world. You would prevent children from being born, thus depriving them not only of life in this world, but of life in the world to come. Pharaoh is a wicked man. I believe that God will not allow him to destroy our people. However, if we lose hope and cease to have children, our people will be no more. We ourselves will give Pharaoh the victory that God would deny him."

Miriam's arguments convinced Amram to change his mind. He remarried Jochebed with great rejoicing. Miriam and Aaron danced around their parents' wedding canopy, while angels proclaimed overhead, "Let the mother of children rejoice!"

That night Miriam had a dream. A man in a white linen robe appeared to her, saying, "Tell your mother and father that a son will be born to them. He will be cast into the waters, yet through him the waters will become dry land. He will perform wonders and miracles without number. He will redeem the children of Israel from slavery and raise them above other nations."

Six months later Jochebed gave birth to another child. Miriam delivered him in secret to hide his existence from the Egyptians. Although the boy was born early, he was large and fully formed. He was the most beautiful child among the Israelites. Jochebed and Amram called him *Tuvia*, meaning *God Is Good*. Miriam called him *Jekutiel*, which means *Trust in God*.

As the infant grew bigger, it became harder and harder for Jochebed to keep his existence a secret. Sooner or later, the Egyptians were bound to discover him.

Jochebed took a desperate chance to save her son. With Miriam's help, she wove a wicker basket just large enough to hold the infant. She lined it with clay and coated the outside with pitch to make it waterproof. Together, she and Miriam placed the basket among the tall reeds that grew along the banks of the Nile. Jochebed returned home, but Miriam remained behind, watching the floating cradle from a distance.

At midday, when the hot Egyptian sun reached its height, Pharaoh's daughter, the princess Thermutis, and her handmaidens came down to the river to bathe. The princess suddenly noticed a basket floating among the reeds. Curious, she sent one of her maids to fetch it. To her surprise, she discovered that it contained a child.

"How came this baby to be floating on the Nile?" the princess asked.

"It must be a Hebrew child!" one of her handmaidens exclaimed. "We should turn it over to the soldiers."

"No!" the princess insisted. "I do not care where this child comes from. I found him; he is mine. I will not allow him to be harmed."

"But who will nurse him?" the handmaidens asked.

Just then, Miriam came forward. She had been watching and listening the whole time. Miriam bowed to the princess and said, "I know a Hebrew woman who has just given birth. Her own child was taken away. She will make a good nursemaid for this one."

"Bring her to me," Thermutis ordered.

Miriam ran home to fetch her mother. Thermutis gave the baby to her, saying, "Take this child to your home. Nurse him and care for him. When he is weaned, bring him to me."

And so it happened that the baby came to be nursed by his own mother and cared for by his own sister. When he was old enough to eat solid food, they brought him to the palace. Thermutis raised him as if he were her own child. She named him *Moses,* which means, *I Took Him from the River.*

Moses' First Test

Moses grew up in Pharaoh's palace, enjoying all the privileges and luxuries of an Egyptian prince. However, his mother and sister continued to visit him. The ties that bound Moses to his people were never broken.

Pharaoh had many wives, and many sons and daughters. He never knew of Moses' existence until the child was three years old. One day he noticed him playing among the royal children. "Who is that lovely boy?" Pharaoh remarked, for Moses' strength and beauty outshined that of all the other princes and princesses.

"He is your daughter Thermutis' son," the Egyptians told Pharaoh.

Pharaoh sent for his daughter. "Why did you not tell me you had a child?"

"He is not mine, Father," the princess said. "I found him when he was an infant. He was floating in a basket in the Nile."

Pharaoh's face darkened. "Perhaps he is one of the Hebrew children. In that case, he must be put to death."

"How could he be a Hebrew?" the princess protested. "Look how beautiful and strong he is! Surely, he is like the heroes of old, sent down by the gods."

Since Thermutis was his favorite daughter, Pharaoh allowed the child to live.

He soon came to love Moses as if he were his own grandchild, holding him on his lap as he sat at the table, feeding him from his own plate, and letting him drink from his own cup. Pharaoh ordered the royal astrologers to cast Moses' horoscope, as was done for all the princes and princesses of Egypt. The astrologers returned with alarming news.

"This child, whom you hold on your lap and cherish as if he were your own, will one day strike the crown from your head. You should put him to death at once."

Pharaoh refused to accept this prophecy. "I will not have Moses killed. You are wrong. You have made a mistake somewhere in your calculations."

"There is no mistake," the astrologers insisted. "If you do not believe us, we can arrange a test to prove we are correct. Take two baskets. Fill one with jewels and the other with hot coals. Present them to Moses and observe him closely. If he reaches out to the coals, he is harmless and our calculations are wrong; you need not fear. But if he reaches out to the jewels, that is a sign that he seeks your crown. In time, he will take it, if you do not put him to death."

Pharaoh ordered that the test be held. Two baskets were filled: one with jewels; the other with glowing coals. Pharaoh's servants placed them before the throne. Pharaoh held Moses on his lap so he could see both baskets and reach for whichever one he chose.

Moses looked first at the coals, then at the jewels. The coals were uncomfortably hot, but the jewels glittered and sparkled like pretty toys. Pharaoh and the rest of his court held their breath as the child lifted his arms and began reaching toward the jewels. But God was watching over Moses. An unseen angel flew down, seized Moses' tiny hand by the wrist, and pushed it into the burning coals. The child shrieked with pain and fright. He put his burned fingers into his mouth to cool them. A piece of coal stuck to his flesh and burned his tongue. Moses' life was saved. However, because the coal had scarred his mouth, Moses grew up to be poor of speech. He stammered and stuttered. No matter how hard he tried, he could never speak clearly.

Moses Flees Egypt

When Moses was twenty years old, Pharaoh appointed him to be one of the governors of Egypt. Moses rode his chariot throughout the land. Day after day he saw the sufferings inflicted on the Israelites by the Egyptians. His heart went out to his people. He felt their misery as if it were his own, for despite his royal dress and high rank, Moses knew he was one of them. Every time he saw an Egyptian beating an Israelite slave, he felt as if the lash were stinging his own flesh.

Whenever Moses saw a group of Israelites engaged in hard labor, he got down from his chariot to help them. He hauled bricks and stones. The Egyptian overseers were outraged, but could do nothing since Moses was the son of Pharaoh and a governor of Egypt.

God looked down from heaven. He saw Moses' compassion for his people and how he tried to help them whenever possible. God said, "Moses proves himself worthy. He will redeem My people from slavery."

But first, God put Moses to a test. One day, as Moses struggled to help a group of Israelites move a heavy stone, an Egyptian overseer came forward and lashed him with his whip. Lashings and beatings were part of a slave's lot. Moses, however, was a prince of Egypt. He had never been struck with a whip before. Enraged, he turned on the overseer and struck him dead.

The Israelite slaves moaned with fear. Moses had killed an overseer. They would surely pay with their lives if the deed became known. Moses buried the overseer in the sand. He said to the slaves, "Sand is silent. It makes no sound when someone steps on it. For your sake and mine, be as silent as sand. Tell no one what I have done today."

The Israelites promised to keep the secret. But God, looking down from heaven, was not pleased. "Moses must learn to control his anger before he can lead My people."

The next day, when Moses drove out in his chariot, he saw two Israelites quarreling. "Brothers, do not fight," Moses said to them. "We must all stand together against the Egyptians."

The two men glared at Moses. "Why should we listen to you?" one sneered.

"Will you kill us as you killed the Egyptian?" the other added.

Moses realized that his crime was no secret. Pharaoh was sure to hear of it.

"The astrologers were right after all," Pharaoh said when he learned of the overseer's murder. "Who but another Hebrew would be concerned about an overseer beating a gang of slaves?" He ordered that Moses be put to death.

Moses left Egypt that night. He escaped from the palace moments before Pharaoh's soldiers came to arrest him.

Moses and Jethro

Moses drove his chariot night and day. He passed the last Egyptian border outpost and continued on into the desert until he came to the land of the Midianites, a tribe of nomads. Seeing a well nearby, he stopped to refresh himself and water his horses.

As Moses sat beside the well, he saw a group of seven young women approaching, herding a flock of sheep. The women drew water from the well for their animals. Before they finished, another group of shepherds appeared. These men did not wait for the women to finish. They pushed them aside, chasing them and their sheep from the well. Then they took the water that the young women had drawn and gave it to their own animals.

Moses became angry. He scolded the shepherds for their selfishness. Although the men outnumbered Moses, his fearlessness and indignation frightened them. They took their sheep and fled. God, looking down from heaven, was pleased. Moses had passed an important test. He showed himself willing to stand up for the weak and oppressed, even when they were not his own people. He also controlled his temper, for he did not use violence against the shepherds or threaten them in any way.

After the shepherds withdrew, Moses drew water for the seven young women. He labored in the hot sun, pulling up bucket after bucket until even the smallest lamb had drunk its fill.

These seven young women were daughters of a prominent Midianite named Jethro. When they returned home, they told their father how an Egyptian stranger had driven away the bullying shepherds and drawn up water for their flocks.

"Where is this man?" Jethro asked his daughters. "How could you leave him standing beside the well after he did so much to help you? Go back. Invite him to our home to share our bread with us."

Jethro's daughters brought Moses back to their father's tent. Moses remained with Jethro for many years. He married Jethro's oldest daughter, Zipporah. In time, they had a son. Moses named him *Gershom,* which means, *I Was a Stranger There.* Even though the Midianites accepted Moses as a member of their own tribe, he still felt like a stranger. His ties to his own people remained strong.

Moses knew that their sufferings would never end as long as they remained slaves to the Egyptians.

The Burning Bush

The time of redemption was approaching. A new Pharaoh took his place on the throne of Egypt. He was even more cruel than his predecessor. He increased the labor of the children of Israel and doubled their punishment. The Israelites cried out to God for help. Their prayers rose to heaven. This time God was ready to answer.

Meanwhile, Moses still tended Jethro's flocks in the desert country surrounding a mountain known as Horeb, or Sinai. One day he noticed a burning bush. This was not unusual. The desert country was filled with dry bushes that caught fire when struck by lightning. However, Moses noticed something strange about this bush. Flames danced on every branch, but the bush was not consumed.

Moses approached to examine this curious sight. Suddenly he heard a still, small voice speaking to him from out of the bush. "Moses!"

He answered, "Here I am!"

"Do not come closer. Take off your sandals. You are standing on holy ground."

Moses slipped the sandals from his feet and stood barefoot on the earth. The voice spoke again. "I am the God of your forefathers, the God of Abraham, Isaac, and Jacob."

Moses drew his cloak across his face. He realized that God Himself was speaking to him.

The voice continued. "I have seen the sufferings of My people in Egypt. I have heard their cries and felt their misery. I will rescue My people from the Egyptians and bring them to a rich land flowing with milk and honey. Go now, for I am sending you back to Egypt to deliver the children of Israel."

Moses gasped. "Who am I that I should go before Pharaoh and tell him to release my people?"

"Do not be afraid of Pharaoh," God said. "I will be with you."

"But what will I tell the children of Israel when they ask who sent me? What will I say when they ask Your name?"

"I AM WHO I AM," said God. "Say to the children of Israel, 'I AM sent me.' Gather the elders of Israel together. Tell them that the God of their forefathers has sent you to bring them out of Egypt. Go before Pharaoh. Tell him to allow My people three days of liberty to worship Me in the desert. Pharaoh will deny your request. Then I will put forth My hand and strike Egypt with wonders never seen. Pharaoh will release you after that. You will go forth in freedom."

Moses was still reluctant to do as God asked. "What if no one believes me?"

"What do you have in your hand?" said God.

"My shepherd's staff."

"Throw it on the ground."

Moses threw his staff on the ground. It turned into a snake. Moses drew back in surprise.

"Do not be afraid. Reach down and take it by the tail."

Moses reached down. As soon as he grasped the snake's tail, it became a wooden rod again.

"What if they still don't believe me?" asked Moses.

God told Moses to put his arm under his cloak. When he drew it out, it was covered with the white sores and scabs of leprosy.

"Put your arm back under your cloak," said God. Moses did. When he drew it out again, his skin was smooth and clean.

"If they do not believe the first sign, show them the second," said God. "If they still do not believe, take a cup of water from the Nile. Pour it on the ground. The water will turn to blood."

In spite of these miraculous signs, Moses still did not want to return to Egypt. "O God, why send me? I am not a speaker. Words come slowly to me. My tongue trips and stammers."

"Who gives human beings a mouth? Who determines if a person can or cannot speak? Can or cannot hear? Can or cannot see? It is I, God Alone! Go now. I will be your mouth. I will teach you what to say."

Moses continued to hold back. "Please, God! Send someone else. Anyone but me!"

God grew impatient with Moses. "Remember your brother Aaron. He helped your mother and sister hide Hebrew babies from the Egyptian soldiers. Aaron is not afraid of Pharaoh, and he is a good speaker. When you go down to Egypt, he will come to meet you. I will tell you what to say. You will tell Aaron. I will teach you both what to do. Do not forget to bring your staff with you. With it, you will perform signs and wonders before the Egyptians."

The Ten Plagues

Moses returned to Egypt. Along the way he saw Aaron coming to meet him. Moses told Aaron what God had said to him from the midst of the burning bush. Aaron gathered the elders of Israel together. Aaron repeated God's words while Moses showed them the miraculous signs. The elders and the people of Israel believed that God had heard their prayers. They bowed down and worshiped, hailing Moses as their leader. They promised to follow him wherever he led them.

Moses, Aaron, and the elders set out to meet with Pharaoh. Along the way the elders lost courage. One by one, they dropped behind and went home. When Moses and Aaron arrived at the palace gate, they were alone.

Sixty thousand soldiers surrounded the palace, all under strict orders to admit no one without Pharaoh's permission. God made Moses and Aaron invisible. An angel led them past the soldiers to Pharaoh's throne.

The two brothers suddenly appeared before Pharaoh. "Thus says the God of Israel. Allow My people to go forth to worship Me for three days in the desert," Aaron said.

Pharaoh flew into a rage. "How dare you come before me without permission! Release the lions!" he shouted. Pharaoh's soldiers let loose the lions that guarded Pharaoh's throne. The savage beasts bounded toward Moses and Aaron to tear them to pieces. Moses raised his staff. The lions rolled at his feet like kittens.

"I know you! You are Moses!" Pharaoh cried. Moses and Pharaoh had grown up together in the palace. Pharaoh had always hated Moses because he feared his father would make Moses king in his place. Now he said, "My father condemned you to death for killing an overseer. I will carry out the sentence." He ordered his soldiers to cut off Moses' head. But God turned Moses' neck to ivory. When the soldiers struck at him, their swords broke.

The frightened Egyptians scurried away as Aaron repeated his words: "Thus says the God of Israel: Allow My people to worship Me in the desert for three days."

"Who is this God of Israel? I know all the gods of Egypt and the gods of the neighboring lands. I never heard of this god, and I will certainly never allow my slaves to leave Egypt."

Aaron spoke again. "Our God, the God of the Hebrew people, has spoken. If you do not heed his words, He will fill your land with death and destruction."

Pharaoh laughed. "I don't believe you! Why are you making trouble for your people? Mind your own business. Don't fill their heads with strange notions about God and freedom, or they will suffer."

The next day Pharaoh summoned the overseers of his work gangs, saying to them, "You once gave the Hebrews straw to mix with mud to make bricks. From now on, let them find their own straw, but their quota of bricks will remain the same. Our slaves are lazy. They want a holiday to go to the desert to worship their god. Give them more work. Then they won't have time to listen to troublemakers."

The overseers obeyed Pharaoh's orders. The slaves no longer received straw to make bricks. Instead, they had to gather their own straw in the fields. Yet each slave was required to make just as many bricks as before. Anyone falling short by even one brick was severely beaten.

The people cursed Moses. "What have you done to us? We were happy in Egypt before you came!"

Moses cried to God, "Why did you send me? The children of Israel suffer more than ever. Pharaoh will not listen to me. He will not let them go. I have only made their misery worse. Better that I had remained in Midian, tending Jethro's sheep."

God spoke gently to Moses. "Do not despair. I told you these things would happen when I spoke to you out of the burning bush. Return to Pharaoh, you and Aaron. Tell him to send the children of Israel forth from Egypt. Pharaoh will ask for a sign. Tell Aaron to throw his rod on the ground. It will become a snake. Then Pharaoh will know that I, the God of Israel, sent you."

Moses and Aaron returned to Pharaoh. Aaron spoke the words that God commanded. As God predicted, Pharaoh refused to believe them. "How do I know your God has sent you? Show me a sign!"

Aaron threw down his staff. It became a snake.

Pharaoh scoffed. "My magicians can do the same." The magicians of Egypt came forward. As each threw his staff on the ground, it became a snake. However, the snake that had once been Aaron's rod swallowed all the others. Aaron picked it up by the tail, and it became a rod again.

In spite of this sign, Pharaoh refused to yield. He dismissed Moses and Aaron, calling them tricksters and charlatans.

Moses and Aaron went down to the banks of the Nile. Aaron struck the water with his staff. At once, all the water in the river turned to blood. So did the water in Egypt's canals and pools. Not even the water in cisterns, tanks, and jars was spared. Only in Goshen, where the Israelites lived, was there water to drink.

This first plague frightened Pharaoh, but he hardened his heart and refused to let the children of Israel go.

Moses and Aaron went down to the Nile again. Aaron stretched his rod out over the water. Hordes of frogs, thousands upon thousands of them, came hopping out of the river. They swarmed into Pharaoh's palace. They jumped on his bed, into his clothes, even into his drinking cup. Frogs infested the whole land of Egypt. There was no escaping them, except in Goshen, where the children of Israel lived.

Pharaoh summoned Moses and Aaron. "Take these frogs away, and I will free your people!" The frogs died all at once. The Egyptians shoveled them into heaps by the thousands. The whole land stank with rotting frogs.

But once again Pharaoh hardened his heart. He refused to let the children of Israel go.

God spoke to Moses and Aaron again. Aaron stretched out his rod and struck the dust. It whirled up into a cloud, filling the whole land with lice. They covered the Egyptians from head to foot. All the people, from Pharaoh on his throne to the poorest beggar squatting in the street, were infested with vermin. They covered animals and cattle. Only in the land of Goshen was there relief from them. The Egyptians cried out in misery, but Pharaoh hardened his heart. He refused to let the children of Israel go.

God brought a fourth plague on Egypt; a plague of wild beasts. Animals never seen before swarmed out of the desert. They attacked people in the streets and in their homes. Weapons were useless; the animals refused to die, even when struck with swords and arrows. Terrified, Pharaoh sent for Moses and Aaron. He promised to free the Israelites if God would remove the plague from Egypt. God heard Pharaoh's words. The animals returned to the desert. But once they were gone, Pharaoh hardened his heart again. He refused to let the children of Israel go.

God struck Egypt with disease. All the animals in the land became sick. The prize horses that pulled Pharaoh's chariot died. So did the sacred animals that the Egyptians worshiped in their temples: the sacred bull, the sacred ibis, the sacred cat, the sacred hippopotamus, and the sacred crocodile. Panic struck the Egyptians. If the gods of Egypt could not protect their sacred animals, how could they protect those who worshiped them? The Egyptians cried out to Pharaoh once more. But again, Pharaoh hardened his heart and refused to let the children of Israel go.

God told Moses and Aaron to take handfuls of ashes from the nearest furnace and fling them skyward. The ashes turned into a cloud of dust that covered the land of Egypt. As the dust fell, it caused the exposed flesh of the Egyptians to erupt in oozing sores and boils. Pharaoh's magicians were helpless, so covered with boils that they could not stand. The Egyptians lay in the streets, groaning with misery. But Pharaoh hardened his heart and refused to let the children of Israel go.

Then God commanded Moses to take his staff and stretch it toward the sky. Dark clouds rolled in to cover the sun. Lightning crackled. Thunder boomed as a mighty hailstorm descended on Egypt. Hailstones broke the limbs from trees and smashed down crops in the fields. Any person or animal caught outside was killed. Only in Goshen did no hail fall.

Pharaoh sent for Moses and Aaron. He promised to free the Israelites if the hail ceased.

Moses stretched his arms toward heaven. The hail stopped.

As soon as it did, Pharaoh forgot his promise. He hardened his heart and refused to let the children of Israel go.

Moses stretched his hand over Egypt again. An east wind arose. It blew all night and all day, bringing a swarm of locusts that blackened the sky. The locusts descended on Egypt, devouring every blade of grass, every leaf, every green, growing thing. Whatever survived the hail, the locusts destroyed. But not in Goshen. Not even one locust landed there.

Pharaoh summoned Moses and Aaron. He humbled himself before them.

"Pray to your God," he pleaded. "Ask Him to remove these locusts, for if they remain in Egypt, there will be famine in the land."

Moses prayed to God for the sake of Pharaoh and the Egyptians. God called forth a mighty west wind that blew the locusts out to sea. Not a single locust remained in the land of Egypt. But once again, Pharaoh forgot his promise. He hardened his heart and refused to let the children of Israel go.

Now God said to Moses, "Stretch forth your hand to heaven, and darkness will descend on Egypt."

So it happened. Darkness covered the land for three days. There was no difference between day and night. Neither the sun, the moon, nor the stars could be seen. The darkness was like a thick blanket. People could not see their neighbors even while standing next to them. Lighting torches or candles did no good. The flames gave off no light. Only in Goshen, where the children of Israel dwelled, did the sun shine.

Pharaoh summoned Moses in haste. "Go at once!" he cried. "Take your people with you. Only their flocks and cattle must remain behind."

"Nothing will be left behind!" Moses told him. "Not a lamb, not a calf, not a hoof or horn will remain. The whole people Israel and all they possess must go forth."

"I give you freedom, and you reject it! Get out! Do not come before me again!" cried Pharaoh. "If I see your face, I will kill you!"

The First Passover

God spoke to Moses. "I will bring one last plague on Egypt. This time Pharaoh will surely let My people go; he will drive them in haste from his country."

Moses came before Pharaoh one last time. He had no fear of death. Nor did he ask Pharaoh again to set the Hebrews free. Instead, he told him what was about to happen.

"Tonight, at midnight, God will pass over the land of Egypt. Every firstborn in Egypt will die, from the firstborn son of Pharaoh sitting upon his throne to the firstborn of the humble maidservant grinding grain, as well as the firstborn of every beast. There will be weeping and wailing throughout the land whose like has not been heard unto this time, and whose like will not be heard again. Only the children of Israel will be safe. Not even a stray dog will bark at them. This will prove it is no accident; God can tell the difference between Egypt and Israel. Your subjects will come running to me. They will go down on their knees and beg me to take my people out of Egypt. And I will."

Moses did not wait to hear Pharaoh's answer. He turned around after speaking these words and walked away without looking back.

God spoke to Moses again, saying, "Gather the people of Israel. Tell them that from this day forth, on the tenth day of the month of Nissan, every household must select an unblemished lamb or kid from their flocks or herds. On the afternoon of the fourteenth day of the month, they are to slaughter it. Sprinkle some of its blood on the doorposts and on the lintel of the house where each lamb is to be eaten. It must not be boiled or partly cooked. They must roast the lamb whole over an open fire, and eat it that night with unleavened bread and bitter herbs.

"This is how you are to eat it—with your belt bound tightly around your waist, with sandals on your feet, and with your staff in your hand; as if you were preparing to go on a long journey. You must do so tonight, too, for on this night I will go through the land of Egypt, striking down every firstborn, both man and beast. The blood on the doorways will mark your homes. When I see it, I will pass over you and your families. I will not strike you dead as I strike the Egyptians.

"You will remember this day forever, and celebrate it as a festival of deliverance for generations to come. For seven days you must eat only unleavened bread. You must cleanse your houses of all leavening as well. In time, when you come to the land I have promised you, your children will ask, 'What is this you are doing?' You must explain to them, 'It is the Passover sacrifice to God, a reminder of when He passed over the houses of our people in Egypt. He struck down the Egyptians, but He protected us.'"

Moses and Aaron gathered the people of Israel together to give them these instructions. They told them to prepare for a long journey, for they were surely going to leave Egypt that night. The people of Israel prayed to God with Moses and Aaron. Then they hurried to their homes to get ready for the events to come.

God fulfilled His promise. That night He struck down every firstborn in the land of Egypt, high and low, from Pharaoh's firstborn son to the firstborn sons of the prisoners sitting in the dungeon. The firstborn of every animal also perished.

A great wailing arose throughout Egypt, for there was not a family in the land that did not lose a beloved father, brother, or son.

Pharaoh awoke in the night to the sound of weeping. His heir, the crown prince, lay dead. Fearing for his own life, he sent for Moses and Aaron.

"Get up! Gather your people! Leave Egypt at once! Take the Israelites and all their belongings. Go wherever you please. Only leave as quickly as you can." Pharaoh threw himself down on his knees before Moses. "Give me your blessing. Protect me from the terror that flies overhead. Don't let me die like my poor son, for I am a firstborn, too."

Moses gave Pharaoh his blessing. Then he and Aaron hurried to join their people. The children of Israel numbered six hundred thousand when they left Egypt. They were organized into twelve tribes based on their descent from the sons of Jacob. These tribes were those of Reuben, Simeon, Levi, Judah, Zebulun, Issachar, Dan, Gad, Asher, Naphtali, Benjamin, and the two half-tribes Ephraim and Manasseh, descended from the two sons of Joseph. A large group of people of other nationalities went with them, for people from all different lands worked as slaves in Egypt. These people had seen the power of God working through Moses. They wished to link their destinies with those of their Hebrew neighbors.

This vast multitude followed the banners of the tribes from the city of Rameses to the town of Succoth, on the borders of Egypt. They walked on foot, driving their flocks and herds before them, carrying everything they possessed on their backs. They left in such haste that the bread they prepared did not have time to bake, so they wrapped their unleavened dough in their cloaks and took it with them.

On the Shores of the Red Sea

The Israelites journeyed through the desert from Succoth to the shores of the Red Sea. God Himself led them, taking the form of a pillar of cloud by day and a pillar of fire by night. When they reached the sea, they waited for God to show them what to do. They could not go back to Egypt, and with the sea in front of them, they could not go forward.

Meanwhile, Pharaoh and his officers recovered from their fright. "Who is going to work for us now that we have let the Israelites go?" they asked each other. Pharaoh realized he had made a mistake. He called for his chariot and set out with his entire army to bring the Israelites back.

The Israelites were camped beside the Red Sea when they looked up and saw a cloud of dust rising in the distance. As the cloud came nearer, they saw it was Pharaoh and his chariot army bearing down on them.

"What have you done to us?" they cried to Moses. "Are there no graves in Egypt that you brought us here to die? Why did we ever listen to you? Better to remain slaves in Egypt than to perish in the desert!"

Moses spoke to them calmly. "Do not lose hope. Stay where you are, and you will soon witness the great miracle that God will perform this day. Do you see the Egyptians coming toward us in all their strength? After today, you will never see them again. God Himself will fight for us. We have but to hold to our faith and keep still."

Moses prayed to God to help the children of Israel. God answered, "Why do you cry to me? Tell the people to go forward. As they enter the sea, take your hand and stretch it out over the water. The sea will divide. The Israelites will march across it as if they were walking on dry ground."

Moses could not believe that he was being given the awesome power to split the sea. He said to God, "At the beginning of Creation, You divided the sea from the land. Surely I, a mere human being, am not able to divide the sea further."

As Moses hesitated, a leader of the tribe of Judah came forward. Nachshon, son of Aminadab, said to the people, "I would rather die than be a slave. If we remain where we are, we will be captured by Pharaoh's army. There is only one way to go—forward, into the sea!"

"But we will be drowned if we walk into the sea!" the people protested.

"Some may die," said Nachshon. "But I do not believe that God brought us here to perish. With God's help, at least some of us will survive. Who will come with me?" Nachshon began walking into the sea. The Israelites held back, unsure what to do. Suddenly, Miriam, Moses' sister, took her tambourine. Beating it with her fingers, she began to dance. At the same time she sang a song of victory.

I sing to the Lord, for He is great!
Horse and rider He has hurled into the sea . . .

The women of Israel trusted Miriam even more than they trusted Moses. While Moses had been growing up in Pharaoh's palace or hiding with Jethro in the desert, Miriam had been with them, delivering their children, caring for them in sickness, comforting them in their misery. Miriam had brought them hope in the midst of despair. The women of Israel picked up their drums, harps, tambourines, and cymbals and began following Miriam in the dance.

> *Your right hand, Lord, is radiant with power!*
> *Your right hand, Lord, smashes the enemy to pieces!*

Step by step, Miriam led the women into the sea. They had no fear, because God and Miriam were with them.

When the men of Israel saw the women following Miriam, they felt ashamed for their own lack of faith. They followed the women forward until the entire people entered the sea.

They kept walking forward until the water rose to their necks. Still, Moses hesitated, frightened by the power that God had placed in his hands. God cried to him, "Why do you wait? The people believe in Me. The water is up to their necks, and still they press forward. How much longer will you delay?"

Moses dared hesitate no longer. He stretched his hand out over the sea. A strong east wind arose. It blew with mighty force until the water parted. A path formed through the middle of the sea. The waters piled themselves like a high wall on either side. The Israelites walked across the bottom of the sea as if they were walking across dry land.

That day saw many miracles. The walls of the sea were transparent. As the Israelites passed between them, they could see all the strange creatures and all the treasures that lay in its depths. Whatever anyone desired was there. If a person wanted riches, he had but to reach through the watery wall to grasp a handful of pearls or diamonds. If a person was hungry, she could reach through the wall and find whatever she wanted to eat. A stream of clear water flowed along the undersea path, providing water for the children of Israel, as well as for their flocks and herds. The Israelites were so entranced by the wonders at the bottom of the sea that Moses had to hurry them along or they might have chosen to remain there forever.

No sooner had the last Israelite crossed, when Pharaoh and his chariots charged onto the undersea path. Unlike the Israelites, they did not find the way easy. It was slick with mud and choked with sharp stones. Horses slipped and fell.

Seaweed clogged the chariot wheels. Axles broke. Wheels fell off. Pharaoh's swift chariot army found itself hopelessly mired.

Then God told Moses to stretch his hand over the sea once more. The waters swept back to their place and covered the Egyptians. Of all that vast host, not a single man, horse, or chariot escaped. All perished at the bottom of the sea.

When the Israelites saw the Egyptians lying dead on the seashore, they sang a song. More than ever, they believed in the power of God and His servant, Moses.

In the Desert

The Israelites now began a long journey into the Wilderness of Shur, a frightful place that extended for hundreds of miles without a single well or shade tree. Its only inhabitants were snakes and scorpions. These creatures were so venomous that if one crawled across the shadow of a bird flying overhead, the bird would die instantly.

The Israelites struggled across the desert. Soon their pots, their jugs, and their goatskin water bags were all empty. Sheep and cattle dropped in their tracks. Children cried for water, but there was none to give them.

Moses pleaded with the people not to lose hope. Scouts reported an oasis ahead. The Israelites arrived, only to find that the water in its wells was so bitter that they could not drink it. They named the oasis *Marah*, which means *Bitterness*.

The people cried to Moses in desperation and fear. "Did you bring us out of Egypt so that we could die here of thirst? Give us water!"

But Moses had no water to give them. Moses prayed to God to show him what to do. God answered his prayer. He showed Moses a laurel tree. The laurel's sap is bitter, but after Moses took a branch from the tree, scratched the Name of God on its bark, and threw it into one of the wells, the foul water became sweet.

The Israelites quenched their thirst and praised God, Who had rescued them once more. They continued across the desert to the oasis at Elim. Here they found twelve wells, one for each of the twelve tribes. Seventy palm trees provided shade; one for each of the elders of Israel. They rested at Elim, filled their skins and water jars, then marched on across the Wilderness of Sin.

Food grew scarce. The Israelites had consumed everything they brought from Egypt. They began to feel pangs of hunger.

"Better that we had died in Egypt!" they cried to Moses and Aaron. "Back there we had meat in our stew pots and as much bread as we could swallow." Hunger and distress had caused them to forget the miseries of slavery. The Egyptians had never given them enough to eat. In Egypt, the flour for their bread was mixed with sand and pebbles. Their only meat came from grasshoppers and locusts that the children caught, for the Egyptians would not even allow them to fish in the Nile.

Moses prayed to God for guidance. God answered, saying, "I have heard My people grumbling. Tell them that they will eat meat this afternoon, and tomorrow morning they will have bread, as much as they can hold. Then they will know that I am truly God."

That evening, just before the sun set, a flock of quail flew into the camp. The Israelites caught the birds easily. There were more than enough for all to eat their fill.

The next morning they awoke to find that dew had fallen around the camp in the night. The dew evaporated, leaving behind a strange, thin, golden crust. It looked like wafers of frost.

"What is this?" the Israelites asked Moses.

"It is *manna*, the food of the angels," he told them. "This is the food that God has provided for you, according to His promise. Gather as much as you require for your daily needs. Remember, on the sixth day you must gather enough for two days, for manna will not fall on the Sabbath."

Manna was a miraculous food. Some gathered more, some gathered less, but every person had as much to eat as he or she required. No one went hungry. Manna required no preparation. It did not have to be peeled or cleaned, baked or cooked. It could be eaten as it was, right from the ground.

Manna had no taste, and yet it had every taste. If a person desired a certain food, the manna would taste just like it. Small children said it tasted like milk. Young men and women thought it had the taste of bread and meat. For old, toothless people it had the taste of honey, and for the sick it tasted like barley mixed with honey and oil.

However, there were limits to manna. It had to be gathered in the early morning, for after the sun came up it melted away like dew. It could not be stored or put away. Anyone who tried to hide an extra portion found it stinking and crawling with worms. Only manna set aside for the Sabbath could be preserved, and then it was preserved perfectly. Flies and insects did not crawl on it. Mice would not nibble it. It remained as fresh as when it was gathered.

In this way, God watched over the Israelites in the desert. He gave them food. He protected them against their enemies. Yet they did not cease to complain. As former slaves, they were used to their masters providing everything. They had no faith in themselves. When faced with difficulty, they became frightened and angry. Then they turned on Moses.

The fierce desert sun burned down. Heat dried up the wells. People fell to the ground, dying of thirst. Instead of seeking new springs, the Israelites hurried to Moses.

"Give us water!" they demanded.

"I have no water," Moses told them.

The people cursed Moses and pelted him with stones. "Is this why you brought us out of Egypt, so we could die of thirst in the desert?"

"Why do you cry to me?" Moses shouted above the uproar. "Pray to God. He is the One Who provides water."

The Israelites would not be satisfied. They threatened Moses, demanding that he give them water at once. Moses appealed to God for help. "What am I to do with these people? They are terrified they are going to die of thirst. They beg me for water, but I have none to give them. They are at the end of their patience. If I don't give them water, they will stone me."

A pile of rocks lay close to the camp. God instructed Moses to lead the people to the rocks. When they gathered there, Moses had the people choose a rock. Moses tapped it with his staff, and water gushed forth. People and animals drank until they quenched their thirst.

As God provided food, He also provided water. A miraculous well appeared. The Israelites called it *Miriam's Well,* in honor of Moses' sister. Miriam's Well was a beautiful fountain shooting streams of water high into the air. It never ran dry. Miriam's Well accompanied the children of Israel throughout their journey across the desert. When they marched, it moved with them. When they camped, it rested close by. The miraculous well never left their side, until they finally entered the land of Canaan.

Soon after this, the Israelites encamped at a place called Rephidim. Suddenly they were attacked by a fierce tribe of desert nomads called the Amalekites. The attack came so swiftly that the people of Israel would have been annihilated had God not covered them with a cloud. The Amalekites could not penetrate the cloud or pierce it with spears or arrows. They camped around it, knowing that the Israelites would have to emerge sooner or later.

The people of Israel asked Moses to lead them into battle. He refused, not because he was afraid, but because an old man like himself would be of better use praying for victory than wielding a sword. He appointed a fearless warrior, Joshua, son of Nun, to command the forces of Israel. Joshua selected the bravest men from among the Israelites and led them out of the cloud to fight the Amalekites.

Meanwhile, Moses, Aaron, and Hur, Miriam's husband, climbed to the top of a nearby hill to watch the battle. When Moses raised his arms, the Amalekites retreated. However, soon his arms grew tired. He had to lower them; then the Israelites retreated. Back and forth the battle went until Moses grew so weary, he could hardly hold up his arms at all. Aaron and Hur sat Moses down upon a stone. Standing on either side of him, they lifted his arms and held them up until sunset when Joshua finally overcame the last of the Amalekites.

Moses took the stone on which he sat and erected an altar to God to give thanks for the victory. He called the place *Adonai Nisi,* meaning *God Is My Banner.*

The Ten Commandments

The Israelites continued their journey. They entered the Wilderness of Sinai and camped before a mountain known as Sinai, or Horeb. The mountain was familiar to Moses. It was here that he had encountered the burning bush.

As the Israelites pitched their tents before the mountain, a party of Midianites appeared. It was headed by Jethro, Moses' father-in-law. He had brought Moses' wife, Zipporah, and their sons to join him.

Jethro marveled that Moses could govern such an unruly mass of people. He noticed that the Israelites brought every little problem to Moses. If one child broke another's bead necklace, they came to Moses. If one man's dog chased another man's goat, they came to Moses. Finally Jethro told his son-in-law, "This is no way to lead a people. You will exhaust yourself trying to settle every little matter, and the Israelites will never learn to govern themselves."

"What can I do?" Moses asked. "The people ask for justice."

"And they will have it. Appoint officers to govern the people. Appoint governors and lieutenants to be in charge of each group of one thousand, one hundred, fifty, and ten. Let them judge the small matters. They can bring the important ones to you."

Moses appreciated Jethro's wisdom. He appointed officers to judge the people. The Israelites no longer had to wait for days to settle small matters, and Moses no longer had to sit in front of his tent, judging the people from morning till night. Moses thanked Jethro for his help. Then Jethro returned to his own country.

Now God summoned Moses to come to the top of the mountain. There He told him, "Go to the people of Israel. Say to them, 'You have seen for yourselves how I dealt with the Egyptians. You have seen how I carried you safely on the wings of eagles and brought you here to me. Now I say to you, if you will listen to My words and keep My laws and My commandments, you will be closer to Me than all the other nations. You will be a nation of priests, a holy people.'"

Moses carried these words back to the elders of Israel. Without hesitation, they said, "We will do whatever God asks."

God ordered Moses to have the people prepare for great events that were to come. They were not to approach the mountain or attempt to climb it. Anyone who did so would die.

On the third day, the Israelites followed Moses out of the camp and stood at the foot of the mountain. A dense cloud of smoke covered the peak. Thunder rolled. Lightning flashed. Loud blasts from a ram's horn split the air.

The top of the mountain appeared to be on fire. A pillar of smoke ascended from the summit like smoke pouring from the chimney of a furnace. The whole mountain shook. The ram's horn blasts grew louder and louder as God Himself descended upon the mountain in all His terrifying glory.

Moses climbed up the mountain to speak with God face-to-face. God gave Moses these Ten Commandments:

1. I AM THE LORD, YOUR GOD, WHO BROUGHT YOU FORTH FROM THE LAND OF EGYPT, FROM THE HOUSE OF SLAVERY. YOU WILL WORSHIP NO OTHER GOD.

2. YOU WILL NOT MAKE IMAGES OR STATUES OF ANY LIVING THING ON EARTH, HEAVEN, OR UNDER THE SEA; YOU WILL NOT BOW DOWN TO THEM OR WORSHIP THEM. FOR I AM A JEALOUS GOD.

3. YOU MUST NEVER USE GOD'S NAME LIGHTLY, FOR I WILL NOT FORGIVE THOSE WHO DO.

4. REMEMBER TO KEEP THE SABBATH DAY HOLY. SIX DAYS YOU WILL LABOR, BUT THE SABBATH IS A DAY DEVOTED TO GOD. NEITHER YOU, YOUR CHILDREN, YOUR SERVANTS, YOUR ANIMALS, NOR THE FOREIGNERS WHO DWELL AMONG YOU MAY DO ANY KIND OF WORK. FOR GOD CREATED HEAVEN AND EARTH IN SIX DAYS, AND ON THE SEVENTH DAY HE RESTED. THAT IS WHY GOD BLESSED THE SABBATH DAY AND MADE IT HOLY.

5. RESPECT YOUR FATHER AND MOTHER, SO THAT YOU MAY LIVE LONG IN THE LAND WHICH GOD WILL GIVE YOU.

6. YOU SHALL NOT COMMIT MURDER.

7. YOU SHALL NOT VIOLATE YOUR MARRIAGE VOWS.

8. YOU SHALL NOT STEAL.

9. YOU SHALL NOT SWEAR FALSELY AGAINST YOUR NEIGHBOR.

10. YOU SHALL NOT COVET YOUR NEIGHBOR'S POSSESSIONS.

Moses received these commandments, as well as many other rules, ordinances, and regulations, so that the children of Israel might walk in the ways of God. When Moses came down from the mountain, he taught these teachings to the people. After listening, they answered with one voice, "Everything that God has told us, we will do!"

The covenant that God made with the children of Israel at the foot of Mount Sinai has lasted to this day.

The Golden Calf

God summoned Moses again, saying, "Come to Me on the mountain. I will give you stone tablets on which I have inscribed all these commandments, rules, and ordinances, so that you may use them to guide the people."

Moses prepared to ascend the mountain again. Joshua went with him part of the way. Aaron and Hur remained behind to govern the people while Moses was gone.

The top of Mount Sinai glowed with fire. A cloud enveloped its summit. The voice of God called to Moses. Moses told Joshua to wait for him. Then he disappeared into the cloud.

During the next forty days God instructed Moses in many things. He told him how to build the Tabernacle, a tent sanctuary where God was to be worshiped. Aaron and his descendants were to be its priests. God described to Moses the garments that Aaron, the high priest, was to wear. He showed him the different kinds of sacrifices that Aaron was to offer on behalf of the people. Through these sacrifices, the Israelites could give thanks to God and obtain forgiveness for their sins. God taught all these things to Moses, writing them down with His own finger on two tablets of stone.

Meanwhile, the Israelites grew restless. Their leader Moses had disappeared into a cloud at the top of a fiery mountain. As the days passed, they began to wonder if he would ever return. What would happen to them without the leader who had brought them out of Egypt? How could they face the dangers of the desert without Moses to guide them?

Fear overcame faith. The Israelites came to Aaron and Hur, demanding that they make another god for them, for Moses was gone and no one knew if he would ever return.

Hur rebuked them with angry words. "How can you be so ungrateful? You have seen God's glory with your own eyes, and yet you still want to worship idols!"

The angry Israelites pelted Hur with stones and killed him. Aaron realized that if he spoke harshly, the people would stone him, too. Aaron was not afraid to die, but he did not wish to compound the people's sin by adding his blood to Hur's. Instead, he bartered for time, hoping that Moses might return before the idol was finished.

"Bring me the golden earrings from the ears of your sons, wives, and daughters," Aaron said. He knew that the faith of the women of Israel was stronger than that of the men. They would never give their precious earrings or those of their children to be made into an idol. This is indeed what happened. However, after their wives refused, the men brought their own earrings to Aaron.

Aaron had no more excuses. He prayed to God. "Lord, I am forced to fashion this idol against my will. The children of Israel are frightened because Moses is no longer with them. They will soon repent of what they are doing. Do not hold this sin against them."

Aaron molded the golden earrings into the shape of a calf. The people bowed down to it, crying out, "This is your god, O Israel, who brought you from the land of Egypt." They brought sacrifices to the golden calf, ate and drank, and lost themselves in revelry.

God looked down from Mount Sinai and saw what was happening in the camp. He said to Moses, "The people you brought out of Egypt have reverted to wickedness. They have turned from the path I showed them. They have made themselves an idol, a golden calf. They bow down to it, offer sacrifices to it. I hear them crying, 'This is your god, O Israel, who brought you out of Egypt!' These people are stubborn, worse than foolish. Do not stand in My way. Let my anger rise up against them and destroy them. You, Moses, are My faithful servant. I will make a great nation out of you."

Moses pleaded with God to have mercy on the children of Israel. "Do not allow Your anger to destroy Your people. If you do, the Egyptians will say, 'It was not God but an evil spirit who led our former slaves into the desert and destroyed them!' Remember your promise to Abraham, Isaac, and Jacob. You swore to make their descendants as numerous as the stars in the heavens and give them the fruitful land of Canaan to be their home forever. Do not forget your promise."

Moses' words quenched God's anger. Moses took the two stone tablets that God had given him and came down from the mountain. Along the way he encountered Joshua, still waiting where Moses had left him.

"Come quickly. We must return. An enemy is attacking," Joshua said. "I hear sounds of battle coming from the camp."

Joshua was mistaken. The cries and screams he heard were not the sounds of battle, but the noise of wild carousing as the Israelites worshiped the golden calf.

Moses and Joshua came down from the mountain. When Moses saw the golden calf and the Israelites dancing around it, his anger flared. He hurled down the two stone tablets. They shattered to pieces at the mountain's foot.

Moses entered the camp, his eyes blazing with anger. No one dared stand in his way as he overturned the golden statue and threw it into the fire. After melting it down, he ground the shapeless lump to powder. He sprinkled it over a basin of water, which he forced the Israelites to drink.

Moses confronted Aaron. "Why did you allow our people to commit this terrible sin?"

Aaron begged forgiveness. He explained how frightened the people had been, how they had murdered Hur, and how he had stalled for time. Moses accepted Aaron's explanation. However, God would not forgive the children of Israel unless the guilty were punished.

Moses stood before the camp and declared in a loud voice, "Whoever is on God's side, come to me!" The whole tribe of Levi joined him. Moses ordered them to take their swords and kill all the idol worshipers among Israel. The three thousand men who urged Aaron to make the golden calf and those who sacrificed to it were put to death.

The next day, Moses said to the people, "I will go before God again and beg Him to forgive you." Moses climbed back up the mountain. He said to God, "I know my people have committed a great sin. Will you not forgive them? If not, take whatever merit I have earned and give it to the people of Israel. If that is insufficient, kill me, too, and erase my name from memory. Let me not be remembered as a prophet who led his people to destruction."

God forgave the Israelites for Moses' sake. He said to Moses, "Go back down the mountain. Lead My people as before." Before Moses returned, God gave him a second set of stone tablets.

When Moses came down from the mountain, his face glowed. Beams of glory extended from his forehead like horns. Aaron and the elders thought he was an angel, at first. Only after Moses called to them, urging them to come forward, did they recognize him.

Moses set the stone tablets before the children of Israel and instructed them in the ways of God.

The Death of Moses

The Children of Israel wandered in the desert for forty years. During that time the people who had been slaves in Egypt passed away. A new generation took their place: young, proud men and women, strong in body and spirit, eager to fight for God to gain the land He had promised their forefathers.

Moses was proud to see them, but he was sad as well, for he knew his life was almost at an end. So was his task. God had chosen Moses to lead the children of Israel to the Promised Land of Canaan. He was not destined to enter Canaan with them.

When Moses knew that his time had come to die, he asked the children of Israel to gather around him. He blessed the twelve tribes, each in turn, and appointed Joshua to be their leader. Then he set out alone, across the plains of Moab to the summit of Mount Nebo. There, on a cliff overlooking the city of Jericho, God showed him the whole land of Canaan, north and south, from the Jordan River all the way to the Great Sea.

"This is the land that I promised to Abraham, Isaac, and Jacob, and all their descendants," said God. "I have let you see it, but you will not enter it."

God kissed Moses on the lips. His soul flew from his body, and he died. God buried Moses in the desert of Moab. The site of his grave is unknown.

There has never been, nor will there ever be, another prophet like Moses, who performed wonders and miracles before Pharaoh in Egypt, and in the desert, and looked upon the Face of God.

The Story of Joshua

After Moses' death, Joshua took command of the Israelite nation. The leaders of the people came to him, greatly worried. "What will become of us?" they asked. "Our leader Moses is gone. Miriam's Well has disappeared. The manna that fed us in the desert no longer falls. The pillar of cloud and the pillar of fire that guided and guarded us day and night is gone. Surely God has abandoned us!"

Joshua's faith in God was stronger than that of Moses'. Moses had sometimes hesitated, unsure whether he could really carry out all that God asked of him. Joshua never wavered. He believed with all the strength of his soul that whatever God promised would be fulfilled.

"God has blessed us, not abandoned us," Joshua told the elders. "The well, the manna, and the two pillars that guided us in the desert have disappeared because we no longer need them. God has fulfilled his promise. He has brought us to the Jordan River. We stand on the edge of the land He promised to our ancestors, a fruitful land overflowing with milk and honey. Prepare yourselves. Be strong, and of good courage. In three days' time we will cross over the Jordan, to take possession of the land that God has given us. For God has ordered us to destroy the cities of Canaan with fire and sword so that the land may be cleansed of idol worship."

Joshua's words heartened the people. They promised to do whatever Joshua asked, and to obey him as they obeyed Moses.

The Fall of Jericho

Jericho, a mighty city surrounded by immense walls so thick that people built houses on them, stood across the river from the Israelite camp. The leaders of the

Israelite army began to wonder if they could ever capture such a powerful stronghold. They came to Joshua, suggesting that he send spies across the Jordan to seek out Jericho's weaknesses.

"Why do we need spies?" Joshua asked. "God said He would deliver Jericho into our hands. Do you not believe Him?"

But the leaders of the army insisted they should send out spies. "Do as the people wish," God told Joshua. So Joshua picked two heroes, the bravest in Israel, to spy out the land. One was his friend Caleb. The other was Phinehas, the son of Eleazar, the high priest of Israel.

Caleb and Phinehas disguised themselves as merchants selling pots. As soon as it grew dark they crossed over the Jordan. In the morning they mingled with the crowds entering Jericho. The two spies drove their donkeys, laden with clay pots, through the streets. "Pots for sale! Pots for sale!" they cried as they walked through the city. In this way they discovered all of Jericho's weaknesses, while no one paid attention to them.

When evening came, Caleb and Phinehas sought lodging in the house of a woman named Rahab. She was a prostitute who lived in one of the houses built on top of the city wall. Her neighbors paid no attention to the two men. Strangers often came to visit her. Rahab noticed the scarred faces and hands of her guests. She suspected they were warriors, not merchants.

"I know who you are," she told them. "You have come from the camp of the Israelites to spy out the city."

Before Caleb and Phinehas could answer, they heard knocking at the door. The king of Jericho's soldiers had come to seek them. "Rahab!" they called out. "Open the door! We have learned that two men are staying with you. They may be Israelite spies. Send them out!"

"They are no longer here," Rahab answered. "They had to leave Jericho before the city gates closed for the night. If they are Israelites, they are surely going to try to cross the Jordan. You can still catch them if you hurry."

After the soldiers left, Rahab said to Caleb and Phinehas, "I know you serve the God of Israel, the Mighty God Who dried up the Red Sea and drowned the Egyptians. Everyone in Jericho is afraid. Our hearts melted and our courage fled when we saw you camped on the other side of the river. We know that God will surely deliver Jericho into your hands. Remember me, I beg you, when you capture the city. As I saved you from the king's soldiers, save my family—my parents, my brothers and sisters—from destruction."

"We will protect you and your family with our lives," Caleb and Phinehas promised her. They gave her a scarlet cord, saying, "When the Israelites come into the city, gather everyone you wish to save into this house. Hang this scarlet cord from the window. All Israel will know that you are under our protection."

"I trust your words," said Rahab. She lowered a rope out the window. Caleb and Phinehas climbed down the wall and escaped from Jericho.

Caleb and Phinehas hid in a mountain cave for three days while soldiers from Jericho searched for them. After the soldiers had given up the search, they came down from the mountains and followed the road that led to the Jordan River. They crossed the river at night, and went immediately to Joshua.

Joshua was pleased to learn that the people of Jericho were losing courage. "God will deliver the city into our hands," he said.

When morning came, Joshua commanded the children of Israel to prepare to cross the Jordan. They gathered in formations behind the banners of their tribes; the fighting men in front, the old men, women, children, and animals in the rear. The Ark of the Covenant, the chest holding the two stone tablets that Moses brought down from Mount Sinai, went before them. As soon as the priests carrying the Ark entered the river, the waters of the Jordan parted. Joshua and the Israelites walked across without wetting the soles of their feet.

Seeing this miracle terrified the people of Jericho. They fled within their walls and shut the city gates. No one could leave or enter. The Israelites camped outside the walls and wondered what to do. The walls of Jericho were so thick and tall that no enemy had ever been able to break through.

Of all the leaders of Israel, only Joshua was not dismayed. "God has promised to deliver Jericho and all the cities of Canaan into our hand. We have but to wait and keep our faith strong. God will tell us what to do."

Sure enough, God spoke to Joshua, saying, "I have delivered Jericho into your hands. Lead your army around the city walls once a day for six days. The Ark of the Covenant will go before you. Priests carrying ram's horns will accompany the Ark. On the seventh day, you must march around the city seven times. The priests will blow on their ram's horns. All the people of Israel will shout at once.

The walls of Jericho will come crashing down, and you will enter the city."

Joshua delivered God's instructions to the Israelites, warning them, "Do not shout, or raise your voices, or yell out our battle cry until I myself give the signal. When I command you to shout, then you must cry out with all your might!"

The next day, led by the priests and the Ark of the Covenant, the Israelites marched around the walls of Jericho in complete silence. The people of Jericho watched from the walls. Some mocked. Others threw garbage or shot arrows. Most stared and wondered. What was the enemy doing?

The Israelites returned to camp after circling the city. They marched around Jericho the day after, and the day after that. Not a word was spoken; not a missile was fired. The Israelites and the people of Jericho studied each other in complete silence.

The seventh day came. The Israelites rose at dawn, assembled their formations, and silently marched around Jericho six times. As the seventh circuit of the walls began, Joshua signaled to the priests, who raised the ram's horns to their lips and blew a mighty blast. At the same time Joshua cried to the Israelites, "Shout! Raise your voices! God has given you the city!"

The Israelites shouted their battle cry; the priests blew on their horns—and the walls of Jericho toppled to the ground. Only the section where Rahab's house stood remained intact. The scarlet cord fluttered from her window.

On that day God fulfilled His promise by delivering the mighty city of Jericho into Joshua's hands. All within its walls perished, except Rahab and her family. From that time on, she worshiped none but the God of Israel.

The Crime of Achan

Because Jericho had fallen on the Sabbath day, Joshua decreed that all the wealth within its walls belonged to God. The children of Israel were forbidden to take anything for themselves. However, a man named Achan, of the tribe of Judah, discovered a golden idol dressed in a costly robe hidden among the ruins. It was small enough to hide under his cloak. He took it away and hid it among his possessions, saying nothing about it to anyone.

After achieving victory over Jericho, Joshua sent a small force to besiege the city of Ai. Here the Israelites suffered a terrible defeat. They fled, leaving hundreds of their comrades lying dead beneath Ai's walls.

Joshua could not understand what had happened. Ai was far weaker than

Jericho. The Israelites should have enjoyed an easy victory. "God must be angry with us," Joshua reasoned. "I am the leader of the people. If I have done wrong in any way, I must ask God's forgiveness."

Joshua went to the Tabernacle and threw himself on the ground before the Holy Ark. He wept, tore his clothes, and prayed.

Joshua lay before the Ark from morning until evening. Finally God spoke to him. "Why have you fallen on your face? You have done nothing wrong. Israel has sinned. Someone among you has violated my commandment. That is why I allowed the people of Ai to defeat you."

The sin had to be made right before the Israelites could have any hope of further victory. But first it had to be discovered. Joshua assembled the people and summoned Phinehas, who had succeeded his father as high priest, to come before him, wearing the breastplate that contained the *Urim* and *Thummin.* These were magical stones representing each of the twelve tribes. They lit up to answer important questions. Joshua examined the twelve jewels. All shined brightly, except the one that represented the tribe of Judah. It alone remained dim.

Joshua had the members of the tribe of Judah cast lots. The lot fell on Achan. "What have you done? Confess your sin!" Joshua told him.

"I have done nothing," Achan insisted. "And there is nothing you can do to me. According to the Laws of Moses, a person cannot be convicted without the testimony of two witnesses. Who bears witness against me? No one! Yet you want to take my life because of the way the lot falls."

The men of Judah rallied behind Achan. "Achan has done nothing! We will defend him!" they cried. Meanwhile, the members of the other tribes were equally determined that he be punished. "Give him up! Achan, confess your sin! God has spoken through the Urim and Thummin!"

It seemed as if war between the tribes would break out at any moment. Suddenly, Achan raised his hand. "Let us not come to blows because of me. I am guilty. Many have died at Ai because of my sin. I do not wish to bring more blood upon my head." He confessed his crime to Joshua. Joshua sent messengers to Achan's tent. They returned with the golden idol and the beautiful robe he had stolen from Jericho.

"I am sorry for what I have done," Achan said to Joshua. "Is there no hope for me?"

Joshua shook his head. "You must die. That is the only way you can atone for your sin. However, because you confessed in time and saved our people from needless bloodshed, I will pray to God to forgive you."

The elders of Israel led Achan to the place of stoning. Joshua prayed for Achan. Then he picked up the first stone. He hurled it with all his strength to give Achan a quick, merciful death. As Achan lay dying, a heavenly voice spoke: "God forgives you, Achan. Because you gave your life to prevent bloodshed, you will have your portion in the world to come."

Joshua told the elders, "I too am guilty of a sin. I sent our soldiers to Ai, thinking God would give them another easy victory. I took God for granted. I will not make that mistake again. God will surely give us the victory, but we must do our best to achieve it."

Joshua outlined a clever plan. Thirty thousand of Israel's bravest soldiers would conceal themselves in the ravines near Ai's western gate. Joshua himself would lead a small force against the city walls. The people of Ai would see that the Israelites were not as numerous as they expected. They would open the gates and charge out to attack. Joshua would pretend to flee, pursued by the soldiers of Ai. When Joshua had lured them far enough away, the thirty thousand Israelites hiding in the ravines would leap out and storm the open city gates.

The plan worked perfectly. Surrounded and overwhelmed, Ai surrendered. The Israelites, with God's help, had won another victory.

The Gibeonites' Deception

Word of Joshua's victories spread throughout the land of Canaan. The inhabitants of the city Gibeon were frightened that Joshua would attack them next. "What can we do to protect ourselves?" they asked each other. "If we resist, the god of the Israelites will deliver us into their hands, as he did with Jericho and Ai. Yet we cannot make peace, either, for the Israelites' god has commanded them to destroy the cities of Canaan with fire and sword."

The Gibeonites thought of a clever plan to trick Joshua into making peace with them. They sent ambassadors to the Israelite camp at Gilgal. The ambassadors dressed in ragged clothes. They put worn-out sandals on their feet. Their empty wineskins were cracked and patched; their pouches were filled with dry, moldy bread. They looked like travelers who had been on a long journey.

"Who are you? Where have you come from?" Joshua asked when they arrived in camp.

"We come from a distant land," the Gibeonites told him. "Word came to us of your triumphs. We heard how you dealt with the Egyptians at the Red Sea; how you overthrew the people of Jericho and Ai. Our rulers sent us to sign a treaty of friendship with you. When we first set out, our clothes were new. Our bread was fresh, and our wineskins full. Look at them now. We pray you, do not send your servants away empty-handed, seeing as we have come so far."

Joshua swore an oath of peace with the Gibeonites. Since they did not live in the land of Canaan, he was not obliged to fight them.

Joshua learned the truth soon afterward when the Israelites entered the land of Gibeon. The Gibeonites did not come from far away at all. "Why did you deceive us?" Joshua demanded. "Why did you say you lived a far distance when you were nearer to us than a three-day journey?"

"Do not be angry with us," the Gibeonites pleaded. "We feared for our lives. We did not want to fight, knowing we would perish. Now we are in your hands. Do with us as you see fit."

"What shall we do with the Gibeonites?" Joshua asked the elders of Israel.

"God told us to destroy the people of Canaan. Kill them!" the elders said.

"But we have sworn an oath before God to live with them in peace," Joshua protested.

"They lied to us. The oath is not binding," said Caleb, son of Jephunnah.

What Caleb said was true. Still, Joshua had no wish to kill unarmed people who offered no resistance. But how could he spare the Gibeonites without violating God's command to destroy all Canaanites?

Phinehas, the high priest of Israel, understood what lay in Joshua's heart. "There is a way to spare the Gibeonites," he said.

"How may it be done?" Joshua asked.

"God has ordered us to destroy the Canaanites because of the violence and corruption that fill their cities," the priest explained. "If the Gibeonites were to give up idol-worship and follow the true and just commandments of the God of Israel, they would be Canaanites no longer. They would become our brothers and sisters. We would have no reason to make war against them."

"Would you give up worshiping idols? Would you devote yourselves wholeheartedly to the God of Israel, following His commandments with devotion, as we do?" Joshua asked the people of Gibeon.

"Gladly!" they exclaimed. "We have seen with our own eyes how God has blessed and protected you. We hope and pray He may do the same for us. From this day forth, we will worship Him alone."

The people of Gibeon joined Joshua and the children of Israel in sacrificing to the God of Abraham, Isaac, and Jacob. From now on they would serve the Israelites by carrying wood and drawing water for the Tabernacle. The Israelites in turn promised to protect them from their enemies.

The Sun Stands Still

The Gibeonites soon needed that help. The kings of Canaan were outraged that the people of Gibeon had joined the Israelites. Five Canaanite kings gathered their armies and besieged Gibeon.

The Gibeonites sent messengers to Joshua, crying for help. Joshua and his army marched all night. They arrived before the walls of Gibeon at dawn, taking the Canaanites by surprise. The Canaanites fought hard because they knew this day was Friday. Once the sun went down, the Sabbath would begin. The children of Israel could not fight on the Sabbath. They would have to put down their swords. Then they would be at the mercy of their enemies.

The battle went on all day. As the sun began to go down, Joshua prayed to God for help. "Let the Sabbath not begin until we have won the victory." Then he cried out in a loud voice for all to hear,

Sun, stand still over Gibeon!
And you, O Moon, in the Valley of Aijalon!

The sun stood still in the sky, and the rising moon did not move from its place until the Israelites overcame the armies of Canaan.

The Israelites won a great victory that day, when God Himself in the heavens fought for Israel.

Judges AND Kings

The Story of Deborah

Joshua divided the land of Canaan among the tribes of Israel, assigning a specific territory to each. Only the tribe of Levi did not receive its own land. The *Levites,* as members of this tribe were called, would live among the other tribes, assisting the priests in serving God.

Joshua died before the conquest of Canaan was finished. No single leader arose after him to take his place. The Israelites soon began squabbling over boundaries and water rights. Without a single leader to settle these arguments, the tribes settled them themselves—usually with the sword. Israel ceased to be a united nation. The tribes fought each other as fiercely as they fought the Canaanites.

Some Israelites wondered if they should fight the Canaanites at all. Canaan was a rich, fertile land, overflowing "with milk and honey" as Moses promised. Surely the gods of this land had blessed its inhabitants. Perhaps the Israelites were making a mistake in worshiping the God of Moses. He was a desert god. They were no longer in the desert. Would they not do better to worship the gods of Canaan?

This is exactly what Joshua had feared would happen if the children of Israel failed to completely conquer the people of Canaan. Israelites began imitating the ways of their Canaanite neighbors. They offered sacrifices to Baal and Asherah, the gods of the land. They danced in the sacred groves and worshiped idols of clay and stone. For a time they prospered. But not for long. God turned away from them and delivered them into the hands of their enemies.

Not all Israelites abandoned the God of their ancestors. Because of them, God did not entirely forsake the children of Israel. From time to time, when hope seemed lost,

God raised a special person—a judge—from among the people. The judges united the divided tribes of Israel and led them to victory over their enemies.

One of the greatest of the judges was a woman. Her name was Deborah.

An Army of Chariots

Jabin, the king of Hazor, was the mightiest of the Canaanite rulers. He possessed an immense army that included a host of nine hundred iron chariots. Jabin's army had never been defeated in battle.

Sisera, Jabin's commander, regarded the Israelites as an undisciplined horde. He had fought them for twenty years. His soldiers drove Israelite armies from the battlefield time and again. Those who did not flee perished under the iron wheels of Sisera's chariots. Sisera chased the Israelites out of the fertile valleys into the rugged hill country where chariots could not go. Only there did the children of Israel find refuge from the forces of Jabin and Sisera.

Many surrendered to despair. How could the Israelites hope to defeat such mighty champions as Jabin and Sisera?

Deborah Rallies the Tribes

One person never lost hope. Her name was Deborah. She was the wife of a man named Lapidoth, who lived in the hill country of Ephraim. Deborah was a woman of courage and wisdom. The scattered tribes of Israel revered her as a prophet.

A palm tree grew on the road between the towns of Ramah and Bethel. Deborah sat beneath that palm from morning to night. People came from all over Israel to ask her for help and guidance. Deborah listened as they spoke of how their homes had been burned, their flocks driven off, their sons killed, and their daughters dragged away as slaves by Sisera's soldiers.

"Do not despair," Deborah told them. "The God of Israel has not forsaken you. The day of judgment is fast approaching. God will deal with Jabin and Sisera as He dealt with Pharaoh at the Red Sea." She sent a message to Barak, the son of Abinoam, summoning him to meet with her.

Barak was a fearless soldier, known throughout Israel as a bold, cunning commander. Even so, he could not hide his dismay when he heard what Deborah expected of him.

"I speak for the God of Israel," Deborah told Barak. "He commands you to gather an army from the tribes of Naphtali and Zebulon. Lead them to Mount Tabor. God will lure Sisera to meet you at the Brook of Kishon, together with his soldiers and chariots. God will deliver Sisera and his entire army into your hand."

Barak was not eager to face Sisera's chariots in battle, despite Deborah's prophecy of victory.

"I will only go if you come with me," he told Deborah. "If you will not go, neither will I."

Deborah looked at Barak with scorn. "Of course I will go with you. However, because you doubted God's promise, you may not claim the glory for the victory. Sisera will be brought down by a woman's hand."

The Day of Battle

Barak summoned all the fighting men of the tribes of Zebulun and Naphtali to gather at Kedesh. Ten thousand answered his call. They followed Barak to Mount Tabor. Deborah went with them.

Word reached Sisera that an Israelite army was forming. He ordered his soldiers and charioteers to march to the Brook of Kishon.

As Sisera's army formed a battle line on the plain below, Deborah looked up at the clouds gathering overhead. She cried to Barak, "Attack! Today God has given Sisera into your power. Do not hesitate. God Himself marches before you!"

Lightning split the sky. Rain fell in torrents. The Brook of Kishon overflowed its banks. Sisera's chariots sank to their axles in the mud. As the Canaanites struggled in the surging stream, the army of Israel charged down Mount Tabor. The Canaanites threw away their weapons and fled. Sisera, Jabin's mighty general, abandoned his chariot and ran for his life. The Israelites pursued, striking down their enemies with sword and spear until none remained alive.

Only Sisera escaped the massacre. He lay facedown in the mud and pretended to be dead. After the battle, he searched frantically for a place to hide.

Sisera and Jael

Sisera wandered aimlessly, terrified and exhausted. At last he came upon a group of tents. It was the camp of Heber, a nomad chief who often visited the court of Jabin. There was peace between the Kenites, Heber's people, and the city of Hazor. *Heber will shelter me from the Israelites,* Sisera thought.

Sisera stumbled to Heber's tent. Jael, Heber's wife, met him at the entrance. "Come in, my lord. Do not be afraid," she said.

Sisera sank to his knees. Jael covered the trembling man with a carpet.

"Give me a little water to drink. I am so thirsty," Sisera pleaded.

"I will bring you milk, my lord." Jael brought Sisera a bowl of goat's milk. Sisera drank. Then he closed his eyes and fell into a deep slumber.

Jael watched him closely. As soon as she was certain he would not awaken, she took a tent pin in one hand, a mallet in the other, and kneeled beside the sleeping general. Jael placed the tent pin against Sisera's head. She raised the mallet. Striking with all her strength, she drove the pin through Sisera's skull.

Suddenly Jael heard voices outside the tent. It was Barak, leading a troop of Israelites. They had followed Sisera's tracks to Heber's camp.

"We are looking for Sisera," Barak told Jael.

"Come in, my lord. I will show you the man you are seeking." Jael held aside the opening to the tent. Sisera lay dead on the carpet, a tent peg pinning his head to the ground.

Thus did Deborah's prophecy come true. The power of Jabin was broken at the Brook of Kishon, and Sisera, the undefeated general, met his death at the hand of a woman.

Deborah judged the people of Israel with wisdom and justice for forty years. As long as she lived, the land knew peace.

The Story of Gideon

After Deborah's death the Israelites resumed their former ways. They worshiped idols and quarreled among themselves. God turned His back on them. He delivered them into the hands of the Midianites.

The Midianites were a tribe of desert nomads. In the time of Moses, they had been Israel's ally. Their chief, Jethro, was Moses' father-in-law. But that was years ago. The Midianites forgot their old ties to take advantage of Israel's weakness. Riding in from the desert on swift camels, they attacked in lightning raids, driving off sheep, oxen, and donkeys. The Israelites had hardly any animals left. They did not dare plant their fields, for fear of the Midianites. The Israelites became poor and hungry. In their distress, they cried to God.

God Summons Gideon

One day a man of the tribe of Manasseh was threshing grain inside a winepress, a large vat carved from a single block of limestone. His name was Gideon, son of Joash. Like all farmers in Israel, Gideon did not dare work in the open for fear of the Midianites. Should raiders suddenly appear, he could duck inside the winepress and hope they would not see him.

Suddenly an angel appeared, sitting under an oak tree that stood close by. The angel spoke to Gideon. "God is with you, Mighty Warrior!"

Gideon looked up in surprise. Was the angel talking to him? He was no warrior, only a poor farmer's son. "If God is with us, why do we live in fear of the Midianites?" Gideon asked the angel. "Where are the miraculous deeds our forefathers told us about?"

Gideon heard another voice. It was God Himself speaking. "Use the strength you have. Save Israel from the Midianites. I Myself am sending you."

Gideon could not believe what God was telling him. "Who am I to save Israel? My family is one of the weakest in our tribe, and I myself am my father's youngest son. Surely there are better men than I."

God insisted. "Do not fear. I will be with you. You will defeat the Midianites."

But Gideon was not convinced. "Give me a sign so I may know these words are true."

"What sort of sign do you want?" God asked.

"I will leave a woolen fleece on the threshing floor overnight. In the morning, if the fleece is wet with dew but the ground around it is dry, I will know that You have chosen me to save Israel."

Gideon spread a fleece on the threshing floor. When he returned the next morning the ground was dry, but the fleece was soaking wet. Gideon wrung enough dew from it to fill a bowl.

However, Gideon still held back. "Forgive me for asking again," he said to God. "Give me one more sign. I will spread the fleece on the ground once more. If I come tomorrow and find the ground wet but the fleece dry, then I will know You have chosen me."

God gave Gideon the sign he asked for. When Gideon returned the next morning he found the ground soaked with dew, but the fleece remained dry.

"For God and for Gideon!"

Gideon sent messengers throughout the land of Israel calling the fighting men of the tribes to join him in attacking the Midianites. Thirty-two thousand warriors answered the summons. They camped beside the spring of Harod. The vast Midianite camp lay below them in the Valley of Jezreel.

God looked over the Israelite army. He said to Gideon, "You have too many soldiers. If you defeat the Midianites with such a multitude, people will say that you outnumbered the enemy. You will get credit for the victory, not Me."

"What should I do?" Gideon asked.

"Say to your soldiers, 'If any man is afraid of dying or being injured, let him go home.'"

Gideon made the announcement. Twenty-two thousand men went home. But

God thought the ten thousand who remained were still too many. He told Gideon to put his soldiers to another test. "Lead them down to the spring to drink. Some of your men will throw their weapons aside, lie on the ground, and lap water directly from the spring. Others will hold on to their weapons. Kneeling, each will cup the water with one hand and drink."

Of the ten thousand, only three hundred held on to their weapons. God said, "I will deliver the Midianites into your hand with these three hundred. Send the rest home."

That night God sent Gideon and his servant Purah to spy out the Midianite camp. As Gideon and Purah made their way through the countless tents, they overheard one Midianite say to another, "I just had a strange dream. I dreamed a barley cake rolled into our camp. It struck a tent so hard that it collapsed."

The second Midianite shook his head. "This is a bad omen. The barley cake is the sword of Gideon. Your dream means that the God of the Israelites will give us into his hand."

When Gideon heard this, all doubt and fear left him. He hurried back through the darkness. Assembling his tiny force, he said to them, "Get up! With God's help, we will overcome the Midianites." Gideon divided his three hundred soldiers into companies of one hundred men. He gave each man a ram's horn and a clay jar with a torch inside. He said to them, "Follow me to the outskirts of the enemy camp. Do as I do. When I blow on my ram's horn, blow on your horns with all your might and cry with me, 'For God and for Gideon!'"

Gideon and his small army circled through the hills until they surrounded the enemy. The Midianites slept soundly in their tents. Suddenly Gideon smashed his jar. He blew his ram's horn, waved his torch, and cried, "For God and for Gideon!"

His three hundred men did the same. They smashed their jars and blew their horns. With torches in one hand and swords in the other, they charged the enemy camp, crying, "For God and for Gideon!"

The Midianites panicked. In the confusion and darkness, they stabbed each other with their swords. Gideon pursued them as they ran. He chased them far beyond the borders of Israel.

◆ ◆ ◆

After the victory, the Israelites wanted to make Gideon their king. "Rule over us," they said to him. "You, and your son, and your descendants. For it was you who defeated our enemies, the Midianites."

Gideon refused this honor. "No, I will not rule over you," he said. "Neither I, nor my son, nor my son's son. God Alone is Israel's king. He Alone will rule us."

Gideon returned to his father's village and resumed his life as a farmer. The Midianites did not trouble Israel again, and the Israelites lived in peace for forty years.

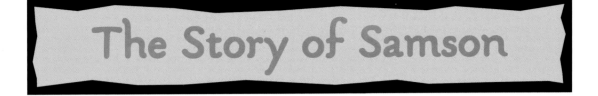

The Story of Samson

Time and again the Israelites refused to learn from their mistakes. They put their faith in idols. Consequently, they had no one to turn to when the Philistines, a great power in Canaan, began to oppress them.

The Philistines were a confederation of five cities that dominated the coastal plain. The cities were Ekron, Ashdod, Ashkelon, Gath, and Gaza. The ancestors of the Philistines came over the sea from Greece. The Philistines were formidable warriors. At one time they nearly conquered Egypt. Unlike the tribes of Israel, they stood united against their enemies. No one in Canaan could stand against them, especially not the weak, divided Israelites.

The Israelites cried to God in their misery, and God did not forsake them. He answered their prayers by raising a judge to fight the Philistines. His name was Samson.

The Birth of Samson

A man named Manoah and his wife lived near the town of Zorah in the territory of the tribe of Dan. They had no children. Manoah and his wife prayed to God to give them a child.

One day an angel appeared to Manoah's wife. The angel said to her, "Prepare yourself, for your prayers have been answered. You must not drink any wine or eat forbidden food, for you are going to have a son. He will be a *nazir;* he will belong to God from his birth. Therefore, do not cut his hair nor let a razor touch his head. For he is the one who will deliver Israel from the Philistines."

Nazirs were people who took special vows of holiness, pledging themselves to

God. Nazirs did not cut or even trim their hair. They did not drink wine or strong liquor. For most, this vow only lasted a period of time. Manoah's child was to be a nazir for life.

Manoah's wife gave birth to a son. They named him Samson. Samson grew up to become a mighty man among the Israelites. He fought the Philistines single-handedly, killing scores of them. He burned their crops by tying torches to the tails of wild foxes, then releasing them to run through the grain fields. He once killed a thousand men with no weapon but a donkey's jawbone. The Philistines attempted to trap Samson within the walls of Gaza; finding the city gates shut, Samson pulled them down and carried them away on his shoulders.

Despite his incredible strength, Samson had a fatal weakness. He was fascinated by Philistine women. He found them far more attractive than the women of Israel.

Word reached Samson about a Philistine woman named Delilah, who lived in the Valley of Sorek. Samson went to visit her and discovered that she was more beautiful than he imagined. He fell in love with her, coming to visit as often as he could. Samson would do whatever Delilah asked.

When the Philistine rulers learned this, they said to Delilah, "Get Samson to reveal his secret. What makes him so strong? Find out how we can overcome him. If you do this for us, we will each pay you eleven hundred silver shekels."

Delilah loved money more than she loved Samson. The next time Samson came to visit, she asked him, "Tell me your secret. What makes you so strong? If an ordinary person wanted to overcome you, what should he do?"

Samson told her, "If someone were to tie me up with seven new bowstrings, my strength would leave me. I would become as weak as an ordinary man."

While Samson slept, Delilah tied him with seven new bowstrings. Then she cried, "Wake up, Samson! Your enemies are here!"

Samson jumped up. He snapped the bowstrings as if they were threads. His strength remained with him, for he had not given away his secret.

Delilah pouted. "Why did you lie? I asked you a question. Why won't you tell me the truth?"

Samson told Delilah, "Very well, I will tell you my secret. If someone were to tie me with new ropes that had never been used, my strength would leave me. I would become as weak as an ordinary man."

When Samson fell asleep, Delilah took new ropes that had never been used for any purpose and tied them around his arms. Then she cried, "Wake up, Samson! The enemy is here!"

Samson jumped out of bed. He snapped the ropes as if they were string.

Delilah began to weep. "You don't really love me, Samson. You treat me like a fool. I ask you a question, and you make fun of me. Why won't you tell me? How can you be captured?"

This time Samson promised to reveal his secret. "If someone were to weave my long hair onto a loom, I would become as weak as an ordinary man."

Delilah waited until Samson fell asleep. As soon as he closed his eyes, she brought out her loom and wove his hair onto it. She fixed it tight with a pin. Then she cried, "Wake up, Samson! Your enemies are here!"

Samson awoke. He shook his head once, and the loom flew to pieces, for he was just as strong as before.

Now Delilah became truly angry. "How can you say you love me?" she cried to Samson. "Three times I asked you a question, and three times you lied to me!" She would not allow Samson to touch her or speak to her. She would not even remain in the same room with him.

After several days Samson gave in. "Calm yourself. Do not carry on so," Samson told Delilah. "If my secret means so much to you, I will tell you what it is. I am a *nazir*. I have been pledged to God since before my birth. I may not cut or trim my hair or beard. A razor must not touch my head. My hair is the source of my strength. If someone were to shave my hair from my head, I would become as weak as an ordinary man."

Delilah sensed that Samson was telling the truth this time. She sent word to the rulers of the five Philistine cities. "Come fast. Bring the money you promised, for Samson has told me his secret." The rulers brought the money. Delilah met them secretly outside the house while Samson was away. She collected the money, carefully weighing each shekel to make sure the full amount was paid. Suddenly she heard Samson returning. "Hide yourselves! Wait here until I call you," she told the rulers and their attendants.

Delilah went inside the house to greet Samson. "Come, my strong one. You have had a long journey. Lie down beside me and close your eyes. It is time to sleep."

Samson fell asleep with his head on Delilah's lap. As he slept, Delilah signaled to one of the attendants waiting outside. The man came in with a razor and shaved off Samson's beard and the seven locks of hair on his head. Samson's vow of holiness was broken; his strength vanished.

"Samson, wake up! The enemy is here!"

Samson awoke at Delilah's cry. Philistine soldiers charged into the house. They seized Samson's arms and legs. Samson tried to shake himself free, but he had no strength. He was as weak as an ordinary man.

Too late, Samson realized that Delilah had betrayed him. He had trusted in his own strength instead of God. Now his strength was gone, and he was a prisoner.

"Let Me Die with the Philistines"

The Philistines bound Samson with ropes and dragged him to Gaza. Once, Samson had walked off with the gates of that city. Now he was so weak, he could barely hold himself erect. The Philistines gouged out Samson's eyes. They believed that a blind man, weak or strong, could never threaten them. Samson became a slave. Bronze shackles were riveted on his wrists; chains bound him to a millstone. Day after day, Samson trudged around in a circle, pulling the heavy millstone like a team of oxen, grinding grain for the Philistines in their dungeon in Gaza.

In his misery, Samson thought that God had abandoned him. But God still remained with Samson. Slowly, his hair began to grow.

Every year the Philistines held a great festival for their god Dagon. Dagon was the god of the harvest. He caused grain to ripen; trees and vines to blossom and bear fruit. This year the Philistines decided to hold a special celebration. For Samson, their most dangerous enemy, had fallen into their hands.

The Philistines gathered in the Temple of Dagon to celebrate their triumph. When the merriment was at its height, they began to sing.

> *A captive is our foe.*
> *Dagon has brought him low,*
> *Who caused us so much woe,*
> *Killed dozens with one blow.*

Someone called out, "Bring Samson here! Let us look at him!"

"Yes! Yes!" cried the others. "We want to see Samson!"

They sent soldiers to bring Samson from the dungeon. Because Samson could no longer see, a young boy held his hand to guide him. They made Samson stand between the two main pillars supporting the temple. The Philistines roared with laughter to see their dreaded enemy so helpless. People flocked from all over Gaza to gawk at Samson. They filled the Temple of Dagon to the walls. Some even climbed up the columns and crawled along the roof beams for a better view.

Samson said not a word as the Philistines mocked him; as they pelted him with half-eaten fruit from their celebration. Silently he prayed, *God, remember me. Give me back my strength just this once. Let me pay back the Philistines for taking my eyes.*

God answered his prayers. Samson felt strength return to his body. He pressed his hands against the pillars. "O God!" he cried. "Let me die with the Philistines!"

Samson pushed against the two pillars with all his might. The Philistines screamed as the walls began to totter. They tried to flee, but it was too late. The pillars collapsed, carrying down the whole temple with them. Three thousand people perished in the ruins that day, among them the rulers of the five cities and all their families.

Thus, even as he died, Samson struck a mighty blow against the enemies of Israel.

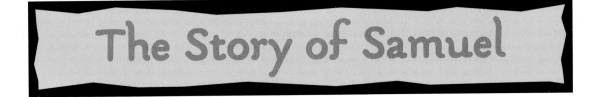

The Story of Samuel

Samuel was the last and greatest of the judges. Like Samson, he was a nazir pledged to God for his entire life. But unlike Samson and the other judges, Samuel was not a warrior. The Israelites revered him because of the power of his spirit and because of his devotion to God. God chose Samuel to prepare the tribes of Israel to become a nation once more. It would be Samuel's task to choose a king.

The Birth of Samuel

A man named Elkanah lived in the town of Ramah, in the hill country of Ephraim. Elkanah had two wives, Hannah and Peninnah. Peninnah had many children. Hannah had none.

Every year Elkanah brought his family to the village of Shiloh, where the Tabernacle stood. There he prayed and offered sacrifices to God. After giving the priests their portion, he would divide the sacrificed animal between the members of his family. He always gave Peninnah generous portions for herself and her children, but he gave Hannah twice as much. Even though Hannah had yet to bear a child, she was the wife of Elkanah's heart and the one he loved best.

Peninnah became jealous. She tried to be a good wife, but no matter how hard she worked to win Elkanah's affection, he still favored Hannah. Peninnah took out her anger on Hannah. She criticized everything she did and everything about her. Cruelest of all, she rebuked Hannah for not having borne a child.

"How long will you keep Elkanah waiting? What is wrong with you that you cannot bear children? I don't know why Elkanah wastes his time with a barren good-for-nothing. He should send you away and find another wife to take your place."

Hannah ran weeping to Elkanah.

"Why let Peninnah vex you?" Elkanah said. "You know I love you. I will never send you away, no matter what she says. Am I not better to you than ten sons? What does it matter to me whether or not you have children?"

These words eased Hannah's misery. But they did not fill the emptiness in her heart. She longed for a child of her own.

Months later, Elkanah and his family made their yearly pilgrimage to Shiloh. After the sacrifice was divided and eaten, Hannah went alone to the sanctuary. She kneeled before the entrance to the shrine and poured out her heart to God.

"O Lord, behold my suffering and humiliation. Hear the prayer of your humble servant. Do not forget me. Give me a child, a son. If You answer my prayer, I promise to dedicate him to You forever. He will serve God all the days of his life."

Eli, the high priest, was sitting beside the entrance. He saw Hannah kneeling in the dust. He watched tears roll down her cheeks while her lips moved silently. Eli assumed she was drunk. He scolded her.

"Aren't you ashamed? How long will you carry on with this drunken behavior? Put away your wine and leave God's presence!"

Hannah turned to face him. "I am not drunk, my lord," she replied. "I have not taken any wine or strong drink. Do not think me wicked. What you see before you is an unhappy woman pouring out her heart to God in grief and pain."

Eli apologized for his harsh words, and blessed her.

"Go in peace. May God grant whatever you asked of Him."

When Hannah left the sanctuary, her tears were dry and her face was no longer sad. She believed God had heard her.

Elkanah and his family arose the next morning. After offering prayers for a safe journey, they returned home.

God answered Hannah's prayer. Within a year she had a son. She called him *Samuel*, which means *I Asked Him of God*.

That year, when Elkanah made his annual journey to Shiloh, Hannah remained at home. She told her husband, "Samuel is still young; he is still nursing. Let me keep him until I need to nurse him no more. Then I will bring him to God's sanctuary, where he will remain forever."

Elkanah told his wife to do as she thought best. He realized how difficult it would be for Hannah to part with her only child. "May God help you to fulfill your vow," he said.

Hannah kept Samuel with her for several years, until he was no longer a baby. When the time came to fulfill her vow, she brought him to Shiloh along with three young bulls, a measure of fine flour, and a jug of wine for a sacrifice. After the offerings had been placed on the altar, Hannah presented her son to Eli.

"Do you remember me, my lord?" she asked the high priest. "I am the woman who came here to pray years ago. You gave me your blessing. God heard my prayer. Now I have come to fulfill the vow I made that day. This is the child I prayed for. His name is Samuel. I have brought him to Shiloh to give him to God. Let him serve God as long as he lives."

Hannah offered another prayer. This time her heart was filled with joy:

> *My heart exults in God!*
> *God exalts my glory . . .*
> *He lifts the poor out of the dust*
> *And the needy from the dunghill*
> *To sit them down with princes*
> *Upon a throne of glory.*
> *The pillars of the earth belong to God.*
> *He sets the world upon them.*
> *God's judgment reaches to the ends of the universe.*
> *He will give strength to His king*
> *And raise up His Anointed One.*

Elkanah and Hannah returned to Ramah. Their son Samuel remained behind to serve in the Tabernacle. Eli, the high priest, became his teacher.

Samuel Hears God's Voice

Eli had two sons of his own named Hophni and Phinehas. Both were wicked men who did as they pleased. They cheated the people who brought sacrifices by taking more than their due from the offerings. They abused the women who served at the sanctuary. No one dared punish them, for they were the sons of the high priest. Eli, old and nearly blind, could do little. He pleaded with his sons to change their ways.

"If one person sins against another, God will judge him," Eli warned them. "But if a person sins against God, who will defend him?"

Hophni and Phinehas laughed at their father's words.

In contrast to Eli's sons, Samuel served God with all his heart. When he was old enough to assist in the Tabernacle ritual, his mother Hannah made him a linen robe of the kind worn by priests. Every year when she came to Shiloh, she brought Samuel a new one. God blessed Hannah. She had many sons and daughters.

Eli taught Samuel the ritual by which the priests of the Tabernacle served God. God had given the ritual to Moses. Moses, in turn, taught it to his brother Aaron, Israel's first high priest.

Although Samuel was still only a small boy, he carried out his duties with great reverence. People bringing sacrifices to Shiloh noticed Samuel's sincere devotion to God. Soon they began to whisper that Samuel would make a better high priest than either of Eli's sons.

Eli's years weighed heavily on him. His eyes grew dimmer and dimmer until he could no longer see at all. Samuel became Eli's eyes. He guided the old priest's hands when he performed the ritual of sacrifice. He took over many tasks that Eli could no longer carry out himself.

One of these tasks was to sleep in the sanctuary until the lamps went out, to prevent the Tabernacle from catching fire. Samuel was asleep in the Tabernacle when he heard a voice calling his name.

"Samuel! Samuel!"

Samuel awoke, thinking Eli had called him. He hurried to the old priest's bedside. "Here I am, Eli. Why did you call me?"

Eli awoke from a sound slumber. "I did not call you, child. I was asleep myself. Perhaps you had a dream. Return to your place. Go back to sleep."

Samuel returned to the sanctuary, but hardly had he closed his eyes when he heard the voice again.

"Samuel! Samuel!"

Samuel arose a second time and went to Eli. Waking slowly, Eli said, "I did not call you, my son. Go back to sleep."

Samuel returned to his bed, but soon after he lay down, he heard that same voice calling his name for a third time. Samuel went again to Eli. This time he found the old priest waiting for him.

"So you have been called again. This is what you must do. Go back to your place, and when the voice calls your name, say these words: 'Speak, Lord, for your servant listens.'" Eli realized that God Himself was calling Samuel.

Samuel returned to the sanctuary. He lay down in the darkness and waited. Again the voice spoke.

"Samuel! Samuel!"

"Speak, Lord, for your servant listens.'" Samuel repeated the words that Eli told him to say.

God spoke to Samuel in the still, small voice with which He had spoken to Moses out of the burning bush.

"Look well, for I am about to perform a deed in Israel that will astonish everyone who hears of it. I will bring down the house of Eli. His sons do not walk in my ways. They do not follow My commandments, and Eli has done nothing to stop them."

Samuel lay trembling in the darkness, listening as God described the terrible punishment about to be imposed on Eli and his family.

After a time, the voice fell silent. Samuel opened his eyes. The night had passed. Sunlight streamed into the Tabernacle. Samuel opened the doors and prepared for the morning's worship. He did not go to tell Eli what God had said. Samuel loved Eli. He feared that hearing such a terrible prophecy would kill the old priest.

When Eli arose from his bed, he sent for Samuel and asked him to repeat the words that God had spoken in the night. Samuel hesitated to answer.

"Tell me what God said. Hold nothing back, for surely God will punish you if you attempt to hide anything from me," Eli insisted.

Samuel repeated God's words. When he finished, Eli lowered his head and sighed. "God has spoken. Let Him do as He sees fit."

The Ark Is Captured

Soon after these events, the Philistines gathered their armies and went forth to make war against Israel. The combined armies of the five Philistine cities had grown even mightier than they were in the days of Samson. They defeated the men of Israel at a place called Aphek, and drove them into the hills.

The people of Israel asked themselves, "Why has God allowed the Philistines to defeat us? Let us bring the Ark of the Covenant down from Shiloh. We will carry the Ark into battle with us. Then our enemies will know that God stands at our side. He will deliver the Philistines into our hands."

They sent word to Shiloh to bring down the Ark. The Ark of the Covenant was the holiest object the Israelites possessed. It contained the stone tablets that God gave to Moses on Mount Sinai. Hophni and Phinehas, Eli's two sons, escorted the Ark to the Israelite camp. When the men of Israel beheld the Ark in their midst, they let out such shouts of joy that the earth trembled.

The Philistines heard the noise and wondered what it meant. Terror seized them when they learned that the Ark had come into the Israelite camp. They remembered what Samson had done to them with God's help.

The Philistine soldiers cried, "Woe is us! God has come into the camp of our enemies. This is the God of Israel, Who smote the Egyptians with terrible plagues and drowned them in the Red Sea." But their leaders calmed them by saying, "Be strong and fight like heroes. Otherwise we will become slaves to the Israelites as they have been slaves to us."

The Philistines did not flee. They fought with strength and courage. On that day God delivered the army of Israel into their hands. Thirty thousand Israelites fell on the battlefield; the rest fled for their lives. The Ark of the Covenant was captured. Hophni and Phinehas, the two sons of Eli, were killed.

When news of the Ark's capture reached Shiloh, Eli fell back in his chair. The chair tipped over, breaking Eli's neck. Thus was God's judgment carried out on Eli and his family.

Samuel Brings Victory

Eli was ninety-eight years old when he died. He had judged Israel for forty years. Now Samuel became judge in his place. All Israel harkened to Samuel's words. They knew he was a prophet as well as a priest, for God spoke to him.

The people turned to Samuel in their woe, for although the Ark was eventually recovered, the Philistines continued to oppress them.

Samuel asked the Israelites, "Do you truly wish to be delivered from the Philistines?"

The people answered, "Of course we do!"

"Then first you must do this. Get rid of your idols. Stop bowing down to false gods. Serve God with all your heart. Worship Him Alone, and He will deliver you from the Philistines."

The Israelites agreed to do all that Samuel asked of them. They stopped worshiping the gods of Canaan. They broke their idols, smashed the pagan temples, chopped down the sacred trees, scattered the altars where they once offered sacrifices to statues of wood and stone. Once the land had been cleared of idol worship, Samuel said, "Let all Israel gather in the town of Mizpah. I will pray for you there."

Men, women, and children—the entire nation of Israel—came to Mizpah. The twelve tribes put aside their feuds and petty quarrels to unite as one people. Samuel offered a sacrifice and prayed on their behalf, while the people fasted and prayed to God for forgiveness for their sins.

When the Philistine leaders heard that all Israel had assembled in Mizpah, they gathered their army and went to attack them, thinking, *Now is our chance to destroy the whole nation!*

The Israelites saw the Philistines coming. "We are lost!" they cried out in fear. But Samuel told them, "Keep praying to God! Do not stop! He will deliver us from the Philistines!"

While the people prayed, Samuel took a lamb and offered it on the altar of sacrifice. The smoke of the offering rose toward heaven. Meanwhile, the Philistine army formed a line of battle. The order to attack rang out. The soldiers drew their swords and pressed forward. They expected an easy victory.

Suddenly, a lightning bolt split the sky. Thunder shook the ground. Earth and heaven trembled. Terror seized the Philistines. They threw away their weapons and ran, pursued by the Israelites. God had delivered the mighty Philistines into Israel's hand. Their powerful army was shattered. Years would pass before they would trouble Israel again.

From that day on, Samuel judged Israel with wisdom and justice. For he walked with God.

A King for Israel

Samuel grew old. The elders of Israel began to worry that he might not live much longer. What would happen after he died? Without a strong leader to unite them, the tribes of Israel might become prey for their enemies. The people might forget God once more, and slide back into idol worship.

The elders came before Samuel at Ramah. They asked him to choose a king to reign over all Israel.

"Why do you need a king?" Samuel asked them. "God is your king. With God as your ruler, you need no other."

"Israel needs a strong leader," the elders said.

"God will raise up another judge after I am gone," Samuel replied.

"That might not be for years," the elders said. "You are old, and your sons do not walk in your footsteps. Choose a king to rule over us, so that we may be like other nations."

Samuel became angry because the elders lacked faith in God and were willing to give up their freedom so easily.

"Do you really want a king?" he asked them. "Let me describe what a king will do. He will take your sons to be his soldiers. He will appoint officers to draft you to do his work. You will be forced to plow his fields, reap his harvest, fashion his weapons of war. He will take your daughters to cook and bake for him. He will take away your best fields, vineyards, olive groves, and give them to his friends. He will take one-tenth of your flocks and herds as his own, and you will serve him. Then you will cry out to God because of this king you wanted. But God will not hear you."

The elders insisted. "We want a king. We want to be like other nations. We want a king to lead us in battle."

Samuel dismissed the elders in disgust. He did not want to choose a king for Israel. He knew that kings brought only trouble and oppression.

However, God spoke to Samuel, saying, "Do not be angry with the people. They are not rejecting you; they are rejecting Me. So they have done since the day I took them out of Egypt. They run to serve other gods, in spite of all I have done for them. You have done all you can, too. You warned them about the nature of kings. Listen now to the elders. Do as they ask. Make them a king."

With heavy heart, Samuel set out to find a king for Israel.

Samuel Anoints Saul

A man named Kish lived in the town of Gibeah, in the territory of the tribe of Benjamin. Kish had a son named Saul. Saul was extremely handsome, as well as exceptionally tall. The average person only came up to his shoulders.

One day two donkeys belonging to Saul's father wandered off. Kish sent Saul to find them. Accompanied by one of his father's servants, Saul set out to look for the donkeys.

Saul and his companion searched the hill country of Ephraim without success. They passed through the territory of the tribe of Benjamin. The donkeys were nowhere to be found.

At last they came to the town of Zuph. Saul was ready to abandon the search. "Let us go home," he told his companion. "My father has probably forgotten about the donkeys by now. If we don't come back soon, he will start worrying about us."

"Let us make one more effort," Saul's companion suggested. "I have heard that a prophet lives in this city. Everyone says he is an honorable man. Why don't we visit him? Perhaps he can tell us something about the donkeys."

"What will we bring him?" Saul asked. "I don't have any money, and we have eaten all our food. I would be embarrassed to ask a favor without being able to offer the prophet something in return."

"I have some silver in my purse," Saul's companion said. "I will gladly give it to the prophet if he can help us."

"Good! We shall go," Saul exclaimed.

Saul and his companion began walking up the hill to the city. Along the way they met a group of young women coming down to draw water.

"Is the prophet still here?" they asked them.

"Yes. He is going to offer a sacrifice today for our town and its people. He is waiting by the altar. If you hurry, you will find him."

Hearing this news, Saul and his companion quickened their pace. As they entered the town gate, they encountered Samuel. The prophet was coming down to meet them. The day before, God had told him, "At this time tomorrow I will send you a young man from the tribe of Benjamin. His name is Saul, the son of Kish. You will anoint him king over Israel. He will save Israel from the power of the Philistines."

As soon as Samuel noticed the tall young man coming through the gate, he heard God's voice speaking to him. "This is Saul, the one I told you about. He will rule over My people."

But Saul knew nothing of this. He did not even realize that Samuel was the prophet he was seeking, for he said to him, "Old One, please tell me where I can find the prophet's house."

Samuel answered, "I am the prophet. Come with me to the altar on the hill-top. Stay with me tonight. Tomorrow morning I will tell you everything you came to learn. Then you can go home. Don't worry about your father's donkeys. They have been found. But as for the honor of ruling Israel, to whom does it belong? Was it not meant for you and your family?"

Astonished, Saul could hardly speak. He had come looking for two donkeys. Now the prophet told him he was going to become king of Israel! "I am from the tribe of Benjamin, the smallest of the twelve," Saul stammered. "My family is the most insignificant in our tribe. Why are you talking to me this way?"

Samuel did not reply. He invited Saul to dine with him as an honored guest. That evening Samuel prepared a bed on the roof of his house so Saul and his companion could sleep in the cool night air.

Samuel awakened Saul at dawn, saying, "Come, get up! It is time to be on your way."

Saul and his companion arose. They accompanied Samuel through the quiet streets. When they reached the outskirts of town, Samuel told Saul, "Send your companion ahead. I must talk with you alone so that I can give you God's message."

Saul sent his companion on. When the prophet and the tall, young farmer were alone, Samuel took a tiny flask of holy oil and poured it over Saul's head. He kissed him and said to him, "Today God has anointed you to be king of Israel. You will rule over God's people and defend them from their enemies."

"How do I know that this is true?" Saul asked.

Samuel said, "When you leave me today, you will pass by Rachel's Tomb. There you will find two men who will tell you that your father has found his donkeys, but that he is now worried about you.

"Later you will pass by Mount Tabor. You will meet three men going to offer a sacrifice to God at Bethel. The first will be leading three young goats. The second will be carrying three loaves of bread. The third will be carrying a jug of wine. These men will greet you and give you two of their loaves, which you must accept.

"At last you will come to Bethel. There you will meet a company of prophets, dancing, singing, playing on the harp, the drum, the flute, and the lyre. God's spirit will enter into you, and you will prophesy with them. From that time on, you will no longer be the man you are now.

"So let it be that when you see these things come to pass, you will recognize them as signs sent to you by God. Then you will know that God is with you."

Everything happened as Samuel prophesied. When Saul met the company of prophets, the spirit of God came over him. He fell into an ecstatic trance. He danced and sang with the prophets.

The people who saw him asked each other, "Isn't that tall young man Saul, Kish's son? What has come over him? Has he become a prophet, too?"

When Saul emerged from his trance he was a changed man. But he did not confide this secret to anyone. He continued on until he reached his home. When he arrived, his uncle asked, "Where have you been?"

Saul answered, "My companion and I went looking for my father's donkeys. We could not find them, so we went to visit Samuel the prophet, hoping that he could help us."

"What did the prophet say?"

"He told us the donkeys were found, and that we could come home." But Saul mentioned nothing about kingship.

Saul Proves Himself a King

After Saul returned home, Samuel summoned all the tribes of Israel to assemble at Mizpah. He said to them, "You turned your backs on God, Who saved you from the Egyptians and from all the nations that oppress us. You say you want a king to rule over you. God has told me to do as you ask. Let us now choose a king to reign over Israel."

The twelve tribes cast lots. The lot fell to the tribe of Benjamin. Samuel told the clans of Benjamin to come near. They cast lots again, and again, and again. The final lot fell to Saul, the son of Kish. But he was nowhere to be found. The Israelites looked everywhere for him. They finally discovered Saul hiding in a heap of baggage. He ran away when they called to him. The Israelites chased him. They brought him back to stand before Samuel. The people marveled at Saul's height, for he stood head and shoulders above all of them.

Samuel described a king's rights and duties to Saul and the people. Then he dismissed them. But many among the Israelites wondered, *Who is this tall fellow? A nobody! A farmer's son! He has never been in battle. How can he save us from our enemies?*

Saul's chance to prove himself came a month later. An army of Ammonites led by their king Nahash besieged the town of Jabesh-Gilead. The Ammonites were a fierce warrior nation. When the people of the town realized they could not hold out any longer, they sent a delegation to Nahash asking under what terms he would allow them to surrender, so that their homes and their families might be spared.

Nahash replied with a sneer, "Here are the terms I give you. Every man in Jabesh-Gilead will have his right eye gouged out. Everyone who sees them will know they were powerless to defend their city. All Israel will be disgraced."

The leaders of Jabesh-Gilead asked for seven days to decide. Meanwhile, they sent messengers to all the tribes of Israel, pleading for help. If no help came in seven days, they would surrender to the Ammonites.

Messengers from Jabesh-Gilead came to Gibeah, where Saul's family lived. Saul was plowing his father's field when they arrived. In the evening, as he led his oxen home, he saw his neighbors weeping.

"What has happened?" he asked them.

The people told him about the desperate message from Jabesh-Gilead. When Saul heard this, he killed both his oxen, cut them to pieces, and sent the fragments through all the land of Israel, along with the message, "Any man who does not come forward to fight with Saul and Samuel will see this done to his oxen!"

The men of Israel put on their armor and sharpened their weapons. They came forth as one to fight with Saul against the Ammonites. Saul sent word to the people of Jabesh-Gilead. "Do not lose hope. Help is coming. You will be rescued before noon tomorrow."

When the people of Jabesh-Gilead heard this news, they said to Nahash, "We will surrender tomorrow. Do with us as you please."

Believing that victory was theirs, the Ammonites celebrated all night. They did not post guards around their camp because they did not think they were in danger. Meanwhile, Saul divided his army into three groups. They crept up on the Ammonite camp early in the morning. All the Ammonites were asleep. The Israelites took them by surprise. They pursued the Ammonites until noon. By then Nahash's army was so decimated and scattered that scarcely two men remained together.

After this victory, Samuel and the people of Israel gathered at the shrine at Gilgal, where they crowned Saul king. The people rejoiced, for now they had a mighty man of valor to lead them.

God Rejects Saul

Saul and his son Jonathan led the armies of Israel against their enemies. Jonathan was even braver than his father. Once Jonathan and his armor-bearer climbed a rocky cliff to take a Philistine army by surprise. They killed twenty enemy soldiers, creating such confusion in the camp that the Philistines thought they were being attacked by an entire army. The terrified Philistines began fighting and killing each other. Saul then led his army into battle and routed the Philistines. Saul and Jonathan won a great victory.

Even so, all was not well in Israel. Samuel had judged Israel for many years. He expected Saul to follow God's instructions exactly, the way he had. However, Saul began making his own decisions. This worried Samuel. He saw the danger he had warned against coming to pass. Saul the king was putting himself before God.

Once the Philistines assembled a huge army of soldiers, chariots, and horsemen to fight against Israel. Saul gathered an army to meet them. The Israelites assembled at Gilgal. Samuel sent word to Saul, ordering him to wait at the shrine until he arrived to make the sacrifice. Only then was he to go into battle.

Saul waited and waited, but Samuel did not come. The Philistines were on the march. Saul's army grew restless. What were they waiting for? Was their king afraid to fight?

The Israelites began to lose courage. One by one, then in troops and companies, they began sneaking away. They went home to hide their families and belongings in case the Philistines overran the country.

Saul saw his army melting away. What was keeping Samuel? Finally he decided to wait no longer. Saul made the offering himself. No sooner had he placed the sacrifice on the altar when Samuel arrived.

"What have you done?" the prophet shouted at Saul.

"I could wait no longer. My army was deserting, and you still were not here. The Philistines can attack at any moment. I dare not lead my soldiers into battle without making the proper sacrifice to God."

Samuel refused to accept Saul's excuse. The king's instructions were clear: He was not to attack the Philistines until Samuel arrived. What was the matter with Saul? Did he not believe that God could bring about a victory? Had not Gideon defeated the Midianites with only three hundred men? Had not Samson killed a thousand Philistines with no other weapon than a donkey's jawbone? Nothing was impossible to God.

"You behaved foolishly," Samuel told Saul. "God wants a king who listens when He speaks. You have disobeyed. God will choose someone else to be king, because you refuse to do what He tells you."

The Israelites won a victory that day, but Saul took no pleasure in it. His heart was troubled. He believed he had done what any responsible leader would do. Yet Samuel said that God had rejected him.

Even so, Saul continued to do what he felt was right, in spite of Samuel.

Saul and Agag

One day Samuel came to Saul to tell him, "God commands you to make war against the Amalekites. He wants to punish them for attacking Israel on the way from Egypt. Go now! Defeat the Amalekites! Kill them all! Destroy everything they possess! Put Agag, their king, to death!"

Saul obeyed God's command. He assembled his army and led it against the Amalekites. It was an easy victory, but Saul felt dishonored by it. The Amalekites were a desert tribe with few possessions. Their king Agag was an old man. Saul decided to hold him for ransom. He also saw no purpose in killing the animals. Why kill a sheep, an ox, or a camel merely because it belonged to an Amalekite? Would it not be better to bring this wealth to Israel?

Saul ordered his soldiers to burn Agag's tents, smash jars and pottery, but save everything of value.

When Saul brought his army home, Samuel came out to meet him.

"May God bless you! I have carried out His command," Saul said.

"Really?" the prophet answered. "Then why do I hear sheep bleating? Why do I hear oxen lowing? Where do all these animals come from?"

"I took them from the Amalekites," said Saul. "We brought back their best sheep and cattle to be sacrificed to God, to give thanks for our victory. I swear that we destroyed everything else."

"You are lying!" cried Samuel. "Have you forgotten how God took you from nothing and made you king over Israel? He commanded you to destroy the Amalekites. Why did you disobey? Why did you keep back goods and cattle, in spite of what God told you?"

Saul began to tremble. "I did obey. I did exactly what I thought God wanted me to do. I made war on the Amalekites and defeated them. I captured Agag, their king. As for these animals, my soldiers, not I, insisted that I bring them to Gilgal as sacrifices."

Samuel felt sorrow and contempt for Saul. Disobeying God was bad enough; trying to put the blame on his soldiers was shameful. "What does God value more?" Samuel asked Saul. "Sacrifices and offerings, or obedience to His commands? It is better to obey God than to sacrifice to Him. It is better to listen when God speaks than to offer up the fat of choice rams. You have rejected God's word; therefore God rejects you. From now on, God no longer considers you to be king."

Samuel turned aside. Saul tried to keep him from walking away by grasping hold of Samuel's cloak. The garment tore. Samuel held up his torn cloak and said, "As you have torn my cloak, so has God torn the kingdom from your grasp and given it to someone more deserving. Do not ask God to change His mind. He is not a human being to lie or waver. What He says He will do, He will do."

Saul fell to his knees before Samuel and wept. "I admit I have sinned. I beg you, do not humiliate me before the leaders of our people. Let us offer a sacrifice together, so that I may worship with you."

Samuel took pity on Saul. They walked to the altar together and worshiped.

After the sacrifice, Samuel demanded that Agag be brought before him. The frightened old man pleaded for mercy. Samuel had none. Taking a sword in hand, he said, "Your sword made women childless, so now your mother will be childless among women."

Without saying another word, Samuel chopped Agag to pieces in front of the altar at Gilgal.

Samuel returned to Ramah. He prayed for Saul and mourned for him. But he could not change what God had decreed. God had turned His back on Saul. He commanded Samuel to choose another king for Israel.

Samuel Anoints David

God spoke to Samuel, saying, "Fill your horn with holy oil and go to the city of Bethlehem. Seek out a man named Jesse. I have chosen one of his sons to be king."

Samuel was afraid to go. "Saul is a troubled man. What if he learns of this? Should he find out that I am going to Bethlehem to anoint someone else as king, he might send someone to kill me."

God told Samuel to take a calf with him. Should anyone ask why he was going to Bethlehem, he could then say, "I am going there to offer a sacrifice to God."

Samuel filled a small goat's horn with holy oil. Selecting a fine calf for the sacrifice, he started for Bethlehem.

When he arrived, the town's leaders asked, "Do you come in peace?"

"Yes," Samuel told them. "I have come to offer a sacrifice to God. I invite all of you to share in the offering with me."

The people of Bethlehem accompanied Samuel to the top of a nearby hill, where he offered the sacrifice. Afterward, the prophet asked them, "Is there a man among you named Jesse?"

One of the town's elders stepped forward. "I am Jesse."

"Do you have any sons?"

"Yes, I have several," Jesse told Samuel.

"I want to meet them," Samuel said.

Jesse gathered his sons together and brought them to Samuel. Eliab was Jesse's oldest son. He was a tall, handsome young man.

Surely he is the one who God has chosen, Samuel thought. He held the horn of holy oil over Eliab's head, but the oil did not flow.

Samuel heard God's voice speaking to him. "Don't be impressed by this young man's face or marvel at how tall he is. He is not the one I have chosen. God sees a person in a different way. You look at his outer appearance. I look into his heart."

One by one, Jesse's seven sons passed before Samuel. They were all tall, handsome young men. Any one might have made a good king. However, when Samuel tried to empty the horn of oil over their heads, the oil refused to flow. God had not chosen any of them.

"Are these all your sons?" Samuel asked Jesse.

"There is one more; my youngest. David is his name," Jesse answered. "He is out in the fields, herding sheep."

"I want to see him," said Samuel. "Send someone to fetch him."

Jesse sent his other sons to bring David back from the fields. David was a beautiful lad, with a glowing complexion. He was handsomer than all his brothers put together. Although he was only a boy, David was not afraid of the prophet. He greeted Samuel as someone he had been expecting. Samuel heard God's voice speaking to him. "Anoint this child. He is the one."

Samuel held the horn over David's head. This time the oil poured down. It ran over David's hair and dripped onto his shoulders, where each drop of oil miraculously became a diamond or a pearl. Far more oil ran out than the horn could possibly hold. Yet it remained as full as it was in the beginning. By this miracle God made known that he had chosen David to be king of Israel from that day forth. God's spirit came down and rested with David, while Samuel returned to Ramah.

The Witch of Endor

Samuel kept the secret of David's kingship. He never told Saul that he had anointed David to take his place. Nonetheless, Saul sensed that God had abandoned him. He became troubled and melancholy, suddenly flying into murderous rages for no apparent reason. No one could comfort Saul when these strange moods seized him. Only Samuel possessed the power to heal the king's spirit. But Samuel remained in Ramah. Saul never saw him again.

After many years Samuel died and was buried in Ramah, the town where he was born. The people of Israel mourned him greatly. Saul mourned him most of all, for with Samuel gone, there was no other prophet in the land of Israel whom he trusted to tell him God's will.

Saul needed to know, for these were dangerous times. The Philistines returned to make war on Israel again. They gathered their army at the town of Shunem. Saul assembled his forces to meet them at Mount Gilboa.

When Saul saw the size of the Philistine army, he became worried. Should he attack, or was it better to wait until reinforcements arrived? Saul regretted the many times he had disobeyed God. Now he desperately needed God to tell him what to do. But God was silent. Samuel could have helped him. But Samuel was dead.

Saul prayed to God to send him an answer, but none came. Neither priests nor prophets nor interpreters of dreams could tell Saul what to do.

In desperation, Saul asked his followers, "Do you know of any woman who can tell the future by means of ghosts or other spirits?"

They answered, "There is such a woman. She is a witch who lives in the town of Endor."

Although Saul had ruthlessly hunted down witches and wizards, he decided to visit this woman in hope of finding answers to his questions. He changed his clothes and disguised his face. Setting out at night with only two servants, he came to the village of Endor. He found the witch's house and knocked.

The door opened. Behind it stood the ugliest woman Saul had ever seen. "What do you want?" she asked him.

"I want you to raise up a spirit from the dead," Saul told her.

The witch hesitated at first. "What makes you think I can do such things? You know what Saul the king has done. He has driven every witch and wizard out of Israel. Those he caught, he killed. How do I know that you are not setting a trap for me, so that I may be put to death?"

Saul answered, "I swear by God Himself that you will suffer no punishment if you raise this spirit for me."

The witch asked, "Whom shall I raise from the dead?"

"Bring me Samuel," Saul told her.

The witch let out a shriek. "You have tricked me! I know who you are! You are Saul!"

"Don't be afraid. I gave my word I would not harm you. Just tell me what you see."

The witch fell into a trance. "I see a spirit rising up out of the earth."

"What does the spirit look like?"

"It resembles an old man wearing a long white robe."

Saul recognized the spirit of Samuel. He fell to the ground and closed his eyes.

The spirit of Samuel looked at Saul and said, "Why have you disturbed my rest?"

"I need your help," Saul pleaded. "The Philistines have come to make war against Israel. God has deserted me. He speaks to me no more, neither by prophets nor by dreams. That is why I called you up from the dead. You must tell me what to do!"

"Why do you ask? The answer is plain," Samuel's spirit replied. "God has deserted you. You disobeyed Him when He told you to kill the Amalekites. Therefore, He has taken the kingdom away from you and given it to another. David, the son of Jesse, is his name. By this time tomorrow night, you and your sons will join me in the realm of the dead. God will deliver the army of Israel into the hands of the Philistines."

The spirit of Samuel faded away. After hearing these terrible words, Saul fainted from fear and weariness, for he had eaten nothing that day. The witch of Endor revived him. She urged him to take a little food. Saul refused. His heart was sick, and he had no appetite. Only when both his servants insisted did he finally agree to eat.

The witch prepared a meal of meat and bread. Saul ate, then returned to the camp at Mount Gilboa.

Saul went out to fight the Philistines the next day. As Samuel predicted, the army of Israel was routed. Saul's three sons were killed. Saul himself was badly wounded. His armor-bearer helped him flee.

When Saul could run no more, he asked his armor-bearer to kill him, so that the Philistines would not capture him alive. The man refused. Saul took his own sword and fell on it, so that he died. When Saul's armor-bearer saw that the king was dead, he fell upon his sword and ended his own life, too.

The Philistines found Saul's body and those of his sons. They cut off his head, stripped off his armor, and nailed his body and those of his sons to the wall of the city of Beth-Shan.

When the people of Jabesh-Gilead heard about the disaster at Gilboa, they sent out their bravest men to rescue Saul's body. They did not forget the debt they owed the king for saving their city from the Ammonites. The men of Jabesh-Gilead crept up to the walls of Beth-Shan under cover of darkness. They removed Saul's body and those of his sons and brought them home to Jabesh-Gilead, where they buried them beneath a tamarisk tree.

David became king in Saul's place. The elders of Israel anointed him at Hebron, as Samuel once had done secretly in Bethlehem.

And David reigned over Israel, for God was with him.

The Story of David

David seemed destined for greatness even when he was a boy. As the youngest of Jesse's sons, it was his task to tend his father's sheep. David played his harp to soothe the flock. David played and sang so beautifully that wild animals came out of the fields to lie at his feet. Birds flew down from the sky to listen, for David's song was as lovely as their own.

This is one of the songs, or psalms, that David wrote as a young boy, watching over his father's sheep on the hills outside of Bethlehem:

> God is my shepherd; I shall not want.
> He lets me rest in green pastures.
> He leads me beside quiet waters.
> He restores my soul.
> He guides me along straight paths for His name's sake.
> Yea, though I walk through the Valley of the Shadow of Death
> I will fear no evil.
> Your rod and staff comfort me.
> You prepare a table for me before my foes.
> You anointed my head with oil; my cup overflows.
> Surely, goodness and mercy shall follow me all through my life.
> And I shall dwell in God's house forever.

Sometimes a good shepherd must fight to defend his flock. One day, as David grazed his sheep on a hillside, he saw a lion coming. David turned to fight the lion, when suddenly he noticed a bear approaching from the opposite direction.

What could David do? He could not fight both animals at the same time. If he fought the lion, the bear would ravage his flock. If he fought the bear, the lion would kill his sheep. He could not call for help. Bethlehem was too far away.

David prayed to God, and God sent him an idea. David fitted a stone into his sling. A sling is a simple weapon—a leather patch attached to two cords. However, in the hands of a skilled slinger, it can throw a stone a great distance with considerable force and accuracy. David was an exceptional slinger, one of the best in Israel. Hiding behind a rock, he flung a stone at the lion. Then he flung a stone at the bear.

The two animals looked around to see what had hit them. The lion saw the bear. The bear saw the lion. They charged at each other, clawing, biting, mauling, until both lay dead on the hillside. David returned to Bethlehem with the skins of both animals on his head. From that time on, people began to say that God had marked David for greatness.

David and Goliath

Meanwhile, Saul's melancholy grew worse. His worried servants knew that music could soothe a troubled soul. They sent for the best harpist in the land to play for the king. That person was David.

David loved and admired Saul. He grieved to see how troubled the king was. He tried his best to cheer him. Saul's spirits rose whenever David played his harp.

Saul came to love David as much as he loved his own son Jonathan.

One cause of Saul's distress was that he had no rest from fighting the Philistines. No matter how many times he defeated them, they came again and again to do battle with Israel. Word arrived that another Philistine army had invaded the territory of the tribe of Judah at a place called Socoh. Saul gathered an Israelite army to meet them. The Israelites encountered the Philistines at the Valley of Elah. Saul's forces encamped in the mountains on one side; the Philistines camped on the other, with the valley between.

The Philistines had a great champion, a giant warrior named Goliath. He stood over ten feet tall. He wore a bronze helmet, bronze greaves on his legs, an iron sword with a double edge, and a breastplate of bronze scales whose weight alone was two hundred pounds. His spear had a huge bronze head with a shaft as long and heavy as the cross beam of a weaver's loom. His shield bearer walked before him, carrying Goliath's immense shield and a pair of javelins.

Every day Goliath walked up and down the length of the valley, taunting the Israelites in the hills. "Why are you hiding up there in the mountains? Come down to fight! Isn't that why we're here? You're Israelites, servants of Saul. I'm a Philistine, your enemy. If you're afraid to come down, choose a champion to fight in your name. Send your best warrior to meet me. If he kills me, then the Philistines will be your slaves. If I kill him, then the Israelites will be our slaves. What are you afraid of? Send a man to fight!"

Before going off to war, Saul had sent David back to his family. David was too young to fight; there was no place for him in the battle line, and Saul would have no time to listen to music. However, three of David's older brothers came to fight.

The two armies faced each other for forty days. Supplies began running low. Jesse sent David to bring food to his brothers. He packed a donkey with ten loaves of bread, a measure of flour, and ten cheeses as a gift to their commander. David was to learn if his brothers were well, and to bring back news from them.

David arrived in camp just in time to see Goliath parading up and down the valley, shouting his daily challenge to the Israelites. The men of Israel trembled to hear his voice.

"Who is this loud, boastful fellow?" David asked his brothers.

"He is Goliath, the Philistine champion," his older brother Eliab said. "Every day he comes to mock us. King Saul has promised a huge reward, along with his daughter Michal's hand in marriage, to the man who kills him. Even so, no one dares fight Goliath."

David grew angry to hear this. "How dare this Philistine dog defy the armies of God!"

David's brothers laughed at him. "What do you propose to do? Are you going to fight Goliath? You're just a shepherd boy who plays the harp. Do you think you are braver than all the mighty warriors gathered here?"

"I will fight the Philistine," said David. "Not for the reward. Not even for King Saul's beautiful daughter. I will fight to restore the honor of Israel. If God is with me, I will defeat the giant."

David marched to Saul's tent. He told the king he was ready to fight Goliath. Saul thought David had lost his wits. "You are only a boy. You are not used to handling weapons of war. Goliath has been a trained warrior since childhood."

"I am not afraid," David said. "When I looked after my father's sheep, I often had to protect them from lions and bears. Once a lion stole a lamb from the flock. I pursued it, caught it by the jaw, struck it down, and rescued the lamb. I was not afraid of any wild animal as long as God was with me. Why should I fear this Philistine?"

Since David was determined to fight Goliath, Saul helped him prepare. He dressed David in his own armor, the finest in Israel. He buckled his sword around David's waist and placed his helmet on David's head. David rattled and clanked. He nearly tripped over Saul's sword.

"This will not do," David told the king. "I am not used to armor. I cannot walk with all this metal weighing my body down. Let me use the weapons I know best. If God is with me, I need nothing more."

David removed the armor. Taking up his shepherd's staff, his pouch, and his sling, he went off to meet Goliath.

Along the way, he crossed a brook. David kneeled and selected five smooth stones from the streambed and put them in his pouch. Then he descended into the valley.

Goliath saw him from a distance. "What!" the Philistine giant roared to the Israelites. "You must think I am a dog to send a child after me with a stick!" He cursed God, David, and all the tribes of Israel with the foulest language imaginable. After that, he banged his spear on his shield until the metal rang. "Come to me, little boy!" he shouted at David. "I'll feed your flesh to the buzzards and jackals!"

David watched him in silence. Finally he said, "You come against me with sword, spear, and javelin. But I come against you in the Name of the God of Israel, Whom you insulted and cursed. Say whatever you like. I am unafraid, for I know that today God will deliver you into my hands. The mighty Philistine champion will be overthrown by a boy armed only with a sling. I will strike you down and cut off your head. The buzzards and jackals will eat your flesh, and the flesh of your companions. Then everyone will know God reigns in Israel. His might does not come from the spear or the sword, but from the Power of His Name. God will decide the battle; and He will put you into my hands."

Goliath bellowed with rage. He drew his sword and charged forward. David reached into his pouch. The five stones he took from the stream miraculously became one shining stone engraved with God's name. David fitted the stone into his sling. He whirled the sling around and around, faster and faster. Goliath towered over David. He raised his sword to strike.

David released his sling. The shining stone whizzed through the air. God's hand guided it to its mark. The stone struck Goliath between the eyes, just below the rim of his helmet. The Philistine champion dropped his sword. His eyes rolled back in his head. He tottered to the right, to the left, then crashed forward on his face like a great tree falling. David picked up Goliath's sword. He raised it high, then swung it down with all his might, severing the giant's head from his shoulders.

The Philistines fled for their lives. Saul and his army pursued them all the way to the gates of their cities.

The Israelites won a great victory that day. When they returned home, the women of Israel came out to greet them, singing,

> *Saul has slain his thousands,*
> *But David, tens of thousands!*

What is this? Saul wondered. *Do the people of Israel honor David more than their king? David has stolen the joy of victory from me. Will he also take my throne?*

Saul became suspicious that David was plotting to overthrow him. Once, he loved David. Now he hated him.

Jonathan and Michal

David was too popular to be attacked openly. Instead, Saul began looking for secret ways to rid himself of his rival.

Saul's daughter Michal had fallen in love with David. David loved her, too, and wished to marry her. It was his right, since Saul had promised Michal to the warrior who killed Goliath. Saul's servants urged David to demand Michal as his bride. But David respected Saul too much to insist.

David said to the king, "I am a poor youth, of no great standing. Whatever glory I have won has come about because God stood with me. I love your daughter Michal, but I am not sure it is fitting for a commoner like me to marry a princess. I have no wealth to give her."

Saul told David, "I would be happy to bring you into our family. As for Michal's dowry, I would be content to have you strike a blow against our enemies. I will put you in command of my soldiers. Bring me the foreskins of one hundred Philistines that you kill in battle. That will be enough." Saul wanted David to endanger himself on the battlefield, where he might be captured or killed.

David did not suspect treachery. He thought Saul was doing him great honor. David and his soldiers went forth and attacked the Philistines. God protected David. He and his men killed more than a hundred. They stripped their bodies of weapons and armor, and cut off their foreskins. For unlike the Israelites, Philistine men were uncircumcised.

Saul pretended to be pleased when David presented him with a sack full of enemy foreskins. David married Michal with great rejoicing. But Saul's fear of David grew even greater.

Saul spoke of his fears with Jonathan, his oldest son. Since Jonathan would be king after him, Saul thought Jonathan would be jealous of David, too. But Jonathan was David's best friend. He knew that his father's fears were imaginary. No one in Israel was more loyal than David.

Saul told Jonathan of a plan to assassinate David. Jonathan was horrified. He pleaded for his friend's life. "Father, I beg you, do not commit this terrible sin against your servant. David has never acted against you. He has always served you faithfully. Do not dishonor yourself by killing an innocent man."

Jonathan's words moved Saul. He told his son, "I will not harm David. As God lives, I will not kill him."

But David was still in danger. At times an evil spirit came over Saul. He could not control his emotions.

One night, while David played his harp, the king fell into a fit of rage. He seized a spear and flung it at David. The spear quivered in the wall, just inches away from David's head. David dropped his harp and fled from Saul's presence. He ran home to Michal.

"Your father tried to kill me!" he told his wife.

Michal, like her brother Jonathan, knew Saul's true feelings toward David. "It may be that you are still not safe. Lie down on the floor. Keep away from the window. I will look to see if anyone is outside."

Michal glanced out the window. She saw shadowy figures moving in the courtyard. "My father's men are out there. I only see a few, but more may arrive tonight. If you are still here by morning, they will kill you."

"What can I do?" David asked.

"I will help you escape." Michal tied the bedclothes together so that David could climb down through the window. He eluded Saul's men in the darkness. In the morning, he made his way to Ramah, where Samuel lived. He knew the king would not harm him while he was under the prophet's protection.

The moment the sun came up, Saul's men burst into David's house. They stormed up the stairs, into the bedroom. Michal tried to stop them. They pushed her aside. A figure lay on the bed, covered by a thick goat hair blanket. The soldiers struck the sleeping figure with their swords. They pulled the blanket aside, thinking to find David's corpse.

Instead, they found a life-size wooden statue, a trophy David had taken from the Philistines. "Why did you deceive my men? Why did you let your father's enemy escape?" Saul asked Michal when he learned what had happened.

"What choice did I have?" Michal asked her father. "David threatened to kill me unless I helped him get away."

Michal lied for David's sake. She wanted her father to think she sympathized with him, so that he would confide in her. Like her brother Jonathan, she longed to find a way to help Saul overcome his senseless hatred.

Saul sent soldiers to Ramah to bring David back. When they arrived, the spirit of God came over them. They danced in a frenzy, threw themselves on the ground, and tore off their clothes. When they recovered their senses, they could not remember why they came. When Saul went to capture David himself, the same thing happened to him. The people of Ramah saw him writhing on the ground and asked themselves, "Has our king become a prophet?"

After that, Saul left David in peace for a while, for he saw that God protected him.

David returned from Ramah, but he was still unsure of his safety. He asked Jonathan, "What have I done to make your father want to kill me?"

Jonathan reassured David that Saul did not seek his life. "He does nothing, great or small, without telling me," Jonathan said. "If he were plotting against you, I would know it."

"Maybe not," said David. "Your father knows that you and I are friends. He would not discuss such things with you, for he knows you would tell me. I am afraid to close my eyes at night or turn my back. I must tell you, my friend, sometimes I fear I am within an inch of death."

"How can I help you?" Jonathan asked.

David answered, "Tomorrow is the Festival of the New Moon. The king will expect me to dine with him. I will hide in the field. If your father asks, 'Where is David?' tell him, 'David went back to Bethlehem to visit his family.' If your father says, 'Good,' and lets it pass, then all is well. But if he becomes angry that I am out of his reach, then I will know he still means to kill me."

"I will do it," said Jonathan. "But if my father is angry, how will I get word to you?"

David had no idea, but Jonathan had a plan. "I will come to the field tomorrow to go target shooting. One of my pages will come with me. I will shoot my arrows, then send the boy to find them. Listen closely to what I say. If I tell him, 'The arrows fell to the side; pick them up,' you will know there is nothing to fear. But if I say, 'The arrows are beyond you,' then run for your life, for my father means to kill you. I will pray to God that you get away. Promise me, David, that you will be my friend as long as I live, and if I should die, that you will always care for my wife and chidren. I know that God is with you, as He was with my father in the beginning."

David swore to be Jonathan's friend forever.

The next morning Jonathan came out to the field. A page came with him, carrying his bow and arrows. Jonathan strung the bow. He fitted an arrow to the bowstring. Then he told the boy, "I will shoot the arrows. You run and fetch them." The arrow streaked across the field. The boy ran after it. He stopped and looked.

"Not there!" Jonathan cried. "The arrow is beyond you!"

At that moment David knew that Saul still meant to kill him, and that he would have no peace until either he or Saul was dead. For indeed, when Jonathan informed his father that David had gone to Bethlehem, Saul became so angry that he flung a spear at his oldest son.

David the Outlaw

David had only one choice if he wished to live. He had to become an outlaw. His brothers joined him. So did desperate men from all over Israel. David's band grew until he had four hundred followers. They hid for years in the barren, rocky wilderness of En-Gedi, always on the move, relentlessly pursued by Saul's soldiers.

By now Saul's hatred for David bordered on insanity. He vowed to wipe out David and anyone who helped him. A spy told Saul that David had visited the village of Nob. Ahimelech, the priest, was David's friend.

Saul surrounded the village. "Why have you conspired against me with David, my enemy?" he asked Ahimelech.

"I have conspired with no one," Ahimelech insisted. "David is not your enemy. Is there anyone in your house who is more loyal? Have you forgotten that he married your daughter Michal? Do you no longer remember how you made him your armor-bearer, the captain of your guard? David is my friend. This is not the first time he has visited Nob. He spoke of no conspiracy, and I know of none."

Saul became enraged. "Traitor! You will die!" He turned to his soldiers, screaming, "Kill Ahimelech! Kill all the priests of Nob." But Saul's officers refused to raise their swords against God's holy priests. Saul turned to Doeg, a foreign mercenary in his service.

"Kill the priests! Kill them all!"

Doeg attacked Ahimelech and the other priests. He did not stop until all were dead. Then he attacked the village. He slaughtered everyone in it, not sparing women, children, or infants in their cradles. Even the animals fell to the sword.

Only one person escaped: Abiathar, one of Ahimelech's sons, who fled to the wilderness to join David.

In spite of this outrage, David still loved Saul. There were times when he had the opportunity to kill him, but he would not do so. Nor would he allow any of his followers to harm Israel's king.

Once Saul pursued David and several of his men into a cave. Saul himself entered the cave to search for them.

"God has put the king into our power!" David's men whispered to him. "Saul is alone. We can kill him or take him prisoner."

"God forbid that I harm the king in any way," David told them. He refused to allow them to lift a hand against Saul. However, when Saul came close to David's hiding place, David reached out and sliced off the corner of his cloak.

David remained in hiding until Saul left. Then he ran out of the cave, crying, "My lord, the king!"

Saul turned around. David bowed and said, "Why do you believe I mean you harm? Had I wished, I could have killed you in the cave. Look at your cloak. I was close enough to cut a piece from the corner; was I not close enough to kill you? God will judge between us, and you must answer to God for your deeds. But as for me, I will never harm you."

Saul wept. "Is that you, David? Now I realize that you are a better person than I am. For you have been loyal to me, but I persecuted you. Surely, you will be king after me. Perhaps God has already given the kingdom to you."

Saul turned away, and David led his followers back to their stronghold.

Time and again David attempted to prove his loyalty. But when the melancholy spirit seized Saul, nothing could convince him that David was not his enemy. He pursued him without rest, until David and his followers were driven to seek refuge in the country of the Philistines.

Only when Saul and Jonathan perished in battle at Gilboa did David find peace. But he did not rejoice. When the news came, he broke down and wept.

> *Your beauty, O Israel, lies dead upon the hills.*
> *The mighty ones have fallen.*
> *Saul and Jonathan led lives of loveliness and grace.*
> *They died together, separated neither in life nor in death.*
> *They were swifter than eagles;*
> *Stronger than lions.*
> *The mighty ones have fallen.*
> *The weapons of war are shattered.*

David the King

David returned to Israel as king. He set about uniting the troubled land. One of his first acts was to honor the people of Jabesh-Gilead for rescuing the bodies of

Saul and Jonathan and burying them with honor. He also made peace with Abner, Saul's general.

David was willing to overlook the past: the days when he lived in hiding, pursued like a wild animal, seeing his closest friends put to the sword. However, some of his followers were not as forgiving. One was Joab, David's bravest commander. Joab never forgot that Abner had murdered his brother Asahel.

Joab sent messengers to Abner, asking for a meeting in Hebron. Suspecting nothing, Abner answered the summons. Joab met him at the city gate. The two commanders stepped aside for a talk. Suddenly Joab drew a dagger and stabbed Abner in the stomach.

David was outraged to hear about the killing. "I and my people did not shed Abner's blood," he declared. "May the guilt fall on Joab and his family." David buried Abner in Hebron. He himself wept at the general's grave. He ordered Joab, his followers, and all the people of Israel to mourn as well.

David led the armies of Israel against their enemies. God was with him. He won every battle. Soon the Edomites, Moabites, Canaanites—even the mighty Philistines—offered to make peace. After years of fighting, Israel's endless wars came to an end.

The Conquest of Jerusalem

With the land at peace, David turned his attention to other matters. Israel still did not have a permanent capital. God told David that the city of Jerusalem was going to be Israel's capital for all time.

God's choice puzzled David. Jerusalem had never been part of Israel. It belonged to the Jebusite people. Impregnable walls surrounded the city, so high and strong that the Jebusites boasted they could defend it with a handful of blind men and cripples. No enemy had ever breached those walls as far back as anyone remembered. On the other hand, choosing Jerusalem made sense. If David selected an Israelite city to be the capital, some would surely complain that David was favoring one tribe over another. Jerusalem, however, belonged to no tribe. Therefore, it could be said to belong to all.

God had another reason for choosing Jerusalem. A rocky outcrop stood in the center of the city. This was Mount Moriah, where Abraham came to sacrifice Isaac; where Jacob wrestled with God the night before he met Esau. This was the spot where Israel began. No other place was as holy.

But how was David to capture Jerusalem? He led an army of thirty thousand men into the hills. They surrounded the city. The Jebusites laughed at them from the walls. They had plenty of food. A secret spring provided fresh water. They had seen invaders come in the past. They knew that all they had to do was wait. Sooner or later, David and the Israelites would grow tired of the endless siege and march away.

However, David did not plan to wait. His general Joab had discovered a secret opening in the rock. The opening hid a spring. A narrow shaft led up through the rock to the city above. This must be how Jerusalem got its water. Joab asked David's permission to try a daring feat. He proposed to climb up the shaft with a small party of men. Once inside, they would open the gates of the city. The risks were great, but Joab was eager to make the attempt. If successful, he would surely regain the trust he had lost by murdering Abner.

Clinging to the slippery rocks, Joab and his men inched their way up the narrow shaft. They reached the top long after midnight. Sure enough, they found themselves inside Jerusalem. All the inhabitants were asleep. The Jebusites put so much trust in the strength of their walls that only a few guards were posted. The city seemed deserted.

Joab led his soldiers through the dark alleys until they reached the main gate of the city. While Joab's men hid in the shadows, their commander walked forward to talk with the guard.

"Good evening. Peace be with you," Joab said, drawing his cloak more closely around his body to hide his Israelite dress.

"Peace be with you," the guard answered. "Why are you abroad this evening?"

"I cannot sleep. I am worried about the Israelites," Joab said.

The guard laughed. "Don't lose sleep over them. They will never enter Jerusalem."

"If they do, I will be ready for them." Joab drew his sword.

"That's a fine weapon!" the guard exclaimed. "May I see it?"

"Of course!" Joab handed his sword to the guard. As the guard examined the sword, Joab asked him, "Whom would you like to kill with that blade?"

"Why, Joab! The Israelite commander!"

"Then you are lucky, because he stands before you. I am Joab."

Before the guard could sound the alarm, Joab drew his dagger and killed him. Joab's men rushed forward to open the city gates. When the astonished Jebusites awoke the next morning, they found Jerusalem in the hands of their enemy.

Joab had won a great victory. David showered him with honors, making him first among his officers.

David made peace with the Jebusites. They accepted him as their king and promised to worship only the God of Israel. David, in turn, promised to honor and protect them as if they were his own people.

Jerusalem now became The City of David. David extended the walls and made the city even greater than it had been before.

Now that Israel had a capital, David ordered that the Ark of the Covenant be brought there. Jerusalem was to become its permanent home.

All Israel gathered to welcome the Ark to Jerusalem. As the Levites carried it into the city, Jerusalem exploded with rejoicing. David himself danced in the streets with the people.

Later, his wife, Michal, said to him, "I am ashamed of you. Why did you make such a fool of yourself, dancing and leaping in the streets with the common people? Have you forgotten that you are the king?"

David replied, "God made me king of Israel. Before Him I will rejoice. If He asks it, I will humble myself still further. You think I disgraced myself, but I believe that the common people whom you despise will honor me even more because I did not hesitate to humble myself before God."

A House for God

David built a beautiful palace in Jerusalem for his sons and daughters, and his growing number of wives. Israel had become a powerful nation. Her neighbors all wished to sign treaties of peace. In those days the rulers of nations sealed a treaty by marrying each other's daughters. David soon had many foreign wives, besides his two Israelite wives, Abigail and Ahinoam. His first wife, Michal, died in childbirth.

One day David looked out the window. He gazed toward Mount Moriah, where the Tabernacle stood. He asked his friend Nathan, "Is this right? I live in a beautiful palace built of fragrant cedarwood. Where does God reside? In a tent!

Surely it is my duty to build God a better house. I will build Him a Temple!"

Nathan was a prophet, a man who spoke with God. He said to David, "Do what your heart tells you. I am sure God will approve."

But God did not approve. That night He spoke to Nathan. "Go to David. Speak these words to him. Thus says God, 'Why do you want to build Me a Temple? I have dwelled in a tent since I brought the children of Israel out of Egypt. I never said to Moses or to any of the judges who came after him, 'Build me a Temple of cedarwood!' I took you, a mere shepherd boy, and raised you up to become king of Israel. I will be with you always, as I will be with your children in days to come. But you are not to build a Temple for Me. You are a man of war. My Temple must be a House of Peace. Your son Solomon, who is not yet born, will be a man of peace. He will build My Temple."

Nathan repeated these words to David. David was sorry that God would not allow him to build a magnificent Temple as he would have wished, but he accepted God's will. He offered a prayer, promising to serve God with all his heart for as long as he lived.

David and Bathsheba

One hot day David climbed up to the roof of his palace to enjoy the breeze from the hills. He looked over the wall and saw a young woman taking a bath in the courtyard of her house. The woman had no idea that someone was spying on her, least of all the king. David should have turned away, but he continued to watch, entranced by her beauty.

"Does anyone know that woman's name?" he asked his attendants.

"She is Bathsheba. Her husband is one of your officers, Uriah the Hittite," they told him.

Uriah was a foreign mercenary in David's service. He was one of David's best commanders. Uriah had served the king loyally for many years.

"Bring her to me."

A messenger summoned Bathsheba to the palace so David could meet her. Bathsheba's intelligence and beauty captivated the king. Even though David already had many wives, he made up his mind to possess Bathsheba.

David knew the laws of Israel did not allow him to take another man's wife while that man still lived. However, if Bathsheba became a widow, she would be free to marry whom she chose. Her husband was a soldier in the king's service. Soldiering was a dangerous profession. If Uriah were to fall in battle, no one would hold the king responsible.

David wrote a secret letter and sealed it with the royal seal. Then he summoned Uriah the Hittite. David gave Uriah the letter, saying, "Deliver this message to my general Joab. Make sure no one else reads it."

Uriah saluted. "Consider it done, my lord."

David smiled as Uriah rode away. Joab was his most reliable general. He could be trusted to follow orders—and to keep secrets.

War had recently begun between Israel and the Ammonite kingdom. Joab commanded the Israelite army besieging the city of Rabbah. Uriah delivered David's letter to him. Joab dismissed Uriah and went to his tent to read it.

David had written these words: "Place the bearer of this message, Uriah the Hittite, in the front rank where the fighting is fiercest. When the enemy attacks, pull your forces back so that Uriah and those with him are cut off. Let them be surrounded by Ammonites and killed."

Joab did not question his orders. He did not know or care what Uriah had done. All that mattered was that the king wanted him eliminated. Joab could arrange that.

The next morning he sent Uriah with a few other soldiers to an exposed position opposite the gates of Rabbah.

"Keep watch on the gate," he told Uriah. "Sound the alarm if you see the Ammonites coming out of the city. I will send reinforcements to drive them back."

Joab's spies had learned that the Ammonites were planning a counterattack. They had assembled their best fighters behind the gates of Rabbah.

The attack came at noon. Uriah sounded the alarm. He sent three messengers to Joab, pleading for reinforcements. Joab did nothing. The Ammonites swarmed over Uriah's position. Only then did Joab attack, driving them back into the city.

That evening Joab sent a messenger to David. He told the messenger, "If the king is upset because so many soldiers have fallen in battle, tell him that Uriah the Hittite is also dead."

The messenger delivered his report, speaking the words that Joab had given him. David replied, "Tell the general not to be troubled by these losses. War is a dangerous undertaking. Men fall by the sword one way or another. He is to continue besieging the city until he captures it."

David could read between the lines of Joab's message. His orders had been carried out. The Ammonites would be blamed for Uriah's death. Poor Bathsheba was now a widow. David was pleased.

Bathsheba went into mourning when she learned her husband had been killed. She mourned him for many days. Uriah was a good man, and Bathsheba loved him dearly.

After the period of mourning, David sent for Bathsheba and offered to marry her. Bathsheba accepted eagerly. What greater honor could any woman have, she thought, than to become the king's wife?

David married Bathsheba with joy and celebration. A year later she gave birth to a child. David was pleased to have another son. He felt that God had blessed him. No one but Joab knew about the crime he had committed. And Joab would never tell.

Soon after Bathsheba's child was born, Nathan the prophet came to speak with David. David welcomed him. "Why has my friend Nathan come?"

"I must talk with the king about a troubling matter," the prophet replied.

"What is it?"

Nathan began. "Two men once lived in a certain city. One was rich; the other was poor. The rich man had many flocks of sheep and goats. The poor man only had one little lamb, but he loved that lamb as if she were his own child. He fed the lamb from his own table and let her drink out of his own cup. He combed her and cherished her.

"One day a traveler came to the rich man's house. The rich man welcomed the traveler as his guest. He ordered his servants to slaughter a lamb for dinner. But instead of taking a lamb from his own flocks, he ordered them to kill the poor man's lamb. So it was done. The poor man's only lamb, which he loved with his whole heart, was taken away and slaughtered for the rich man's table. Now I ask you, O King, what punishment does the rich man deserve?"

David shook with anger. "Why, that man deserves to die! At the very least, he should be forced to pay the poor man four times the lamb's value."

Nathan pointed his finger at the king. "You are the man."

David fell back in his seat. The prophet's piercing eyes fixed him in an unwavering stare. "Listen to God's words," Nathan continued. "'I took you from your father's house and raised you up as My anointed king. I sheltered you from your enemies and made you ruler over the whole house of Israel. If that were not enough, I would have done still more for you. Why then did you turn away from My commandments? You murdered Uriah the Hittite. You struck him down with the sword of the Ammonites and took his wife as your own. You used treachery and violence against Uriah. Therefore, treachery and violence will never leave your house.'"

David began to weep. He thought no one knew about his crime. But God knew. David tore his robe. He threw himself at Nathan's feet, crying in anguish, "God, forgive me! I have sinned against You!"

"God forgives you. You deserve to die, but God will spare your life. However, your newborn son, Bathsheba's child, will not live."

With these terrible words, Nathan turned his back on the king and left.

Nathan's prophecy came true. The newborn prince died. David's treachery against Uriah would be repaid tenfold by treachery within his own family. For evil acts, like poisonous weeds, spread their venom across generations.

Absalom, My Son!

As David grew old, his many sons began pondering their future. Who would succeed him as king of Israel?

Jealousy turned to violence. Amnon, David's oldest son, raped his half-sister Tamar. Tamar's brother Absalom pretended to forgive Amnon. But at a feast when Amnon was drunk with wine, Absalom ordered his servants to stab Amnon to death.

Such lawlessness among his own children shocked David. Even so, he could not bring himself to punish Absalom. Absalom was David's favorite child. He was extremely handsome, as David had been in his youth. His most striking feature was a glorious head of red-gold hair whose flowing curls reached his waist.

Everyone assumed that Absalom would become king after David. Indeed, that was David's hope. But Absalom did not want to wait. He began plotting against his father.

First, he needed the support of the people. Absalom got up every morning and went to the gates of Jerusalem, where the king's judges sat. He stood with the people waiting to have their cases heard and asked them, "Where are you from? Why have you come here?"

The people were flattered to have a royal prince speak to them. They told Absalom about themselves and the injustices that had brought them to Jerusalem. Absalom would nod in sympathy.

"It is too bad that you have to travel such a long distance, and wait in such a long line to get the justice you deserve," Absalom told each one. "Do you know why this is so? It is because my father, the king, doesn't really care about you. The judges he appoints don't care, either. Now, if I were king, matters would be different. You wouldn't have to wait in line all day to speak to a judge. You would come right to me. I myself would hear your case, and I would rule in your favor, because I love you. Remember, Absalom is your friend."

Of course, this was nonsense. It was impossible for the king to hear all the cases in the land, and Absalom knew it. However, he was so handsome and spoke so sincerely that the people believed him. When they bent down to kiss his hand in gratitude, Absalom would raise them up and embrace them. "Remember Absalom, your friend who loves you."

In this way Absalom began stealing the people's hearts away from David. He also attracted support from powerful people in the land. The day arrived when Absalom felt strong enough to challenge his father for the throne. He said to David, "Permit me to go to Hebron, to worship God at the graves of our ancestors." David, suspecting nothing, granted permission.

As soon as Absalom arrived in Hebron, he sent messengers to his supporters throughout the land of Israel. "When you hear the ram's horn blow, cry out, 'Absalom is king in Hebron!'"

The ram's horns sounded. First by the hundreds, then by the thousands, people gathered their weapons and flocked to Hebron to help Absalom fight against David.

Word of the uprising reached Jerusalem. At first, David could not believe what his officers told him. Absalom, his beloved son, had risen against him? Why?

But there was no time to look for answers. David gathered his army and left Jerusalem. He dared not remain in his own capital. If Absalom's supporters within the city suddenly were to rise up, he could be surrounded and captured.

David crossed the Jordan River. He paused to organize his forces. Joab, his general, remained loyal. So did a detachment of Philistine mercenaries. David wanted to lead his soldiers into battle, but his officers would not allow it. "It does not matter if we are defeated," they told David. "You can raise another army and fight again. However, if you are killed or captured, then our cause is lost."

David promised to remain behind to pray for his army's success. As his troops marched into battle, he begged them not to harm Absalom. In spite of his son's treachery, David still loved him.

The two armies met in the dense Forest of Ephraim. Both sides suffered heavy losses; men fell by the thousands. At first it seemed the victory would go to Absalom, but slowly David's generals gained the upper hand. Absalom's soldiers began to flee.

Seeing the battle was lost, Absalom thought only about saving himself. He mounted a swift mule and galloped away, abandoning those who had fought for him. Absalom rode through the forest. His beautiful hair streamed out behind him in the wind.

The mule passed beneath the branches of a giant elm tree. Absalom's wind-blown hair became tangled in the branches, pulling him from the mule's back. The mule galloped on, leaving Absalom hanging by his hair between heaven and earth.

One of David's pursuing soldiers came racing back to Joab. "I have seen Absalom," he cried. "He hangs by his hair from a great elm."

"You saw him?" Joab asked. "Is that all you did? Why didn't you kill him? I would have paid you ten pieces of silver for his life."

"God forbid!" the soldier replied. "I would not have harmed Absalom for a thousand pieces of silver. Have you forgotten what the king told us before we went into battle? 'Do not harm Absalom, for my sake!' How could I disobey the king?"

Joab turned away in disgust. He knew that if Absalom were allowed to live, David would surely pardon him, and just as surely, Absalom would rebel again. Joab knew what had to be done, even if David refused to recognize it.

Accompanied by ten soldiers from his bodyguard, he went searching for Absalom in the forest. When he found him, he took three spears and drove them, one by one, through Absalom's body. Then Joab's soldiers drew their swords, thrusting and hacking at Absalom until he died. Joab ordered his soldiers to cut Absalom down from the tree. They threw his body into a deep pit and covered it with stones.

Joab sent two messengers to bring David news of the victory. When the first arrived, David asked him, "Is Absalom safe?"

The messenger replied, "I do not know, my lord. I heard a great commotion behind me when I left the camp, but I do not know what it was."

David asked him to step aside. The second messenger arrived. "I bring good news! God has overthrown those who rose against you!"

"Is Absalom safe?" David asked him.

The messenger hesitated, then replied, "May all your enemies and those who wish you harm meet the fate of Absalom."

At that moment David knew his son was dead. He tore his clothes, threw himself in the dust, and wept, "O Absalom, my son, my son! O my son Absalom! I wish I had died instead of you. Absalom! My son, my son!"

Joab arrived to find David weeping. "Raise yourself from the dust!" the general shouted at the king. "Is this how you thank the brave men who fought for you? Do you love your enemies more than those who risked their lives for their king? If we had died and Absalom had lived, would you be pleased? Get up! Your soldiers are waiting."

David knew a king's duty. He got up, washed his face, put on a new robe, and went out to congratulate his victorious army.

But David never ceased mourning for Absalom. For the rest of his life, a day never passed when he did not close his eyes and weep.

"O Absalom! My son, my son!"

The Story of Solomon

Who would be king after David died? David had placed all his hopes on Absalom, and Absalom had betrayed him. None of David's other sons was fit to be king. They were all foolish, lazy, greedy, and cared nothing about the people.

With one exception—Solomon. Solomon, Bathsheba's second child, was David's youngest son. Even when he was a small boy, Solomon proved he had the intelligence and compassion for people that made a good king.

Boiled Beans

Solomon liked to accompany his older brother Absalom to the gates of Jerusalem. Here they observed how the royal judges dispensed justice to the citizens of Israel. Absalom only pretended to care about the common people and their problems. Solomon, however, was genuinely interested. He tried to learn as much as he could about the laws of the land and the means by which a good judge reached a fair decision. Absalom told people what they wanted to hear. Solomon asked penetrating questions. He wanted to learn the truth.

After Absalom's death, Solomon continued to go to the city gates by himself. He listened to the people and, whenever possible, tried to help them.

Once, Solomon saw a farmer standing by a wall, crying. "What is wrong?" Solomon asked him.

"Woe is me!" the man said. "The king's judge has ruled against me. I must sell my farm and everything I own to pay my debt. My family and I will be left penniless. And all for one egg!"

An egg? Solomon asked the farmer to tell him his story. The farmer began:

"Five years ago, my neighbor and I were working in the fields. We stopped for lunch. My neighbor had some hard-boiled eggs. I asked if I could have one. He said I could, if I promised to repay him for the egg, as well as any profit that might come from it. I agreed.

"Years passed. One day he came to my door. 'I have come to collect the debt you owe me,' he said. I didn't know what he was talking about, until he reminded me of the egg. 'You're right. I remember now,' I told him as I handed him an egg.

"'And the rest?'

"'What else do I owe? I borrowed an egg, and I gave you one.'

"My neighbor shook his head. 'My friend,' he began, 'must I remind you of your promise? You agreed to pay me for the egg *as well as any profit that might come from it.* One egg hatches one hen. In one year's time a hen might lay a hundred eggs. The hundred hens that come from those eggs might each hatch a hundred chickens . . . ' He went on and on. The final result after five years was tens of thousands of hens worth twenty-five hundred silver shekels. 'That is what you owe me,' he said.

"'This can't be right!' I protested. 'How can I owe so much money for borrowing a single egg?' We came to Jerusalem and went before the judge. The judge listened to each of us in turn. He ruled that my neighbor was correct. Ignorance was no excuse. I should have realized the bargain I was making. Now I have to pay my neighbor every last shekel. Woe is me! I am ruined. And all for one egg!"

Solomon knew the judge to be a fair man. Still, it didn't seem right that a poor farmer should lose everything he owned just for one egg. He told the farmer, "This is what you must do. Tomorrow morning the king will go out for his daily ride around the city. Boil a pot of beans and wait for him in a certain field. When you see the king's chariot go by, walk back and forth across the field, flinging the boiled beans here and there. The king will stop to ask what you are doing. Tell him this." Solomon whispered the words into the farmer's ear.

The next morning King David got in his chariot to ride around Jerusalem. As he drove past a certain field, he noticed a farmer carrying a steaming pot of boiled beans. The farmer walked back and forth along the furrows, sowing the beans with a wooden spoon.

"Who is that man? What is he doing?" David asked his attendants. They told him how the farmer had come to Jerusalem for justice, and how the judge had ruled he must repay twenty-five hundred silver shekels for borrowing one egg.

David shook his head. "I feel sorry for the farmer, but the ruling is just. Poor man. He has lost his wits." David stopped to talk with the farmer. "What are you doing?"

The farmer bowed to the king. "I must pay my neighbor hundreds of shekels for an egg I borrowed five years ago. I am trying to raise money by sowing a field of beans. When the beans are ripe, I will sell them. That will pay some of my debt."

David shook his head. "All your labor is for nothing. Foolish man, don't you realize that boiled beans can never sprout."

The farmer looked David in the eye. "And can a boiled egg hatch chickens?"

David gasped. The farmer was right. The judge had overlooked one important fact. The original egg was boiled. Nothing could have hatched from it! The farmer owed his neighbor nothing more than the single egg he borrowed.

"Who told you to say that?" David asked the farmer.

"A small boy spoke to me as I stood by the city gate. He was a polite, handsome little fellow. I do not know who he is, except he was dressed like a prince."

David recognized his son Solomon. When he returned to the palace, he ordered Solomon to come before him.

"Who are you to interfere with the king's justice?" David asked sternly.

Solomon looked at his father. "Is it justice when a poor farmer has to pay twenty-five hundred shekels for borrowing an egg?"

At that moment David realized Solomon was not only wise, he also cared deeply about justice and the welfare of all the people in the kingdom, from the highest to the lowest.

Thank God for giving me such a son! David thought to himself. *He alone is worthy to succeed me on the throne.*

Solomon Becomes King

That night David spoke to Bathsheba. "I have made my decision. Our son Solomon will be king after me and sit upon my throne."

Bathsheba was disturbed to hear this. "Is this decision wise, my lord?" she asked David. "Solomon is the youngest and weakest of your sons. Will the people accept him? Will your other sons accept his rule, or will they rebel against him as Absalom rebelled against you?"

David told her not to fear. "God will be with Solomon. Before I die, I will make clear to all Israel that he is the one chosen by God to succeed me."

David summoned the three most important people in the land: Zadok, the high priest; Nathan the prophet; and Benaiah, son of Jehoiada, the captain of his body-guard. He told them, "Dress Solomon in royal robes. Put him on my favorite mule and escort him to Gihon. There Zadok the priest and Nathan the prophet will anoint him as the king chosen by God to rule over all Israel. You will blow the ram's horn and all the people will proclaim, 'Long live Solomon, king of Israel!'"

So it was done. When Zadok held the horn of holy oil over Solomon's head, the oil ran down like water pouring from a fountain. At that moment all Israel knew that God had chosen Solomon. The people blew on their ram's horns with all their might and joyously proclaimed, "Long live Solomon! Long live the House of David! Long live Israel's king."

The Death of David

David had chosen his successor. His last task was done, and now his life was almost at an end. David was not a perfect man. He was guilty of many sins. But he loved God and always tried to do his best. And God loved David, in spite of his mistakes. For that reason, God granted David a great favor. He told him when he would die.

"You will die on the Sabbath day," God said.

David was an old man, but young or old, no one wishes to meet the Angel of Death. However, David knew that the Angel of Death has no power over a person who is studying God's Holy Law.

As soon as the Sabbath began, David would immerse himself in God's teachings. He did not eat or sleep. He pored over the ancient scrolls, studying the laws of Moses. He did not cease from his studies until the Sabbath ended.

The Angel of Death complained to God. "How am I to complete the task You set for me? Every person is given a certain number of years. When that number is filled, I come to take their souls. David has already lived out his portion. Yet I cannot take his soul. Every Sabbath, when I come to fetch it, I find him studying Your commandments. He never ceases to study until the Sabbath is over. Then I cannot touch him, because You decreed that David would die on the Sabbath day."

God agreed with the angel. No person can live forever, and David had used up his rightful portion of years. It was time for him to die. God told the angel how to take David's soul in the quickest, kindest way.

◆　　◆　　◆

The Sabbath was almost at an end. David sat in his library, studying as usual. Outside his window, the sun was going down. But David did not see it. He did not lift his eyes from the scrolls.

Suddenly, he heard a rustling in the garden. David lifted his head. He heard the sound again. What was that? The Sabbath was nearly over. David thought there could be no harm in having a look.

David rose from his chair and walked into the garden. He did not see the Angel of Death, perched overhead in a tree. David put his foot on the marble staircase. Suddenly, the stone crumbled. David fell back against the pavement. The angel swooped down and took his soul with a kiss.

When the Sabbath ended, servants brought David's dinner to the library. He was not there. They found him in the garden, lying on the marble pavement. His eyes were closed, and a look of great peace covered his face.

David, Israel's greatest king, was dead.

The Wisdom of Solomon

All Israel mourned David, but none more than Solomon. He prayed to God. "My father David was a great king, both in war and peace. I am only a small boy. There is so much I do not know, so much I need to learn."

God answered Solomon. "Do not be afraid. I am with you always. I will grant you one wish for your father David's sake. What will you ask for? Wealth and power? Riches and fame? Long life and the death of your enemies? Speak, and I will grant it."

Solomon said, "I have only one wish. Give me a wise and understanding heart. Teach me the difference between right and wrong. Help me to become a good king."

Solomon's wish pleased God. "You thought only of your people. You requested nothing for yourself. Therefore, I will give you what you asked for, and what you did not ask for. I give you wisdom. You will be known forevermore as the wisest of kings. You will have riches, fame, long life, and victory over your enemies. For are all these not the fruit of wisdom?"

God fulfilled His promise to Solomon. Israel became a mighty nation, even greater than it had been in the time of David. And Solomon became known as the wisest of kings.

Once two women came before Solomon. Each carried a tiny infant. The two babies looked exactly alike, except only one was alive. The other was dead.

The first woman said to Solomon, "My neighbor and I live together in one house. I had a baby. Three days later, she had one, too. Her child died in the night. She came to my room while I was sleeping. She took away my baby and replaced it with hers.

"I awoke the next morning. When I tried to feed my baby, I discovered he was dead. I looked at my neighbor nursing her child and realized it was my own. Then I knew what had happened. She had stolen my living baby and left me her dead one. I beg you, Solomon, give me justice! Make her give my child back to me!"

Solomon turned to the second woman. "What do you have to say?"

"She is lying," the woman answered. "Her son died. The living baby is mine."

Solomon asked his attendants, "What do the judges of the land say?"

"They do not know how to decide this case," he was told. "Both women say, 'The living baby is mine. The dead one is yours.' The women resemble each other, and the children are similar in appearance. Only God knows who is telling the truth!"

Solomon nodded. "I will settle this case. Bring me a sword." One of his bodyguards stepped forward. "Cut the living baby in two," Solomon told him. "Give half to one woman; give half to the other."

The soldier picked up the baby. As he drew his sword, the first woman cried out, "No! Do not hurt the child! Let my neighbor have him!"

But the second woman only murmured, "The king's decision is just."

"Put down your sword," Solomon told the soldier. "Give the baby to the first woman. She is his mother. She would rather give up her child than see him harmed in any way."

Word of Solomon's wise decision spread throughout the land. The people of Israel marveled at his insight and thanked God for giving them a righteous king to rule over them with justice, mercy, and wisdom.

Solomon Builds the Temple

Before David died, he told Solomon how much he wanted to build a Temple to God in Jerusalem. "God would not allow me to build His House," David said. "I am a man of bloodshed; I spent my whole life making war. You, my son, are a man of peace. Your very name, *Solomon*, means *Peaceful*. God will always be with you. When you are established on your throne, build Him the House He deserves."

But how was the Temple to be built? What would it look like?

Solomon prayed to God for answers. God gave him the information he needed, describing the Temple to Solomon in great detail, with all its dimensions and furnishings. There was only one question that God did not answer. How was Solomon to cut the great marble blocks needed to build the Temple's walls? God told Solomon that no iron tools must be used to build the Temple. Iron is a metal of war, and God's Temple must always be a House of Peace.

After Solomon became king, he sent messengers to the neighboring country of Tyre asking Hiram, its ruler, to send skilled craftspeople and precious fir and cedarwood for the Temple's construction. For no one was as skilled in the working of wood, stone, and metal as the people of Tyre.

Solomon raised a force of thirty thousand men from among the people of Israel. He sent them to Tyre, ten thousand at a time, to labor for a month under the direction of Hiram's overseers. They cut down cedars and firs in the mountains of Lebanon and carried them to the coast, where they tied the logs into rafts. They sailed these rafts to the port of Joppa. Here the logs were taken apart and carried over the Judean hills all the way to Jerusalem.

Solomon spared no expense. He ordered the finest stone and marble from quarries all over the world. The huge blocks for the Temple's walls and courtyards were cut and polished at the quarry. Ships carried them to Israel. Enormous teams of men and oxen hauled them over the hills to Jerusalem. In this way Solomon fulfilled God's command that no iron tool should be used to build the Temple. The carefully shaped stones and timbers were put together like the pieces of a giant puzzle. The clang of metal was not to be heard on the Temple Mount. Nor was any iron tool—neither hammer, nor ax, nor chisel—to be found there during the whole time the Temple was being built.

The work of building God's House took seven years. During that time not a single workman died. Not one person fell sick, or was even slightly injured. However, on the day following the Temple's dedication, everyone who had worked on the building—Judean and Tyrian—was suddenly taken into Paradise. In this way God rewarded those who built His House, and also insured that no one would ever build a similar Temple for any pagan god.

The Queen of Sheba

The fame of Solomon's wisdom spread as far as the distant land of Sheba. Sheba's queen was wise as well as beautiful. She gathered her attendants and journeyed to Jerusalem to see if everything she heard about Solomon was true.

Solomon sent a chariot army to escort the queen to his palace. As the queen approached the borders of Israel, she saw what she thought was another sun shining. As it came closer, she realized that it was an army of shining chariots driven by men in armor of silver and gold. Their commander was the most splendid of all. The queen came forward and bowed to him, for she thought he was Solomon.

"Most Gracious Queen," the officer said, "why do you bow to me? It is I who should bow to you, for I am only Benaiah, son of Jehoiada, Solomon's servant."

The queen of Sheba and all her attendants exclaimed, "If such is the glory of Solomon's servant, imagine the glory of the king himself!"

Benaiah escorted the queen back to Jerusalem, where Solomon had built a special palace for her. It was made entirely of glass. A river flowed beneath the floor. When Solomon came forward to greet the queen, she thought he was walking on water. The queen of Sheba raised her own robe so as not to get it wet. She laughed with surprise when she realized she was walking on glass. *I see that Solomon's wealth is even greater than I expected,* the queen thought to herself. *Now I will learn if he is as truly wise as others say.*

The queen said to Solomon, "My Lord, it is said that you are the wisest of kings. May I ask you some riddles to test your wisdom?"

"All wisdom comes from God," Solomon replied. "Ask whatever you will. With God's help, I will answer."

The queen began, "What water comes neither from the rocks, nor from the heavens? Sometimes it is as sweet as honey, sometimes as bitter as wormwood. Yet it always comes from the same source."

"Tears," answered Solomon.

The queen asked another riddle. "She is buried in the ground while still alive. The more she decays, the more alive she becomes. Those who buried her will profit from their labors. Who is she?"

"A seed," said Solomon.

The queen of Sheba marveled at Solomon's wisdom. "The stories are true.

Solomon is indeed the wisest of kings. Tomorrow, I will test you again. For now, it would please me most if you would show me the wonders of Jerusalem."

Solomon lifted the queen into his chariot. He drove through Jerusalem, showing her all his palaces, along with the treasures they contained. They stopped to offer sacrifices at the new Temple. Its magnificence astounded the queen. "Surely, this building could not have been built without God's help. Praised be the God of Solomon! I will worship Him, too!" From that day on, the queen of Sheba worshiped no other god but the God of Israel.

The next day the queen of Sheba invited Solomon to join her for breakfast at her glass palace. Six thousand boys and girls served the first course. All the children were stunningly handsome, and they all looked alike. They wore the same clothes. Their hair was combed the same way. They even wore the same earrings in both ears.

"Tell me, Solomon," the queen of Sheba began. "Which of these children are boys and which are girls?"

"Bring bowls of almonds!" Solomon commanded. When the huge bowls arrived, he said to the children, "Help yourselves. Take as many as you wish."

Some of the children filled their aprons with almonds. Others took only two handfuls. Solomon turned to the queen of Sheba. "The ones who filled their aprons are girls. The ones who took only as much as they could hold in both hands are boys. The girls are accustomed to wearing aprons and using them to carry things. The boys have never worn aprons until today. They don't know how to use them."

The queen of Sheba smiled. "Your answer is correct. You have identified the boys and the girls. Indeed, your wisdom is even greater than I expected. Allow me to ask you one more riddle. If you answer correctly, I will return to my country knowing that Solomon is the wisest of kings."

"Ask whatever you wish," Solomon said.

The queen of Sheba sent the six thousand children from the hall. They soon returned, each child carrying a delicate flower. "Do you see these flowers?" the queen asked Solomon. "Only one is real. The others are artificial. Which is the real flower, O Wisest of Kings?"

Solomon walked among the children. He stooped to examine the flowers. To his surprise, he could find no way to tell them apart. They looked alike, felt alike, smelled alike. They each had the same tiny blemish on the underside of one petal. Try as he might, Solomon could not identify the real flower. He was about to give up when he heard a buzzing at the window.

"Open that window," Solomon said. A bee flew in. She drifted from flower to flower. Suddenly she crawled into one and began buzzing loudly.

Solomon turned to the queen of Sheba. "The bee has given you the answer. She is wiser than I. She has identified the real flower for you."

"But it is a truly wise king who knows to call for help when he needs it," said the queen.

The queen of Sheba stayed with Solomon for the rest of that year. When she left Jerusalem to return to her own country, she gave him a present of 120 talents of gold, as well as baskets of rare spices and precious stones whose like had never before been seen in Israel. Many Israelites accompanied the queen on her journey home, including several priests and Levites whom Solomon sent to spread the worship of the God of Israel among the people of Sheba.

The End of the Kingdom

It is said that the queen of Sheba married Solomon before she left for her own country. This may have happened, for Solomon, like his father, David, had many wives from distant lands. One was the daughter of Pharaoh, king of Egypt. Not all these women wished to serve the God of Israel. They still worshiped the gods of their native lands.

Solomon tried to please his wives by building temples to their gods on the soil of Israel. Luxurious temples to foreign gods sprang up around Jerusalem. Foreign priests came from Egypt, Moab, Edom, and Ammon to serve them. The Israelites saw the princesses worshiping idols in their temples. Many became attracted to these strange gods and began worshiping them, too. Solomon did not try to stop them. Nor did he seek to stop the priests from spreading pagan worship throughout the land.

God became angry with Solomon. He spoke to him, saying, "Tear down these temples! Drive out the priests! Send your wives away if they continue to worship idols! There must only be One God in Israel, the Holy God of Abraham, Isaac, and Jacob!"

But Solomon refused to listen. He was growing old, and his wives had great influence on him. When God saw that Solomon failed to obey, He said to him, "You have neglected My commandments and ignored My decrees. Therefore, I will remove the kingdom from your family and give it to one of your servants. This will not happen during your lifetime. For the sake of your father, David, it will only occur after your death. Also, for David's sake, I will leave one tribe to your descendants, and they will continue to rule in the city of Jerusalem."

God began preparing the seeds of his promise. One of Solomon's most trusted officers was Jeroboam, son of Nebat, who belonged to the tribe of Ephraim. Solomon appointed Jeroboam to oversee all the men of Ephraim who worked for the king.

One day Jeroboam was returning home from Jerusalem when he met a prophet named Ahijah, who lived in Shiloh. "Come with me. I wish to speak with you," Ahijah said.

Jeroboam followed him to an open field. After making sure they were alone, Ahijah took off his cloak and tore it into twelve pieces. He gave ten to Jeroboam, saying, "These are yours. For God says, 'I will tear the kingdom from Solomon's hands and give it to Jeroboam, son of Nebat. He will possess ten tribes, but Solomon's sons will only possess one." The extra tribe was the tribe of Levi. Levi had no territory of its own, but was scattered throughout the land of Israel.

Ahijah told Jeroboam that these events would come to pass after Solomon's death. But Jeroboam could not wait. He led the men of Ephraim in revolt against Solomon. However, God remained true to His promise. The kingdom was not to be taken from Solomon during his lifetime. Solomon's soldiers defeated Jeroboam. His followers were put to death. He himself was driven into exile in Egypt. Only after Solomon's death did he return to Israel.

Solomon ruled Israel for forty years. He died, and was buried in Jerusalem, close to the tomb of his father, David.

The Kingdom Divides

Rehoboam, Solomon's oldest son, took his place on the throne. He inherited a troubled realm. All was not well in the land of Israel. The common people had paid a heavy price for the magnificent palaces that adorned Jerusalem and the armies of chariots that protected the borders. Farmers and shepherds from all over the land had been forced to work for the king, neglecting their own fields and flocks. The tribes from the northern part of the kingdom were especially angry, since they lived far from Jerusalem and received little benefit from the wealth pouring into the capital. These northern tribes were ready to listen to any leader who promised relief from their heavy burdens.

One such person was Jeroboam. As soon as he heard that Solomon was dead, he returned to Israel and gathered his supporters in the town of Shechem. He sent a message to Rehoboam, asking him in the name of the people to lower taxes and reduce the number of days they were required to work for the king.

Rehoboam, unlike his father, Solomon, and his grandfather David, had little sense or compassion. He was a foolish young man, inexperienced in the ways of government, and more inclined to listen to flatterers than to the words of wise counselors. He asked Jeroboam for three days to prepare an answer.

Rehoboam first asked his father's ministers what to do. They told him, "The people's demands are just. Speak to them as a friend, promise them what they want, and they will follow you forever."

Unfortunately, Rehoboam was too proud to follow this sensible advice. He refused to humble himself for any reason. He asked his companions what they thought he should do. These young nobles knew nothing about the mood of the common people. Instead, they told Rehoboam what he wanted to hear.

"Who is king in Israel?" they asked him. "How dare this unwashed rabble demand anything of you! Say to them, 'My little finger is thicker than my father's thigh. The yoke my father laid on your shoulders will seem light compared to the one I will place upon them. My father beat you with ordinary whips; I will lash you with the cat-o'-nine-tails!'"

Three days later, when the people assembled to hear Rehoboam's answer, he used exactly those words.

The people cried out in rage, "What share do we have in the House of David? To your tents, Men of Israel! David's descendants can look after themselves!" They left Shechem and hurried home to prepare for war.

Their anger needed only a spark to ignite a rebellion. It came within days. Rehoboam sent one of his officers into the countryside to draft villagers for a work gang. The villagers exploded with rage. They stoned Rehoboam's officer to death. Rehoboam had to jump in his chariot and flee to Jerusalem for safety.

The kingdom established by David was no more. Israel split into two nations. The southern part, centered around Jerusalem, became known as Judah. The northern part continued to call itself Israel.

Jeroboam, Israel's new king, considered how to preserve his country's independence. If his people continued bringing sacrifices to Solomon's Temple in Jerusalem, their hearts would naturally be drawn to their southern brethren. Sooner or later, they would seek to reunite in one kingdom. To prevent this, Jeroboam erected other temples in the north to rival the one in Jerusalem. He encouraged his people to worship idols, including two golden calves resembling the one the Israelites forced Aaron to make when Moses went up on Mount Sinai.

By encouraging the worship of foreign gods, Jeroboam hoped to break the bonds of kinship that united Israel and Judah. He succeeded, but at a terrible cost.

Within a few generations, the same problems that led to the breakup of David's kingdom began causing trouble in the northern kingdom as well. Its rulers thought little about the welfare of their subjects. They sought to increase their power by extending their nation's borders, leading to endless petty wars between Israel and her neighbors. Taxes rose. The gulf between rich and poor widened. Injustice and oppression increased, along with idol worship. The common people languished in misery and confusion.

God heard their cries. He had not forgotten the northern kingdom. He sent Israel a prophet, one of the greatest who ever lived.

His name was Elijah.

Prophets

The Story of Elijah

King succeeded king in the northern realm of Israel as ambitious generals plotted against each other to seize the throne. Jeroboam's son Nadab and his entire family were murdered by Baasha, son of Ahijah. Baasha's son Elah was assassinated by Zimri, who was in turn overthrown by Omri.

Omri proved to be a strong ruler. His son Ahab succeeded him. Israel became a powerful nation. Ahab married Jezebel, the daughter of the king of Sidon. To please her, he built a temple and offered sacrifices to Baal, the god she worshiped. Ahab allowed Jezebel to invite priests of Baal into the kingdom. Jezebel encouraged them to spread the worship of her god throughout Israel. When God's prophets and other holy people protested, Jezebel ordered Ahab's soldiers to kill them.

Altars to Baal sprang up on every hillside. People brought sacrifices to his temple. They worshiped in his sacred groves. Even King Ahab bowed down to Baal.

God said, "The people have turned away from the True God, Who brought their ancestors out of slavery in the land of Egypt. They bow down to idols and offer sacrifices to statues of wood and stone. I will punish the land of Israel. They will cry out to their gods, but their idols will not save them."

The Key to Rain

A man lived in the village of Tishba, in Gilead. His name was Elijah, and he was a prophet. Elijah's soul burned with love for God. He hated idols and the foreign priests who spread their worship among the people. Most of all, he hated Jezebel for luring King Ahab into abandoning the God of his ancestors. God spoke to Elijah, saying, "This is My judgment on Ahab and his kingdom. Because he and his people have turned from Me and followed false gods, I will lock up the heavens. Drought will dry up the land. No rain will fall until the people return to Me."

God told Elijah to leave his home and go to the desert. "How will I live? Who will feed me? Where will I get water?" Elijah asked. God told him not to worry. "I will provide for you," He said.

Elijah traveled eastward. He found a cave that overlooked a stream. Elijah drank from the stream, and every morning wild ravens brought him food. Elijah lived this way for three years.

Meanwhile drought stalked the land. God had given Elijah the key to the rain. As long as he possessed it, the waters of heaven remained locked in the clouds. No rain fell. Crops withered in the fields. Animals died for lack of water. The people cried out to God to save them.

God told Elijah, "The people have returned to Me. Open the clouds and let the rain fall."

Elijah refused. He said to God, "Let me hold the key to the rain a while longer. The people have not repented. They are merely thirsty. As soon as the rains fall, they will return to their idols."

Elijah's lack of compassion angered God. "If the people are to go without water, so will you." The stream dried up. Elijah had to leave his cave. Hungry and thirsty, like all the others in the land, he wandered to the village of Zarephath. God led him to the house of a woman whose husband had recently died. His name was Amittai. He had stopped eating and drinking so his wife and son could have food and water.

Elijah came to the door. He begged for water and something to eat. Hardly any food remained in the house; a little flour and oil, and a few cups of water. Even so, Amittai's widow invited the stranger in and baked him a little loaf of bread. Elijah blessed her. "Because of your kindness, you will never lack for food. The flour in your jar will never run out. Your oil and water jugs will never be empty until the rain falls once more from heaven."

Famine worsened in the land. Sickness spread through the villages. People died, and there were none left to bury them. Plague came to Zarephath. Elijah's blessing could not protect the widow's little boy from coming down with a fever. She nursed him all night, but in the morning he died.

Elijah tried to comfort the grieving mother. Instead, she cursed him, blaming the prophet for all her sorrows. "Why did you come to my house? Why do you talk to me about God? God has sent me nothing but misery. First my husband died, now my child. Once, I was a happy woman with a fine family. Now I have nothing. You cannot help me. God has abandoned me."

The widow's words broke Elijah's heart. How could he hope to explain God's ways to her when he himself could not understand why she suffered so? He had prayed to God to help the little boy. His prayer went unanswered. Nonetheless, Elijah's faith remained strong. He did not give up. He stepped outside the house and walked a distance away so that no one could hear him. Stretching his arms toward heaven, he prayed to God again. "I can still help the widow's child. Give me the key to raising the dead, so that I may restore him to life."

God answered, "There are three keys to the universe: the key to the rain; the key to birth; and the key to raising the dead. You already have the key to the rain. If I give you the key to raising the dead, you will possess two keys and I will only have one. You will be mightier than God. That cannot be."

Elijah understood what God was telling him. He had caused the people of Israel to suffer too long. Elijah handed back the key to the rain, saying, "Give me the key to raising the dead. I will borrow it only long enough to save this child."

God gave Elijah the key to raising the dead and took back the key to the rain. Elijah returned to the house. He saw that the widow had fallen asleep, still holding her dead child in her lap. Elijah gently lifted the boy from his mother's arms and carried him to the upstairs room where he slept. The prophet laid the child on his own bed with his face toward the ceiling and his arms reaching out to either side. Elijah lowered himself on top of the boy: arm to arm, belly to belly, face to face. He breathed into the boy's mouth, praying, "O God, let this child's soul come back to him!" Elijah did this three times. After the third time, the boy opened his eyes and came back to life. Elijah led him downstairs to his mother.

The little boy whom Elijah brought back from the dead grew up to become a prophet. His name was Jonah.

The Miracle on Mount Carmel

God spoke to Elijah. "The time has come to leave your hiding place. Go to Ahab. Make yourself known in Israel. The drought is about to end. Then all will know that I am God."

Elijah left Zarephath and traveled toward Samaria, the capital. Along the road he encountered Ahab, riding in his chariot.

Ahab recognized Elijah at once. He blamed the prophet for the drought that afflicted the land. "Is that you, Troubler of Israel?" the king cried.

Elijah answered, "It is not I who brings trouble to Israel, but you and your family. You have disobeyed God's commandments. You bow down to idols. God has sent me to prove to you and all Israel, once and for all time, who is the real God. Call your people. Tell them to assemble on Mount Carmel. Gather the 450 priests of Baal who eat at Jezebel's table. Let them come too. Let them see with their own eyes the power of God."

Ahab accepted Elijah's challenge. He summoned the people of Israel and the 450 priests of Baal to gather on Mount Carmel. Sleek, well-dressed, clever with words, the foreign priests felt certain they could defeat Elijah in any challenge he might offer. Did they not enjoy the favor of King Ahab and his wife Jezebel? Who was Elijah but a half-mad prophet dressed in animal skins! What could he do that they could not immediately surpass?

The Israelites gathered around to witness the contest between Elijah and the priests of Baal. Elijah explained what was about to happen.

"The priests of Baal and I will each build an altar to the God we worship. I have brought two young bulls. Let the priests of Baal choose whichever one they like. Let them kill it, cut it in pieces, and arrange the pieces on the wood on top of their altar. I will do the same with the other bull. However, neither of us will set fire to the wood. Instead, they will call upon Baal and I will call upon the God of Israel. Whoever sends down fire from heaven to consume the offering is the True God."

"That is a fair test," the people agreed.

Elijah invited the priests of Baal to choose their bull. They made their selec-tion, but the animal lowered his head and refused to go with them. Elijah whispered in the bull's ear, "Do not be afraid. I promise your death will be swift and painless."

"I am not afraid to die," the bull told Elijah. "I am angry that I am going to be sacrificed to an idol while my brother's death will glorify God's Name. Why should he be honored while I am disgraced? He is no better than I."

"You are mistaken," Elijah said. "By putting these priests to the test, you will glorify God as much as your brother. I promise you that by this evening you will both frolic in the pastures of heaven."

Only then did the bull allow himself to be sacrificed. But Elijah had to lead him to the altar. The bull refused to submit to the priests of Baal.

The priests of Baal killed the bull. They cut his body into pieces and laid them on the wood covering the top of the altar. Then they began to pray: "O Baal, Ruler of the Universe, answer our prayer. Send down fire to consume these sacrifices."

The priests hoped that Baal would send down fire. But in case he didn't, they arranged for one of their number to hide inside the altar. As his companions raised their voices, he was supposed to light the offering. But God knew about the trick. He sent a poisonous snake slithering through the altar stones. The snake bit the priest, who died without a murmur.

The other priests prayed. They waited for fire to consume the offering. Nothing happened.

The priests of Baal prayed louder. They lifted their arms toward heaven as they danced around the altar.

"Great Baal, hear the voices of your servants! O King of heaven, send down fire!"

Still, nothing happened. Elijah, standing with the crowd of Israelites, mocked them.

"You need to shout louder. Remember, Baal lives far away in heaven. Perhaps he is busy with something else and not paying attention. Maybe he is asleep. Or on a journey. Or perhaps"—Elijah raised his voice so that the people could hear him over the frantic cries of the priests—"he is no god at all, but an idol made of wood and stone! Shout as loud as you can; he will never hear you!"

The priests of Baal danced around the altar in a frenzy, shrieking and crying out their god's name. They threw off their clothes. They slashed their flesh with blades of iron and flint until their bodies ran with blood, for they believed their god enjoyed licking the blood of human beings. The people of Israel turned away in disgust, but the priests of Baal continued. Weeping and wailing, they circled the altar until the last one dropped from exhaustion.

Now Elijah stepped forward. "Come closer to me," he said. As the people approached, he picked twelve stones from the ground—one for each of the tribes of Israel—and built them into an altar. He dug a trench around the altar deep enough to hold two bushels of grain. After arranging the wood on top of the altar, he killed the remaining bull, cut it to pieces, and placed them on top of the wood.

Then he said, "Bring me four jars filled with water. Pour it over the wood and the sacrifice."

The people brought water and poured it over the altar.

"Do it again," Elijah said.

They did it again.

"Do it a third time," said Elijah.

A third time it was done. The water soaked the wood and the sacrifice. It ran down from the altar, filling the trench.

By now it was almost evening. Elijah raised his eyes toward heaven. His face glowed with unearthly light as he looked into the setting sun and spoke these words:

"God of Abraham, Isaac, and Jacob, show us today that You are the True God in Israel. I am your faithful servant. I have done as You commanded. Answer my prayer. Let these people finally understand that You Alone are God."

As Elijah finished praying, a fiery beam came down from heaven. The people gathered on the mountain fell to the ground in terror. The priests of Baal covered their faces. Only Elijah stood erect, staring with unblinking eyes as the fire from heaven consumed the sacrifice, the altar stones, and the water-filled trench as well.

The people saw and believed. "The God of Israel lives! He is the True God!"

"Kill the priests of Baal! Do not let them get away!" Elijah commanded.

The Israelites threw themselves on the priests. They dragged them down to the brook Kishon, where they killed them all. The stream ran red with their blood. Not a single one escaped.

Then Elijah said to Ahab, "Eat and drink. Now is the time to celebrate the end of the drought. God is going to send rain."

Ahab returned to his tent. Elijah remained at the top of Mount Carmel. He sat on the ground with his face between his knees and prayed. After a while he said to one of the people with him, "Look to the west. Tell me what you see."

The man returned. "I see nothing. The sky is clear."

Elijah told him, "Go back and look again." He sent the man six times. Each time he returned, saying he had seen nothing. When he came back the seventh time, he told Elijah, "I see a small gray cloud in the distance, no bigger than a man's fist."

"Go tell Ahab to get in his chariot and ride," said Elijah. "God has unlocked the heavens. A mighty rain is coming. The king must hurry or he will be trapped by the rising waters."

The heavens opened. All the rain that had been stored in the clouds for three years poured down at once. The drought ended. The people of Israel cried with joy. Elijah ran in front of Ahab's chariot to guide him safely home through the storm.

The Still, Small Voice

On that day the God of Israel triumphed over the false priests of Baal. But victory came at a heavy price. When Jezebel learned how her beloved priests had been slaughtered like sheep, she swore to have revenge on Elijah and the God he worshiped.

"As Elijah did to the priests of Baal, so I will do to Elijah and all who worship the God of Israel!"

Jezebel sent soldiers to break down the altars to the God of Israel. They killed anyone who sacrificed to Him, as well as any prophet who fell into their hands.

Elijah's courage left him. He fled to the neighboring kingdom of Judah to save his life. Even there he did not feel safe. He left the city and wandered in the desert. Elijah walked through the stony wastes until he was exhausted. When all his food and water were gone, he threw himself beneath a tree and begged God to end his life.

Elijah lay on the ground with his eyes closed, waiting for death to take him. After a while he fell asleep. Suddenly he felt someone touch him. He opened his eyes and saw an angel.

"Get up! Eat!" the angel said.

Elijah looked around. He saw a loaf of bread and a water jug lying next to him.

The loaf was warm, as if it had just come from the oven. The water in the jug was as cool as melted snow. Elijah ate and drank. Refreshed, he lay down beneath the tree and went to sleep again.

The angel appeared a second time. "Get up! Eat! A long journey lies ahead of you."

Elijah awoke to find another loaf and another jug of water resting in the same place. He ate and drank. Then he got up and started walking.

God guided his footsteps. At the end of forty days Elijah came to Mount Sinai, the holy mountain where Moses received the Ten Commandments. He did not eat or drink during that entire journey. The two meals of miraculous bread and water brought by the angel sustained him for forty days.

Elijah climbed to the top of the mountain. He found a cave and went inside. There he remained.

After many days God spoke to him. "Elijah! Why are you hiding in this cave?"

Elijah answered, "I am sick at heart. My soul is weary. I tried my best to serve You, but it is all in vain. The children of Israel ignore Your commandments. They throw down Your altars. They have killed all Your holy prophets. I am the only one left because I escaped in time. If I were to go back, Ahab and Jezebel would kill me."

God said, "Elijah, stand outside the cave. Open your eyes. See what happens."

Elijah stood outside the cave. A strong wind began to blow. It blew away huge boulders as if they were dry leaves, and opened up great cracks in the mountain. But God was not in the wind.

After the wind came a mighty earthquake. The mountain shook, and the earth trembled. But God was not in the earthquake.

Then a fire came down from heaven. It consumed every bush, every tree, every growing thing. But God was not in the fire.

At last Elijah heard a still, small voice. He knew this was the voice of God speaking to him. It said:

"Go back to Israel. The people need you to guide them. There are still seven thousand men and women there who remain faithful to Me. They have not bowed down to Baal, or kissed his statue."

"Shall I go alone?" Elijah asked.

"No. Along the way you will meet a young man named Elisha, son of Shaphat, from the town of Abel Meholah. Take him with you. He will be like your own son, and you will anoint him to be a prophet, too. Go quickly, for Ahab and Jezebel have committed a great sin. They have murdered a man named Naboth and stolen his property."

Elijah returned to Israel. God was with him, guiding his footsteps and protecting him from those who might do him harm. As he passed by the village of Abel Meholah he saw an unusual sight. A young man of enormous strength and stature was plowing a field, walking behind a yoke of twelve oxen. He looked as mighty as Samson. Elijah stopped and asked his name.

"I am Elisha, son of Shaphat," the young man said.

Elijah threw his cloak over his shoulders. "Come. Follow me."

Elisha recognized the prophet of God. "I will. Only give me time to say good-bye to my parents. Then I will follow you."

"Go," Elijah said, "but consider your decision carefully."

Elisha did not hesitate. He sacrificed two of his oxen to God. Then he broke up the plow and the ox yokes. Using them as fuel, he boiled the meat of the sacrifices and invited his family and neighbors to eat. After finishing the meal, he turned his back on his old life and went to follow Elijah.

Naboth's Vineyard

God told Elijah to hurry, for a terrible crime had just taken place in Samaria, Ahab's capital. On early summer evenings, after the heat of the day had passed, it was the king's custom to harness his horses to his chariot and ride around the city. Ahab often stopped to rest in a fine vineyard belonging to a man named Naboth. The king enjoyed sitting beneath the grape arbors, eating fresh grapes and drinking new wine. One day he said to Naboth, "I wish this vineyard belonged to me. Let me buy it from you. Name your price, and I will pay it."

"I am sorry," Naboth told him, "this vineyard is not mine to sell. I inherited it from my father. By the laws of Moses, I must pass it on to my children."

Ahab persisted. "I will give you another vineyard, a better one, to leave to your children."

Naboth replied, "God forbid that I should sell my forefathers' inheritance!"

Naboth did not mean to insult the king. He had no choice. According to the law of Israel handed down from Moses, a person who received the inheritance of a field or vineyard did not really own it. He only had use of it during his lifetime. After his death, the property had to pass to his chidren. Inherited property could not be sold to anyone, not even the king.

Ahab knew this, but not being able to get something he wanted upset him. Discouraged and angry, he returned to his palace. He took to his bed and refused to come down for dinner. His wife Jezebel went up to see what was wrong.

"Why are you so glum? Why won't you eat your dinner?"

"It is because of Naboth, who owns the vineyard I admire. I offered him money. I offered him another vineyard, bigger and finer than his own. He refused. He even had the arrogance to say, 'God forbid that I should sell you my vineyard!'"

Jezebel laughed. "Is this what upsets you? Are you not king in Israel? Who is Naboth to refuse you? Forget your troubles. Get up and eat. If you really want that vineyard, you will have it. I will get it for you."

Ahab put aside his anger. He dressed and went down to join his wife at dinner, pleased that the coveted vineyard would soon be his. He did not ask Jezebel how she meant to obtain it. He did not wish to know.

The next day Jezebel sent secret letters to the governors of Samaria. She ordered them to arrest Naboth on charges of blasphemy and treason. Jezebel signed the letters with Ahab's name and sealed them with his signet ring.

The governors hastened to carry out Jezebel's orders. They arrested Naboth and brought him to stand trial before the people. Two witnesses bribed by Jezebel swore they heard Naboth curse God and King Ahab. Outraged, the people dragged the poor man outside the city walls and stoned him to death.

When Jezebel heard that her orders had been carried out, she said to Ahab, "Rejoice! The vineyard is yours. Naboth is dead, condemned for blasphemy and treason. His property belongs to you."

Ahab went to Naboth's vineyard with a glad heart and claimed it as his possession.

God spoke to Elijah. "Go to Ahab, king of Israel. He is sitting in Naboth's vineyard."

Elijah and Elisha went to Samaria. They found the city in an uproar over Naboth's death. "Who would believe it? Naboth dwelled among us as our friend and neighbor. We thought he was an upright man. But in his heart he was a traitor and blasphemer."

Elijah listened patiently while the people spoke. Then he asked them, "Who accused Naboth of blasphemy?"

The people named the two witnesses.

"Are these men of good character?"

The people fell silent. Naboth's accusers were known throughout the city as liars and scoundrels.

The prophet continued. "When did these two hear him speak those words? Did judges question them closely to determine if their accusations were true?"

Again no one answered. No one had really questioned the men. Elijah raised a frightening doubt. Had the people of Samaria put an innocent man to death?

"You are guilty of a great sin," Elijah told them. "From now on, when a person is accused of a serious crime, the judges must always take into account the character of the witnesses. There must be at least two witnesses, and the judges must question them separately about each detail of their accusation. Only when that is done can they be believed."

Elijah left Elisha and went to confront Ahab alone. He found him in Naboth's vineyard. Ahab sat beneath the vines, munching a bunch of grapes. A shadow fell across the pavement. The king looked up and saw the prophet.

"How did you find me, my enemy?" Ahab snarled, throwing the grapes aside.

Elijah pierced him with a look of fire. "Are you a robber, to murder a man and take his belongings? Woe to you, Ahab! Because you have done evil in God's sight, God will bring evil on you and your family. At the place where the dogs licked Naboth's blood, so will they lick your own. Your sons will perish. Their bodies will be eaten by dogs and vultures. As for Jezebel, carrion dogs will devour her, too. Nothing will remain but her hands, her skull, and the soles of her feet."

Ahab cried out in anguish. The king fell facedown in the dirt. He wept and begged for mercy. The crown fell from his head and rolled toward Elijah's sandal. The prophet kicked it aside. He turned his back on Ahab and walked away.

All that Elijah prophesied came to pass. Ahab fought a battle with Hazael, the ruler of the neighboring kingdom of Aram. An arrow struck Ahab between his breastplate and the skirt of his armor. Ahab slumped in his chariot. He cried to his charioteer to hold him up so that his soldiers would not see their king had been wounded. Ahab's blood gushed from the wound. It dripped through the leather webbing that formed the floor of his chariot.

Ahab died that evening. His soldiers left the battlefield to carry his body back to Samaria. They washed his blood-soaked chariot outside the city wall, on the spot where the crowds stoned Naboth to death. Ahab's blood stained the very cobblestones that were once stained with the blood of Naboth. Packs of stray dogs came to lick it. The first part of Elijah's prophecy had come true.

So did the second. Ahab's son Joram succeeded to his throne. An officer named Jehu assassinated him and threw his body into the vineyard that once belonged to Naboth. Crows and vultures devoured Joram's corpse, as Elijah had foretold.

Jehu drove his chariot to Samaria to take possession of the capital. Jezebel, the old queen, was still alive. As Jehu drove through the city gates, she screamed down at him. "Traitor! Assassin! Murderer of your king!"

Jehu called to the officers standing beside her at the window, "Who is with me? Throw her down!"

The officers seized Jezebel and flung her out the window. Jehu drove his chariot over her. His horses trampled her body beneath their hooves. Jezebel's blood splashed on the palace walls.

Her body lay in the street for hours as Jehu took control of the capital. His soldiers hunted down and killed the last survivors of Ahab's family. Afterward, he told his officers, "Find that cursed woman Jezebel and bury her. We must not forget that she is a king's daughter."

By then the carrion dogs had devoured nearly all that remained of Jezebel. Jehu's officers could only find her skull, her hands, and the soles of her feet.

Thus did God destroy the House of Omri because of the crimes of Ahab and Jezebel. However, Elijah did not see all his prophecies fulfilled, because by then he had been taken into heaven.

The Fiery Chariot

It happened this way. Elijah was dwelling in Gilgal when God spoke to him.

"Elijah, the time has come for you to leave the world."

"Take me, God!" Elijah said. "I am not afraid of death."

But God did not plan for Elijah to die. "You have been my faithful servant. The Angel of Death will have no power over you," God said. "I Myself will carry you up to heaven in a whirlwind of fire."

God told Elijah to leave Gilgal and go to the shrine at Bethel. As Elijah prepared for the journey, his disciple Elisha said to him, "Where are you going, Master? Let me go with you."

"No," Elijah said. "God has told me to go to Bethel. I must go alone."

But Elisha did not want to remain behind, for he feared he might never see Elijah again. "As God lives and as you live, I will not leave you," Elisha said.

Elijah could not force Elisha to remain behind, so he permitted the young man to go with him. Together they traveled to Bethel. When they arrived after many days, the prophet's followers came out to greet them. They saw the look on Elijah's face and realized this was the last time they would ever see him.

"Do you know that God will soon take our master from us?" they said to Elisha.

"I know. Speak no more of it," Elisha replied, for his heart was heavy.

Later that day Elijah told him, "Wait here in Bethel. God is sending me to Jericho."

Elisha repeated what he said before. "As God lives and as you live, I will not leave you." So Elijah and Elisha traveled on to Jericho together.

When they arrived, Elijah's friends and followers told Elisha, "Do you realize that God will soon take away our master?"

"I know it. Speak of it no more, I pray you," Elisha said again.

Elijah spoke to Elisha a third time, saying, "Stay here in Jericho. God has told me to go across the Jordan River."

Elisha repeated the words he had spoken twice before. "As God lives and as you live, I will not leave you."

Elijah set out with Elisha from Jericho to walk to the Jordan River. Fifty of his friends and followers watched from a distance to see what would happen. The two prophets came to the river. Elijah removed his cloak. He rolled it up and struck the waters with it, as Moses struck the Red Sea with his staff. The waters of the Jordan parted. Elijah and Elisha walked across on dry ground.

Elijah turned to Elisha. "Little time remains. In a few moments I will be taken from you. Tell me now, what can I do for you before I am carried away?"

His heart breaking, Elisha said, "Master, give me a double portion of your holy spirit."

"That is not in my power to do, for it depends on God's will and not my own," Elijah said. "I will do what I can. I will give you a sign. If you see me when I am taken away, God will grant your request. But if you do not see me, it has been denied."

Elisha embraced his master. "That is enough."

They continued together. Suddenly Elisha heard a roar overhead. He looked up and saw a chariot of flame drawn by horses of fire coming down from the sky. Elijah stepped into the chariot. A fiery whirlwind carried him up through the cloud. Elisha cried out in ecstasy. He tore his clothes and rolled on the ground.

"My father! My father! I see the chariot and the horsemen of Israel!"

When Elisha emerged from his ecstatic trance, the horses and the fiery chariot had disappeared. All trace of Elijah had vanished. Only the prophet's cloak remained behind. It had slipped from his shoulders when he entered the chariot. Elisha lifted Elijah's cloak from the ground and wrapped it around his own shoulders. Then he crossed back over the Jordan. The waters closed behind him.

The people who had come from Jericho met Elisha on the other side of the river. When they saw him coming toward them wearing Elijah's cloak, they fell to their knees, proclaiming, "Elijah's spirit rests on Elisha!"

Elisha walked in Elijah's footsteps. He carried on his master's work and became a great prophet in Israel.

Because Elijah never died, he continues to watch over the people of Israel. Whenever they are in need, he comes to them as a friend and redeemer. At the end of time, Elijah will return in his fiery chariot to herald the coming of the Messiah, the savior sent by God to rule the world in peace and justice forever.

The Story of Jonah

God raised a new nation in the east. Its name was Assyria. Assyria's capital, Nineveh, was located near the city of Ur, the birthplace of Abraham. The Assyrians were a ferocious, warlike people who terrorized their neighbors. Their powerful armies laid waste to entire cities, so that not one stone remained standing on another. They cut off their captives' heads to build pyramids of skulls. Others they skinned alive, or impaled on tall poles, leaving them to die miserably. The unfortunate survivors were sold into slavery or driven into exile.

Having conquered her neighbors, Assyria turned west. The tiny kingdoms of Israel and Judah lay in her path. God sent prophets to warn their people to cease worshiping idols and return to Him. He also sent a prophet to the Assyrians.

The prophet's name was Jonah. He was the son of Amittai, the husband of the widow of Zarephath. Jonah was the little boy whom Elijah brought back to life. When he grew up, he became a prophet, too. One day God spoke to him.

"Jonah," God said. "Go to the city of Nineveh, the capital of Assyria. Preach to the people there. Give them this warning: Turn from your wicked ways, or God will destroy you!"

Jonah did not want to go to Assyria. He did not want to preach to the people of Nineveh. Like most of the inhabitants of Israel, Jonah hated and feared the Assyrians. He knew what they had done to the neighboring kingdoms, and what they threatened to do to his own country. Let the arrogant people of Assyria see their capital laid waste! Let them suffer the same misery they had inflicted on others! Jonah did not want to give the Assyrians a chance to repent. He wanted God to destroy them.

Instead of obeying God's command and traveling to Nineveh, Jonah went to the port city of Joppa. There he boarded a ship bound for Tarshish. Tarshish was a city in Iberia, on the western end of the Great Sea, as far in the opposite direction from Nineveh as a person of Jonah's time could travel.

As soon as Jonah's ship passed beyond sight of land, a mighty storm arose. Masts and spars splintered under the blasts of the wind. The frantic sailors flung the cargo over the side to lighten the vessel. Having done all they could, everybody onboard sank to their knees and cried aloud to the gods they worshiped.

"Save me, Marduk!"

"Great Baal, protect me!"

"O Isis, do not let me drown in the sea!"

The captain noticed that one of his passengers was missing. He went below to look for Jonah and found him lying on a bale of cloth, snoring away.

"Wake up!" the captain shouted. "This is no time for slumber. Get up on deck with the crew and your fellow passengers. Call upon whatever god you worship. Pray to him to save us, lest we perish in the storm."

Jonah went up on deck. When he arrived, one of the sailors said, "Perhaps someone among us has angered the gods. Let us cast lots to find out who it is." The passengers and crew cast lots, and the lot fell on Jonah. The sailors asked him, "Who are you? What country do you come from?"

Jonah answered, "I am a Hebrew. I worship the God of Israel, the Ruler of Heaven, Who made the sea and the dry land."

The sailors asked, "What did you do to make your god angry?"

Jonah told them how God had commanded him to go to Nineveh to preach to the people there, and how he had tried to flee to Tarshish rather than obey.

The storm grew worse as he spoke. Dashed by wind and water, with their vessel threatening to break apart beneath their feet, the sailors cried to Jonah, "What must we do to calm the sea?"

"Throw me overboard. That will make the sea calm again. God has sent this storm because of me."

The sailors did not want to drown a helpless man.

"To the oars!" the captain cried. "We will do our best to row back to port."

The sailors and passengers pulled at the oars with all their might, but the shrieking wind blew them farther out to sea. Realizing they had no choice, the captain and crew took hold of Jonah. "God of Israel," they cried, "we deliver this man into your power. Do not blame us for his death, and do not let us perish because of him."

With these words they cast Jonah into the sea. At once the ocean became calm. The ship sailed on as before. The frightened sailors offered sacrifices to the God of Israel and vowed to worship Him.

Jonah and the Great Fish

As Jonah sank beneath the waves, God summoned a giant fish from the depths of the ocean. The fish was as long as a thousand ships tied bow to stern. Its scales were plates of gold and silver, each as wide as a warrior's shield. They gave off beams of light, as bright as the sun.

God commanded the fish to save Jonah. The fish swallowed the prophet. For three days and three nights Jonah lived inside the fish. Together they traveled beneath the oceans of the world. Looking through the fish's eye, Jonah beheld all the treasures and wonders that lay at the bottom of the sea. He saw the sea monster Leviathan, the ruler of the oceans. He saw the wreckage of Pharaoh's chariots and the bones of his soldiers. From a distance, he glimpsed the smoldering fires of Gehenna, where the wicked are punished for their sins.

After a time Jonah grew weary of the sea. He prayed to God to release him from the fish. God heard Jonah's prayer. He ordered the fish to vomit the prophet out upon dry land.

Jonah stood alone on the shore. His clothes were torn to rags, his hair and beard were covered with salt, and he stank from fish. Yet his first act was to praise God.

> *I called to God in my sorrow, and He answered me.*
> *You threw me into the depth of the sea.*
> *I will sacrifice to You with gratitude and thanksgiving.*
> *I will redeem all my vows, for God has delivered me.*

God answered Jonah, saying, "Go to Nineveh, that great city, and speak the words I will tell you to say."

This time Jonah obeyed. He arose at once and started for Nineveh.

Jonah in Nineveh

Jonah reached Nineveh after a long, long journey. The city's size amazed him; it was bigger than all the cities of Israel and Judah put together. Indeed, it took three days for a messenger on horseback to ride from one end of Nineveh to another. Jonah entered through the western gate and began walking. One week later he reached the city's center.

"Citizens of Nineveh!" he cried. "God has sent me to speak to you! Open your ears to the words of God!"

People gathered around to listen. Jonah addressed them, speaking the words that God made him say.

"Hear my voice, people of Nineveh! God has seen your wickedness. Only forty days remain. Unless you turn from your wicked ways, this great city and all who dwell within its walls will be destroyed!"

The Assyrians harkened to Jonah's words. The king of Assyria proclaimed a day of fasting. Everyone in the land, from the king sitting upon his throne to the beggars lying in the street, dressed in clothes made from rough sacks. They humbled themselves before God by heaping dust and ashes on their heads. They fasted, prayed, and promised to turn away from violence and sin.

God saw that the people of Nineveh had truly repented. He forgave them, and canceled the punishment he had prepared.

Jonah and the Gourd

Everyone in Nineveh rejoiced. But not Jonah. The prophet did not want God to spare the city. He hated the Assyrians. He had looked forward to seeing them destroyed. Jonah cried to God, "This is why I fled to Tarshish. I knew that if I prophesied to the people of Nineveh, they would repent and You would forgive them. Now they are not going to have to suffer for their crimes. My heart is sick with anger and bitterness. I wish I were dead!"

God spoke gently to Jonah. "Is it really right for you to be so angry?"

Jonah did not answer. The prophet left the city. He climbed to the top of a hill overlooking its eastern wall. There he built himself a shelter out of scraps of wood. He sat beneath it while he watched to see what would happen.

The hot sun scorched Jonah's head. God created a gourd, a plant with broad leaves, to shield him from the sun. The gourd grew overnight, and in the morning when the sun came up, Jonah relaxed in its shade. But the next day at dawn God created a worm to gnaw the plant's roots. The gourd withered and died. When the sun arose, God sent a burning east wind blowing out of the desert. The sun's rays beat on Jonah's head, while the hot, dry wind baked his skin and choked him with dust. Jonah cried out in anguish, "I wish I were dead!"

"Why are you so angry?" God asked. "Are you upset about the gourd?"

"I have a right to be angry. I loved that gourd. It brought me comfort and shade. I miss it terribly."

Then God said to Jonah, "You grieve for the gourd, a simple plant. You didn't water it; you didn't cultivate it. You did nothing to make it grow. It came up overnight and it died in a night. How then can you expect Me not to have pity on the great city of Nineveh? One hundred and twenty thousand people live here, including little children still so young they cannot tell their right hand from their left. And what of all the animals?"

The Story of Amos

Ashepherd named Amos lived in the Judean village of Tekoa. Amos was a simple man who spent his days tending his flocks and looking after his fields and orchards. He was not a prophet, nor had anyone in his family ever been a prophet. One day while Amos was alone in the fields, God appeared and showed him a vision.

Amos' Visions

A mighty swarm of locusts descended from the sky. They covered the earth as far as Amos could see, devouring crops, trees, and every green leaf until nothing remained.

"What does this vision mean?" Amos asked.

God answered, "I am going to raise up a mighty nation, as numerous as locusts, to destroy the kingdom of Israel."

Amos cried out in terror, "God, forgive them! Do not destroy all of Israel! Have mercy on the children of Jacob, so weak and small!"

God pitied Israel for Amos' sake. He promised Amos, "It shall not be."

A while later God showed Amos another vision. A rain of fire poured down from the sky, consuming land and sea. Amos cried aloud, "God, have mercy! Do not let this happen! How can the children of Jacob survive, so small, so few!"

God relented again. He promised Amos, "It shall not be."

Then Amos saw another vision. God stood on a wall, holding a string with a lead weight in His hand. He asked Amos, "What do you see?"

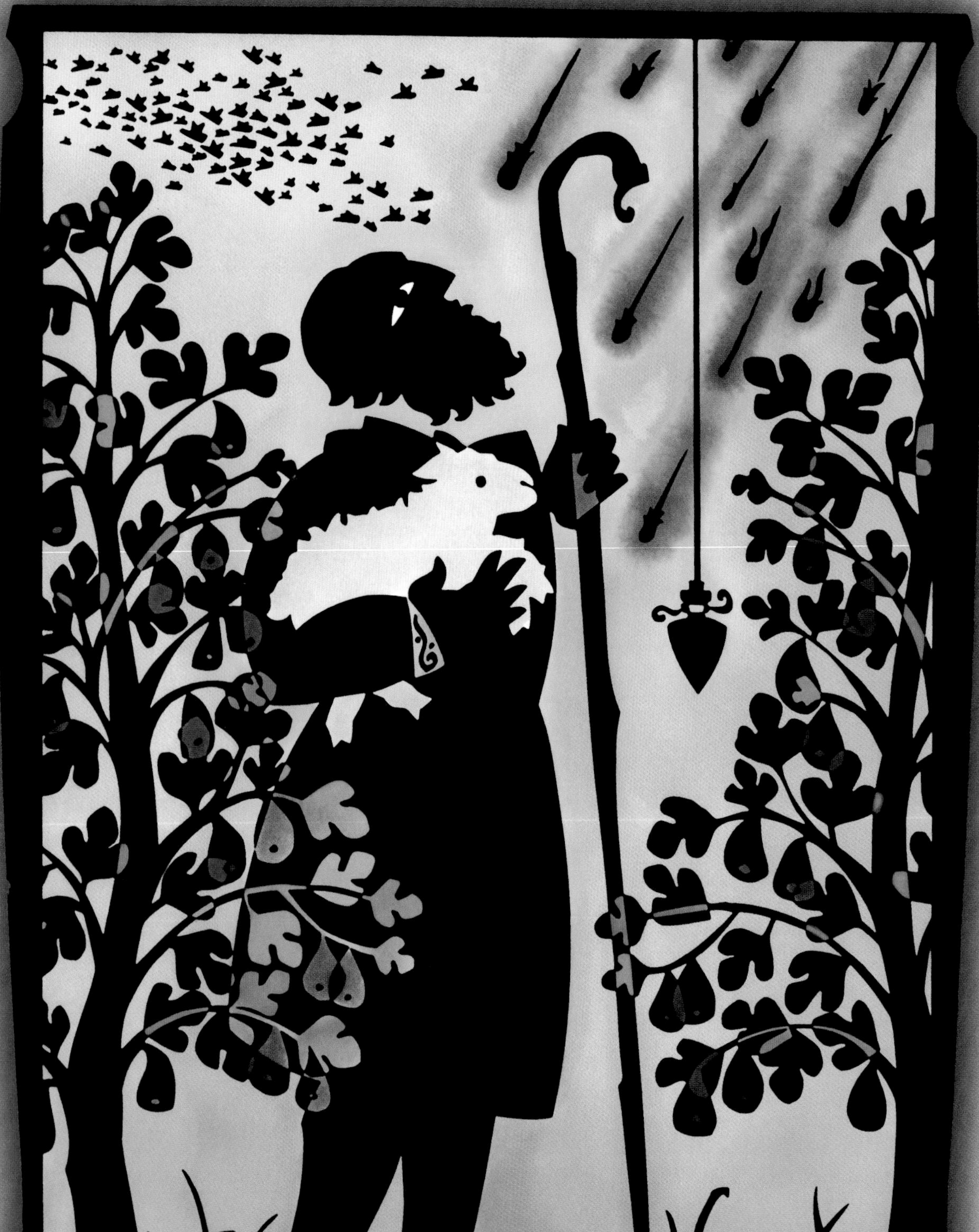

Amos answered, "I see a plumb line, such as stonecutters or bricklayers use to tell if a wall stands straight."

God continued. "With this plumb line I am measuring the hearts of My people Israel as a builder measures the straightness of a wall. If a wall is not straight, it cannot stand. The builder must pull it down. My people's hearts are not straight. I will pull them down. No more will I forgive Israel's sins, their wickedness and idol worship. I will demolish the hill shrines. I will raze the temples. I will deliver the royal family to their enemies."

God's words and the frightening visions terrified Amos. He realized that if the people of Israel did not change their ways, God would destroy them. As with the locusts and the fire, it would be a devastation so complete that nothing would survive. The people of Israel had to be warned. God had chosen Amos to tell them.

Amos in Samaria

Amos left his home and crossed the border into Israel. He took along nothing but a staff, a goatskin water bottle, and a sack with barley cakes and goat cheese as food for his journey.

When Amos arrived in Samaria, Israel's capital, he was astonished by both its wealth and corruption. Shrines to pagan idols flourished, yet not one altar to the God of Israel was to be found. The rich dwelled in shining marble palaces adorned with gold and ivory, while in the streets and in the countryside, the poor had to pawn the clothes they wore to buy food. Families who could not pay their debts were sold into slavery. Amos stopped by the city gates to watch the king's judges administering justice. He was shocked to see the judges openly asking for bribes. Justice in Israel was bought and sold. The judge's decision went to the person who paid the most.

Outraged, Amos understood why God's patience was nearing an end. He walked to Samaria's heights, where the splendid palaces of the nation's leaders stood. There Amos preached the fiery words that God placed in his mouth:

Woe to you, living comfortably in Zion.
All of you, safe and smug, on Samaria's hill.
Loafing on beds of ivory, sprawling on soft couches,
Stuffing yourselves with mutton and veal.

You strum on the harp and imitate King David.
You swill wine by the bucket
And rub yourselves with expensive oils
Without a moment's thought to the nation's ruin.
The day is coming when you will drag yourselves into exile as slaves.
That will be the end of your merrymaking.
For God has said, "I loathe your arrogance.
Your palaces disgust me. I will abandon this city and everyone in it to their fate."

Amos preached until his voice grew hoarse, but no one listened. No one in Samaria wanted to hear that God cared more about honesty and compassion than beautiful temples and elaborate sacrifices. Discouraged, Amos started back to Tekoa. God appeared to him on the road and told him to go instead to the shrine at Bethel.

Amos and Amaziah

The temple at Bethel had been erected by Jeroboam, Israel's first king, to lure his people away from worshiping at Solomon's Temple in Jerusalem. The priests at Bethel served idols in the shape of two golden calves. Amos stood at the gates to the shrine. He mocked the people coming to sacrifice to the idols:

Come to Bethel to sin against God!
Come to Gilgal and sin even more!
I despise your feasts.
I take no pleasure in your sacred ceremonies.
Bring your sacrifices and offerings. I won't accept them.
I will not look at the beast you bring to the altar.
Spare me your songs. I scorn the music of your harps.

"You say God doesn't want our sacrifices. What does he want?" someone shouted. Others took up the cry. "Tell us, Prophet! What must we do to make God happy?"

Amos told them:

Let justice flow like a river,
And righteousness like a mighty stream.
Come to Me, not to Bethel.

Come to Me, not to Gilgal.
For the shrine at Gilgal will be erased,
And the temple at Bethel will be in ruins.
Turn to God if you want to live,
Or a fire will consume Israel
And no one will be able to quench it.

This time someone heard Amos all too well. Amaziah, Bethel's high priest, was outraged. How dare this lunatic shepherd preach against the royal sanctuary and its priests! Amaziah stormed out of the temple and struck Amos in the face. The prophet fell to the ground. The priest, red-faced with anger, stood over him, shouting, "Get out, you so-called prophet! Go back to Judah! Did the people there hire you to preach against Israel? Leave Bethel at once and don't come back! How dare you spread false prophecies here! This is a holy place, a royal sanctuary!"

Amos rose from the dust. He brushed himself off, then answered quietly, "You are mistaken, Amaziah. I am not a professional prophet or seer. No one pays me to prophesy; I do not make any money from it. I am a simple shepherd, and I own an orchard of fig trees. That is all the wealth I have. One day, as I was tending my flock, God appeared to me. He showed me visions and told me, 'Go preach to My people Israel.' And so I did. Listen now, Amaziah, to what the future holds for you. You tried to stop me from preaching God's word to Israel. Therefore, says God, the time is fast approaching when your wife will sell herself to get food to survive; your children will perish by the sword. Strangers will cast lots for your property. You, the haughty high priest of Bethel, will die in chains, a miserable slave in a foreign country. All the people of Israel will be taken captive and driven far from their native land."

Amos turned his back on the trembling priest and walked away.

Before Amos returned to Tekoa, God showed him another vision. The prophet saw a basket filled with ripe fruit. "What do you see, Amos?" God asked.

Amos replied, "I see a basket of fruits, the kind that grow at summer's end."

"At the end of summer the orchard stands bleak and barren. So, too, will Samaria stand blighted and bare. I am going to bring an end to Israel. On that day the people will wail and moan. Corpses will cover the land. I will darken the sun at noon. I will turn their feasts into funerals; their songs into moans and laments. Their bodies will be covered with sackcloth. Every head will be bare."

Amos saw a vision of frightening destruction. He saw the Temple in Jerusalem shaking in the midst of an earthquake. God stood on the altar. He spoke with a mighty voice, louder than the earthquake's roar.

"I will strike the lintel, and the Temple will shake. No one will escape. I will pursue them as deep as the grave or as high as the heavens. I will pull them down from the heights of Mount Carmel and chase them to the bottom of the sea. I am God, Commander of Legions. I touch the land, and it melts. The inhabitants perish. Water rises. All is swept away. I am God, Who calls forth the waters of the ocean and pours them on the land. God is My Name!"

Amos fell to his knees, shaking with terror. If God would destroy His own house, what hope could there be for the nations of the earth? Thousands of years before God had destroyed the world in a great flood. Might he do it again?

"Is there no hope at all?" Amos cried out.

God answered, "The end of time is coming when the circle will be complete. The one who sows the seeds will meet the one who harvests the grain. The person who treads out the grapes will meet the person who plants the vines. When the mountains run with juice and the hills melt, I will bring Israel back from exile. My people will rebuild the ruined cities. They will plant vineyards and drink wine from their own grapes. They will tend orchards and eat their fruits. I will anchor them so firmly on their land that no one will ever uproot them again. So says God."

Amos had completed his mission. He returned to his home in Tekoa, to his sheep and fruit trees. He had done what God commanded him to do. The future lay in God's hands.

The Story of Hosea

Hosea, son of Beeri, was an ordinary man. He lived in a small village in Israel. Hosea was neither rich, young, nor handsome. But he had a beautiful wife, a lovely young woman named Gomer. Hosea loved her with all his heart, but Gomer did not love him. Being a wife and mother bored her. She wanted beautiful clothes, daring friends, exciting things to do. A group of handsome young men urged her to leave her dull husband and come with them to the city. Gomer abandoned her family and ran away.

Hosea was heartbroken to learn that Gomer had left him. He asked his friends what to do. "Divorce her," they told him. "You never should have married that worthless woman. You are better off without her."

"My children cry for their mother," Hosea pleaded.

"And she abandoned them! Be sensible, Hosea. Forget Gomer. You'll never see her again. Find a decent woman to marry."

Hosea Searches for Gomer

But Hosea could not forget the wife he loved. He set out for the city, determined to find Gomer and, if possible, to persuade her to come home.

Hosea walked through the streets and alleyways. He stopped every person he met to ask, "Have you seen my wife? She is tall and slender, with beautiful dark hair. When I saw her last, she wore a green dress and silver bracelets. She had gold rings in her ears. Her name is Gomer. Have you seen anyone who looks like that? Can you help me?"

The people shook their heads. "No. That is nobody we recognize."

But one day a man told Hosea, "I think I saw a woman like that down at the slave market. You'd better hurry. They may be bidding on her now."

Hosea ran to the slave market. He saw his beautiful wife standing on the auction block. Her green dress was in rags. Her earrings were gone, as were the bracelets, now replaced by iron shackles. Gomer lowered her face as the slavers bid for her.

"Five silver shekels . . . do I hear ten? Ten it is! Do I hear fifteen?"

"Fifteen silver shekels . . . and full measures of barley and wine!" Hosea cried.

Gomer looked up. She recognized her husband's voice. Her eyes met Hosea's. Gomer turned away in shame.

"Fifteen shekels is the bid. Do I hear twenty? Twenty? Sold—for fifteen shekels!"

The slave master unlocked Gomer's shackles. Hosea tried to embrace her, but Gomer would not let him touch her. "I am not worthy of your love," she told Hosea. "I do not understand why you want me back, or why you paid such an enormous sum to set me free."

"How did you come to be a slave?" Hosea asked.

"My so-called friends who lured me to the city never cared about me at all. They only wanted the little money I had. After they spent it, they sold me into slavery. You should have let me remain a slave. It is what I deserve."

"No, I could not do that. I would have paid the slave master any amount to set you free. Even though you broke my heart, I never stopped loving you. I forgive you fully and completely. Come, my beloved, let us go home. Our children are waiting."

Gomer went back to the village with Hosea. They lived together, in love and devotion, for the rest of their lives.

God Calls Hosea

God saw how Hosea's love for his wife overcame the sorrow and anger of her betrayal. "This is the man I am looking for," God said. He spoke to Hosea.

"Hosea, prophesy to the people of Israel. Speak the words that I will put in your mouth."

"I am no prophet," Hosea protested.

God said, "I will make you a prophet and you will serve Me, as did my servant Amos. You loved Gomer even when she betrayed you. So, too, do I love Israel. Though My people turn from Me and abandon My commandments, I never cease to love them. They run after false gods like Gomer ran after her false friends. They will suffer for it, as she did. Yet I love them still. One day I will redeem them from the chains of slavery and exile, and bring them home."

Hosea traveled through the towns and cities of Israel, speaking words of rage and doom.

Israel is like a wild vine, growing out of control.
Its fruit multiplies, as do the altars to false gods.
The land prospers, and with it, the pagan temples.
Are they all crazy? Have they all gone mad?
God will overthrow these heathen shrines.
He will demolish these pagan temples.
Samaria's royal house will be swept away
Like trash dumped in a river.
Thistles and thorns will grow upon the altars.
The hills and mountains will cover them.

People trembled to hear these words. "Has God abandoned us?" they cried. Hosea assured them there was still hope. God was always ready to forgive.

How can I abandon you, My children?
How can I turn my back on you, O Israel?
My heart is torn apart.
My emotions are tangled.
Let Me not release my anger.
Let Me not destroy my children.

"What if we change? What if we keep God's commandments and live as He wants us to do?" someone called out. "Will he forgive us?"

"He will do more than forgive. Thus says God," Hosea told them:

I will make a new covenant for Israel's sake
With birds and beasts and swarming insects.
Bows and swords I will break,
Weapons of violence I will sweep from the earth

So that all creatures may live without fear.
I will betroth myself to you in justice and righteousness,
In kindness and mercy.
I will betroth myself to you in devotion;
Then you will know that I am God.

The Downfall of Israel

Hosea held out hope for a new beginning. But it was not to be. The people of Israel did not listen to him any more than they listened to Amos. They refused to change. They continued their old ways, pursuing wealth and worshiping false gods. And so the terrible prophecies of Amos and Hosea came to pass.

Assyria's armies came west to attack the kingdom of Israel. Samaria fell. The shrine at Bethel was sacked. The entire population of the northern kingdom was led off into captivity. The exiles mingled with the surrounding nations. They adopted their languages and worshiped their gods. Within a few generations, they vanished forever.

But according to one legend, the lost tribes of the Northern kingdom still exist. They inhabit a mysterious country on the other side of a magical river called the Sambatyon. For six days each week this mighty river rushes through its gorge in a wild torrent, tossing huge stones high in the air. But on the seventh day, the Sabbath, it rests.

At the end of time, God Himself will lead the exiles back across the Sambatyon River. On that day, Hosea's prophecy will be fulfilled.

I will bring Israel back to the land once more.
I will have mercy on those who were denied mercy.
I will say to those who were not My people,
"You are my people."
And they will answer,
"You are our God!"

The Story of Isaiah

At the time Hosea preached in Israel, a young man from a noble family entered the Temple in Jerusalem, Judah's capital. The priests and Levites greeted him as he passed. They knew him well. His name was Isaiah, son of Amotz. Isaiah was a member of Judah's royal family, a descendant of David and Solomon.

Isaiah often came to meditate at night in the Temple, for his soul was deeply troubled. Though born to wealth and privilege, he could not erase from his mind the scenes of misery he saw every day. So many poor people filled Jerusalem's streets. Hungry, sick, and completely without hope, they cursed the sun each morning for bringing them another day of life. Meanwhile his cousins, the royal princes, could spend as much on a pair of earrings as a farmer earned in a year. To them, wealth was an endless river. They had but to dip in their buckets to take as much as they wanted. Isaiah knew that every drop came from the sweat of the poor. The taxes that paid for jeweled gowns and ivory bracelets were squeezed from the people who worked the land. Protesting was useless. Justice in Judah was bought and sold like a sack of barley. Farmers were cheated out of their crops; workers out of their wages. Tales of a king like Solomon sitting on his throne, giving justice to the people, seemed no more than a legend.

Surely God could not be pleased to see such corruption and injustice in His holy city. What about the old stories of Nathan and Elijah? Didn't God demand righteousness and justice from His People?

Whenever Isaiah asked these questions, the Temple priests assured him that God was indeed content. He must not take the old stories too seriously. Inequality had existed since the world began, and Jerusalem was no worse than other countries. As long as the priests offered the proper sacrifices and the Levites sang the appropriate hymns, God was happy.

Yet deep in his bones Isaiah could not help feeling that something was terribly wrong in Judah. That is why he came to the Temple at night, after the day's sacrifices were done, to stand in darkness and silence before the altar. Perhaps one day God would speak to him.

The Vision of the Burning Coal

As Isaiah stood alone in the sanctuary, he saw a vision. God sat on a throne of light that filled the whole Temple. Fiery angels attended Him. Each angel had six wings. One pair covered their mouths; a second covered their feet; and with the third they flew, calling to each other in ringing voices, "Holy, holy, holy is God, Commander of Legions! His glory fills the world!" The noise they made caused the Temple's doorposts to vibrate. The whole building became filled with smoke.

Isaiah cried, "Woe is me! I am doomed! I am an unworthy man. I live among unworthy people, and behold! My eyes gaze upon God Himself!"

Suddenly one of the fiery angels took a glowing coal from the top of the altar and pressed it against Isaiah's lips. Isaiah's heart stopped beating. He felt his soul leave his body. It was as if he had died.

Then he heard the angel say, "Look! This burning coal has touched your mouth. Your unworthiness has been erased. Your sins are removed."

God Himself spoke. "Who shall I send? Who will speak for Me?"

Isaiah answered: "Here I am! Send me!"

The Tale of the Vineyard

Isaiah, once a prince, became a prophet of God. He left his palace, took off his elegant robes, and gave away his jewelry. Now he walked through the streets of Jerusalem dressed in plain rough clothes. Wherever people gathered, no matter how ragged and dirty, Isaiah spoke to them, telling stories like this:

I once had a friend who owned a vineyard.
He planted it on a fertile hill.
He turned over the earth, removed the stones,
And planted it with carefully selected vines.

He built a tower in the middle of the vineyard

So he could watch over it.

He carved a wine vat out of limestone to press the grapes

When they were ripe.

My friend had great hopes for his vineyard.

But instead of sweet, juicy grapes

The vineyard brought forth wild, sour ones.

Isaiah turned to the people who had gathered to listen. He spoke with the voice of his friend, asking them,

Now tell me, people of Jerusalem,

Citizens of Judah,

What shall I do with this vineyard?

What more could I have done for it?

It should have brought forth sweet grapes,

But it only produced sour ones.

"What did your friend do?" the people asked.

Isaiah answered,

I will tell you what I will do with this vineyard.

I will pull down the fence to let animals eat the grapes and trample the vines.

I will let it go to waste, unpruned and unweeded.

Nettles and briars will overgrow the vines.

I will tell the clouds not to rain on it.

"What is the point of this story?" a beggar cried from the back of the crowd. "I, too, had a vineyard. I had to sell it to pay my taxes. Now I barely have enough to eat. Why should I care about someone else's vineyard?"

Isaiah looked at the beggar. "I will tell you why this vineyard is important," he said.

Israel is God's vineyard,

Judah is the field He cherishes.

He looks everywhere for justice,

But finds only violence and corruption.

Instead of righteousness,

> *He hears only the cries of victims.*
> *Woe to those who buy house after house,*
> *Who gobble up field after field.*
> *Until no place is left for the poor to live.*
> *Are you the only ones who live in this land?*
> *Even an ox knows its master.*
> *Even a donkey knows who provides its hay.*
> *But Israel does not know.*
> *The people show no understanding.*
> *They are a wicked nation, heavy with guilt.*
> *A nest of poisonous snakes; spoiled children.*
> *They have forsaken their God.*
> *They have turned away from the Holy One of Israel.*

A group of well-dressed young noblemen passed by. "Look!" one called to his companions. "Is that cousin Isaiah? The stories are true. He really has gone mad. He thinks he's a prophet!"

"Has God spoken with you today, Isaiah?" the others cried with scorn. "Tell us, cousin, what were His words?"

Isaiah turned to face them. "I will tell you what God said to me:

> *They will hear but not understand.*
> *They will see but not realize.*
> *They have hardened their hearts.*
> *Dulled their ears. Dimmed their eyes.*
> *So that they neither hear nor see nor comprehend.*

"Beware, Isaiah! Such talk is treason," the young men shouted.

People in the crowd took up the cry. "Traitor! False prophet!"

A stone flew past Isaiah's head. Filth from the gutter spattered his clothes. The commotion drew a detachment of soldiers. The crowd hurriedly dispersed.

Isaiah walked away, discouraged. He spoke the words God put in his mouth throughout the streets of Jerusalem, but no one listened. He might as well have preached to one of the statues in the pagan temples.

"Prophet!"

Isaiah turned. A group of children had followed him down the winding street. They were all half-starved and dirty. Like so many homeless people in Jerusalem, they survived as scavengers, rifling the trash heaps outside the city walls for food. "We heard you speak," one ragged boy said. "We believe your words come from God. Teach us. Tell us what we can do."

Isaiah gathered the children around him. They went to the market, where he brought bread and fruit for them to eat. Afterward, he took them to a fountain, where he washed their hands and faces. The prophet and the children sat down together beside the fountain. As the water trickled into the basin, Isaiah spoke these words. People passing by stopped to listen:

Wash yourselves. Cleanse your bodies.

Turn from evil.

Stop doing wrong.

Begin doing right.

Strive for justice. Help the oppressed.

Abhor violence.

Respect the rights of the powerless.

Defend those who have no one to fight for them.

Because God says, "Come, let us reason together.

Though your sins be as red as scarlet,

They shall become as pure as snow.

Though they be as red as crimson,

I will turn them white as wool.

If you will follow God's ways,

You will eat of the fruit of the land.

But if you turn against Him, you will die by the sword."

So speaks the voice of God.

"Why talk to us?" one of the market women scoffed. "Speak to the king's officials. Tell them to defend poor people's rights. See what happens."

The crowd gathered around the fountain laughed. Someone threw an overripe pomegranate at Isaiah. It splattered on his cloak. A tall girl dipped the hem of her ragged dress in the fountain and wiped the mess away.

"Do not give up. Others may not listen, but I know your words come from God."

"So do we," a few of the other children said. The rest had wandered away.

There is hope, Isaiah thought. *Not everyone has shut his heart to God. But the ones who listen are so few, and they are among the weakest, the most powerless in the land. What can be done to reach the souls of Judah's leaders?*

Isaiah asked God to show him a way.

Two Smoldering Torches

God spoke to Isaiah. "Go to Ahaz, king of Judah. He needs your help. Tell him to put his faith in God and not to fear his enemies."

Isaiah hurried to the royal palace. Dozens of crazy prophets came there every day, claiming to have messages for the king from one god or another. The guards at the gate ignored them. Isaiah might have been crazy, too, but he was also the king's cousin. He was taken to Ahaz immediately.

Ahaz rose from his throne. "Cousin Isaiah! I am thankful you have come. Is it true you are now a prophet? Then, perhaps you can help me. Our kingdom is in grave danger. I don't know what to do."

"I can only speak the words God puts in my mouth," Isaiah said. "Tell me what is wrong. If God sends an answer, you will hear it."

"The Assyrians are on the march again. They have conquered Babylon and most of Aram, leaving nothing behind but ruined cities and piles of corpses. I feared Judah would meet the same fate, so I paid tribute to the Assyrians. Peace comes at a heavy price. The Assyrians demand more of our wealth every year. Pekah, the king of Israel, and Rezin, who rules what is left of Aram, invited me to form an alliance with them against the Assyrians. I refused at first. How could three tiny nations hope to defeat mighty Assyria? Pekah and Rezin would not accept my refusal. Their armies have crossed our borders and are coming to besiege Jerusalem. They threaten to do away with me and put a puppet king on the throne who will do their bidding. Help me, Isaiah! What should I do? Jerusalem's walls are strong, but the nation is not prepared for war."

"Listen to God's words," Isaiah told the king. "Stand fast. Do not be afraid of your enemies. Pekah and Rezin are nothing but two smoldering torches. They will soon be gone. You need not fear them. God is with you."

"I am pleased to hear that," said Ahaz. "However, I cannot rely on God alone. I have sent a messenger to Tiglath-Pileser, the king of Assyria. I have agreed to become his vassal if he will defend Judah against her enemies. It is the only way for our kingdom to survive."

"You are making a terrible mistake!" Isaiah exclaimed. "Tiglath-Pileser is a dangerous ally. Why bind Judah to Assyria? Why not put your faith in God? He is mightier than any king. Do you not believe my words are true? If you need proof, ask God for a sign. He will send you one."

"I don't want to test God," Ahaz answered. "That would show I do not have faith."

"Perhaps you do not," Isaiah replied. "Although you will not ask for a sign, God will send you one. A certain young woman in your court is going to have a child. She will give birth to a son. She will call his name *Immanuel*, meaning *God Is with Us*. Before this child is weaned, these two kings you so greatly fear will be swept away. Their countries will become wastelands. However, by bowing to Assyria instead of God, you will expose our nation to even greater danger. God is warning you: *'Since you have turned away from God's quiet waters, I will bring Assyria upon you like the mighty and numerous rivers of the Euphrates. It will break through its channels and overwhelm its banks, sweeping through Judah in a mighty deluge.'* It is not too late. Call back your messenger."

Ahaz refused. In spite of Isaiah's warning, he agreed to submit to Tiglath-Pileser in exchange for Assyria's protection. Pekah and Rezin did lay siege to Jerusalem, but soon they had to return home to face an Assyrian attack. Both were defeated in battle. Israel and Aram were laid waste. Their cities were destroyed, and their populations slaughtered. The survivors were led off into exile as slaves.

Judah was saved. Ahaz kept his throne but, as Isaiah predicted, he was now king only in name. Assyria had become the nation's real ruler.

The Siege of Jerusalem

Ahaz did not live long to enjoy his small success. He died, and his son Hezekiah took his place upon the throne of Judah.

Hezekiah and Isaiah had been friends since childhood. The king knew the valuable advice the prophet had given his father. If Ahaz had listened, Judah would still be a free nation. Hezekiah would not have to ask the Assyrian ambassador to approve every important decision.

The Assyrians did not care what god the Judeans worshiped as long as they paid their tribute and did not try to act independently. Isaiah urged Hezekiah to purify his kingdom. "Do away with idol worship. Cleanse the land of corruption and wickedness," the prophet told the king.

Hezekiah listened. He and his people needed God's help if they ever hoped to free themselves from the Assyrians. First, they had to prove themselves worthy. Hezekiah sent soldiers to tear down the temples to foreign gods. He banned all idol worship in the land of Judah. He punished evildoers and removed corrupt judges and officials. The people of Judah praised God, the king, and the prophet Isaiah. They believed that soon God would help them overthrow their Assyrian overlords.

The opportunity came sooner than anyone expected. A secret embassy from the king of Egypt arrived in Jerusalem.

"My master, Pharaoh, pledges to support his brother, the King of Judah, should he wish to rise up and join Egypt against the Assyrians," the Egyptian ambassador told Hezekiah.

"Allow me to consider Pharaoh's proposal with my ministers," Hezekiah said.

Hezekiah called a meeting of Judah's ruling council. His ministers unanimously approved an alliance with Egypt. "With Pharaoh's mighty armies fighting beside us, we will drive out the Assyrians. Judah will be free again."

Suddenly Isaiah burst into the council room. He was completely naked. Not one stitch of clothing covered his bony frame. "Look at me!" the prophet commanded. "Do you see that I am naked? The Egyptians will be naked, too. The Assyrians will lead them off in chains, without a rag to cover themselves. Why won't you listen? Trust God, not foreigners! Egypt cannot save you. But God can! Listen to His words:

Woe to those who put their faith in Egypt
And rely on the power of horses and chariots!
The Egyptians are human beings, not immortals.
Their horses are flesh and blood, not divine creatures.
When God puts forth His hand, your ally will stumble.
You who relied on him will go down, too.
You will both perish together.

Isaiah pleaded with the king not to enter into a dangerous alliance with the Egyptians. Day after day he walked naked through the palace and the streets of Jerusalem. Everyone who stopped to stare heard him say again and again, "People of Judah! Turn to God! Put your faith in Him! Not the Egyptians!"

But Hezekiah's faith was not as strong as Isaiah's. He thought the time had come to gamble for Judah's freedom. "Judah will stand with Egypt against the Assyrians," he told Pharaoh's ambassador.

"And Egypt will stand with you," the Egyptian promised.

Hezekiah's decision meant war.

Sennacherib, Assyria's king, invaded Judah. One by one, its cities fell. The Assyrians burned them to the ground and dragged off their inhabitants into slavery. Hezekiah sent desperate messages to Pharaoh, pleading for help. None arrived. Too late, he realized his cousin Isaiah had been correct. The Egyptians were a broken reed. Pharaoh was afraid of the Assyrians.

Hezekiah had only one choice. He sent messengers to Sennacherib, begging for peace. He promised to pay any amount of gold or silver if the Assyrians would spare his kingdom.

Sennacherib's answer plunged Hezekiah even deeper into despair. The Assyrians demanded an enormous tribute, nearly all the wealth in the kingdom! Hezekiah agreed to pay. He handed over all the gold and silver from his palace. He surrendered the treasures stored in the Temple. He even removed the gold plate from the Temple's doors. Solomon's splendid Temple now stood bare and desolate, as if it had been stripped by an enemy.

Sennacherib's messenger weighed the tribute. Then he announced, "The Great King also demands that the traitor Hezekiah surrender himself."

"Never!" cried Hezekiah. He knew that torture and death awaited him as Sennacherib's prisoner. He shut the gates of Jerusalem. Soon word came that the Assyrians had captured the city of Lachish. Now they were coming to besiege Jerusalem itself.

The Assyrians surrounded Jerusalem so completely that not a dog or a cat could go out or come in. They impaled their prisoners, both men and women, on stakes within sight of the city's walls to terrify its inhabitants. Sennacherib's officers surveyed Jerusalem, choosing the best point for an attack. Meanwhile, his engineers constructed huge battering rams and siege towers.

The people of Jerusalem watched these preparations with growing fear. They had never seen such might. Unless a powerful ally came to their aid, they had no hope of defeating the Assyrians. But they had no allies.

Sennacherib tried to divide the people of Jerusalem against each other. He sent one of his officers, an official named Rab-shakeh, to speak to them in their own language. Rab-shakeh stood before the gates, where the people gathered on the walls and towers could hear him. He delivered this speech:

"Citizens of Jerusalem, listen to the words of Sennacherib, the Great King of Assyria. Don't listen to Hezekiah when he calls on your god to save you. The nations we conquered had their gods, too. They prayed to them, sacrificed to them, wept before their altars. It did no good. Not one of those gods ever saved his people from us. Look north to your brothers in Israel. Where are the gods of Samaria? Did they save their kingdom? Why do you think your god can save Jerusalem?"

The people on the walls turned to each other in confusion. Perhaps Rab-shakeh was right. Better for them to surrender and live, even as slaves, than to die miserably. And they would surely die if they continued to defy the Assyrians.

Isaiah walked among them, speaking calmly. "Don't listen to this Assyrian," Isaiah told the people. "Put your faith in God. God Himself will defend Jerusalem. I promise that not one of Sennacherib's soldiers will ever set foot within its walls."

"How can you be so sure?" the people asked him.

"Because I have faith," Isaiah said. "Show God that you have faith, too. He will not fail you."

Encouraged by these words, the people of Jerusalem shouted back at Rab-shakeh, "We will not surrender our king or our city! We will not open our gates to Sennacherib! We trust in the God of Israel! He will deliver us! We are ready to die for him!"

Hezekiah called on the people of Jerusalem to renew their faith in God. The king himself, guided by Isaiah, led the way. He took off his royal robes and dressed in rough cloth made of dusty old sacks. He sat in the dirt, pouring dust and ashes on his head. Hezekiah prayed to God to forgive his sins and the sins of his people. "Isaiah was right. I should have listened. I should have trusted You instead of Pharaoh. If I had, my people and I would not be in fear of death. Forgive me, God of Abraham, Isaac, and Jacob! God of my ancestors, forgive me!"

God heard Hezekiah's prayer. He sent Isaiah to him with words of courage.

"Do not be afraid of these Assyrian blasphemers," Isaiah told the king. "Sennacherib will soon return to his own country by the way he came, there to die by an assassin's sword. He will never trouble Jerusalem again. God has said,

'The king of Assyria will never enter this city. He will not shoot an arrow into it, nor come before it with his shield, nor build siege works against it. I Myself will defend it, for My sake, and for the sake of My beloved servant David.' So says God."

Isaiah's prophecy came true. That night God sent an angel flying over the Assyrian camp. A sudden plague struck the Assyrians. Sennacherib's army perished overnight. Sennacherib fled, fearful the plague might strike him, too. He mounted his chariot and galloped for home, not stopping until he crossed Assyria's borders. While he was gone, his sons had plotted against him. They waited for him in the temple of Ashur. When Sennacherib came to offer a sacrifice of thanksgiving for having escaped from Judah alive, they cut him down with their swords.

As for the people of Jerusalem, when they awoke the next morning they saw flocks of crows and vultures hovering over the enemy's tents. Not one living soul was left in the entire camp. Sennacherib's mighty army had vanished, leaving only piles of corpses.

Hezekiah and Isaiah walked together to the gates of the Temple. There the king led the priests, the Levites, and the people of Judah in offering thanks to the God of Israel, Who had delivered them from death and slavery.

"Praise God, Who has once again fulfilled His promise, as He did in the time of our ancestors," said Hezekiah. "He has preserved and protected us in the face of our enemies. Let us praise His glorious name forever and ever!"

Isaiah and the people of Judah answered, "Amen!"

The Story of Jeremiah

After Hezekiah's death the people of Judah returned to their old ways. Conditions grew worse than before. Manasseh, Hezekiah's successor, openly worshiped idols. He set them up in the Temple itself. Prophets and priests who spoke out against him were killed or driven out of the country. Manasseh even ordered Isaiah put to death. By the time the king died, the God of Israel was nearly forgotten.

Josiah, Manasseh's grandson, worked hard to undo his grandfather's misdeeds. He rebuilt the Temple, cleansing it of all traces of idol worship. He tore down the pagan shrines and drove all foreign priests out of the country.

Unfortunately, Josiah died in battle while still a young man. A series of weak kings took his place, all of whom were puppets to the Egyptian Pharaoh. Temples to foreign gods reappeared in Jerusalem. The kings could do nothing about it. For the sake of harmony they joined the Egyptian ambassadors in offering sacrifices to the gods of Egypt. Many Judeans joined them.

Jeremiah Receives the Call

While these events were taking place, God appeared to a young man named Jeremiah. He lived in the village of Anathoth, a few miles northeast of Jerusalem. Jeremiah came from a distinguished family of priests. His ancestor, Abiathar, was high priest during King David's time.

Like Amos and Hosea, Jeremiah did not want to be a prophet. However, God did not give him a choice. He spoke to him, saying, "I chose you for My own even before your body formed in your mother's womb. I consecrated you before your birth, to be a prophet to the people of the world."

Jeremiah pleaded with God. "Do not make me a prophet. A prophet's life is more bitter than wormwood. Manasseh hunted prophets like wild beasts. He killed Isaiah. Amos was driven out of Israel. What good is it to speak words of truth when no one listens? Who would heed a young man from a tiny village? I am like Moses. I hardly know how to speak. I am like a little child. Who will listen to me?"

God said, "Do not say, 'I am like a little child'! You will go where I send you and speak the words I tell you to say. Do not be afraid. I will be with you. I will protect you."

God reached out and touched Jeremiah's lips. Jeremiah felt a new soul enter his body. He felt as if he were being born for a second time. "Behold!" said God. "I have placed My words in your mouth. Today I place in your power all the nations of the earth. They are yours to raze and uproot; to demolish and destroy; to build and to sow."

The Two Visions

A vision appeared before Jeremiah's eyes. He saw the branch of an almond tree just about to burst into bloom. "The almond is the first tree to bloom after winter is past," said God. "I am early, too. I will not hesitate to carry out My promise."

The vision slowly disappeared. A second took its place. Jeremiah saw a cauldron heated by a raging fire fanned by the wind. The cauldron leaned to the north. The liquid inside seethed and bubbled, as if about to overflow. "Danger will boil up out of the north to overwhelm the people of this land," said God. "I am summoning the kingdoms of the north to gather before the gates of Jerusalem. I will judge those who have neglected Me by worshiping other gods and offering sacrifices to idols."

"If all these things are doomed to come to pass, what is the good of sending me?" asked Jeremiah.

God answered, "A small hope remains. Be strong. Speak loudly. Tell the people everything I say to you. Do not be afraid, for I Myself will stand beside you. You will be like a fortified city, an iron pillar, a bronze wall. The kings and princes of Judah, the priests and even the common people will turn against you. They will mock and persecute you, but they will not win. Because I am with you. I will protect you from them."

Jeremiah's Mission Begins

Jeremiah left Anathoth and walked to Jerusalem. As he passed through the city's streets he saw people everywhere worshiping idols.

Unlike Amos, Jeremiah spoke to them gently. "Remember the days of our forefathers, when Israel worshiped God with a new bride's devotion?" he asked them. "God says:

> Remember when you were young,
> How you loved Me then
> Like a bride on her wedding day.
> You followed Me through the desert,
> Through a barren land.
> Israel was devoted to Me in those days,
> The first among nations.
> No one who harmed her went unpunished.
> I destroyed her enemies.

"Look at all that God has done for us!" Jeremiah exclaimed. "He brought our ancestors to this rich and fruitful land. He defended us against our enemies. Why, then, do you turn your backs on Him to worship foreign idols? God is angry. Listen to His words!

> My people sold their glory for useless idols!
> It is astonishing! Shocking beyond words!
> My people have forsaken a spring of pure, living water
> For a muddy cistern, a broken one
> That cannot hold anything.

"It is not as simple as you believe," a perfumed courtier remarked. "People of many lands live in Jerusalem. Foreign embassies come here all the time. Why shouldn't they have temples to worship their gods in their own way? If Judah is to survive, we need alliances with other nations, no matter what gods they worship."

"Isaiah taught us to put our trust in God, not foreigners," Jeremiah replied.

"Listen to God's words:

> *Why run off to Egypt to drink the waters of the Nile?*
> *Why run off to Assyria to drink from the Euphrates?*
> *Your own wickedness will punish you.*
> *Your own treachery will condemn you.*

"That is what you say!" a merchant with jeweled earrings scoffed. "God has protected us in the past. He will continue to protect us in the future. Judah may not be perfect, but she is better than other nations." The people in the crowd nodded as they walked away, leaving Jeremiah alone in the street.

"I spoke the words You told me to say, yet the people did not listen. What more can I do?" he asked God.

God answered: "Are you surprised? Do you think it is easy to make people change their ways?

> *Can the leopard remove her spots?*
> *Can those who are used to doing evil*
> *Suddenly do good?*

"When you speak to the people next time, tell them this:

> *I will scatter you like straw before the desert wind.*
> *This is your fate. I will not change it.*
> *Because you have turned your back on Me,*
> *Trusting in false gods.*

Jeremiah trembled to hear these words. He dreaded what might happen to him when the time came to say them.

At the Temple Gates

God commanded Jeremiah to stand at the Temple gate. When people came to offer sacrifices, the prophet warned them, "Listen to the voice of God, people of Judah! Change your ways! You keep saying, 'Trust in God's Temple. God's Holy Temple will protect us.' 'It is a lie!' says God. 'I don't want your sacrifices. I want you to change your hearts. Deal with each other honestly. Do not oppress the weak and helpless. Do not shed innocent blood. Do not worship false gods. If you will only follow My commandments, you will stay in this land forever, the land I promised to your forefathers.

"'But do you listen? Not at all! You steal, you murder, you lie, you sacrifice to idols—and then you come and stand before Me in this holy place, thinking, 'We are safe.' Safe to do what? To continue your wickedness. You have turned My Holy Temple into a nest of thieves.

"'Remember the shrine at Shiloh, where the Tabernacle stood in the days of Samuel! Look at it now, a barren waste. I destroyed it because of the wickedness of My people. As I did with Shiloh, so will I do with this Temple here, the one that bears My name. I will drive you from My sight, as I drove out your brothers and sisters, the people of Israel.'"

Jeremiah's Trial

The people turned on Jeremiah in rage. What was he saying? That God's holy Temple would be destroyed? An angry mob attacked Jeremiah. "What do you mean, our Temple will be like Shiloh? Jerusalem will become a wasteland? Liar! How dare you speak these words! Kill the prophet! Kill him!"

The Temple guards arrested Jeremiah. They dragged him before the royal judges. "This man should be put to death. He has prophesied against God's Temple and slandered its holy priests. We heard him with our own ears," the angry priests cried.

The judges asked if the prophet had anything to say for himself. Jeremiah replied, "I am innocent. True, I have spoken words that angered the priests, but God Himself told me to say them. His message is clear. Change your ways, obey His commandments, and He will not bring about the destruction He promised. I am in your power. Do with me what you like. Only remember: If you put me to death, you will be guilty of shedding innocent blood. I did not choose my words. God told me what to say."

The Temple priests clamored for Jeremiah's death. But the judges disagreed. "A prophet can only speak the words God puts in his mouth," they decided. "A man who speaks in God's name does not deserve to die. Jeremiah is innocent. Set him free."

The priests were outraged. "He spoke against the holy Temple! He should be whipped!" they screamed as soldiers led Jeremiah away.

The priests spread the word that the prophet had cursed the Temple and called on God to destroy the whole land of Judah. Within days Jeremiah became the most despised man in Jerusalem. It grieved Jeremiah to be rejected by everyone. But God still needed him. Soon He sent him forth with another message.

The Tale of the Jug

God told Jeremiah to buy a clay jug and take it to the Valley of Ben-hinnom, opposite the Potsherd Gate on the south side of the city. The valley was one vast trash heap. All of Jerusalem's garbage came through the Potsherd Gate to be dumped here.

Holding the jug in his hand, Jeremiah stood amidst piles of trash and began preaching. A crowd gathered to listen. Jeremiah warned them the time was coming when this valley would be called "The Valley of Slaughter." The inhabitants of Jerusalem would be butchered by their enemies. Their bodies would lie in heaps, pulled apart by vultures and jackals. Starving parents would cook the flesh of their own children. People would devour each other before being killed themselves.

The people trembled to hear this shocking prophecy. When Jeremiah finished, he shattered the jug on a stone. "So says God," the prophet declared. "I will shatter your nation and your city like this jug. No one will be able to put the pieces back together. The corpses of the dead will be dumped in this polluted valley. There will be no place left to bury them. All of Jerusalem will become a Valley of Slaughter!"

A passing priest overheard Jeremiah speak. Outraged, he ran to the Temple and reported the prophet's words to Pashur, commander of the Temple guards.

"So Jeremiah is back again!" Pashur said. "This time he won't get off so easily." When Jeremiah climbed out of the valley, soldiers seized him, whipped him, and put him into the stocks. Jeremiah stood in the pillory all night, his back bloody and torn. Passersby cursed and spat upon him.

Pashur came by the next morning. "Have you learned your lesson, Jeremiah? If so, I am ready to release you."

Jeremiah refused to take back his words. Pashur released him, anyway. Jeremiah limped home. When he was alone, he poured out his heart to God.

Everyone laughs at me. Everyone despises me.
I must bring a message of doom and destruction.
Everywhere I go I am mocked for speaking God's words.
Why was I born? To know only sorrow and misery?
To live out my days in shame?

Yet Jeremiah also knew that terrible danger faced the nation. Only by turning to God could the people of Judah hope to survive. God needed a man of enormous courage to deliver His message. That was why He chose Jeremiah.

The Coming Disaster

Beaten, scorned, arrested, Jeremiah continued preaching. His words grew more urgent as a new nation, Babylon, arose. The Babylonians had conquered what was left of Assyria. Now they were ready to challenge Egypt.

Jehoiakim, Judah's king, grew tired of being a puppet. After the Babylonians defeated the Egyptians in battle, he decided to switch sides. Jeremiah condemned such intrigue. Jehoiakim was gambling with the lives of his people. If he guessed wrong, Judah would suffer. Outraged, the king ordered the prophet to be silent. He banned Jeremiah from the Temple and forbade him to preach anywhere in Jerusalem.

Jeremiah could no longer speak God's words. However, he could still write them. Jeremiah asked his friend Baruch to copy his words on a parchment scroll. Baruch stood at the window of Jeremiah's house and read the scroll to the people gathered outside.

News of Jeremiah's defiance reached the king. Jehoiakim was furious. His officers ordered Baruch to bring them the scroll. When Baruch appeared, they ordered him to read it.

The king's officers listened to Jeremiah's words with alarm. What were they to do? If the king heard these prophecies, he might put Jeremiah to death. What greater sin could there be than killing a prophet for speaking God's own words?

The officers told Baruch to give them the scroll. Then they warned him to take Jeremiah and to go into hiding.

Jehoiakim grew more and more angry as he heard the scroll read. After listening to each section, Jehoiakim cut it from the scroll and threw it into the fire.

When the whole scroll was burnt to ashes, Jehoiakim ordered his officers to arrest Baruch and Jeremiah.

They were nowhere to be found. The king's soldiers searched in vain. God told Jeremiah to take another scroll and write down the same words that had been burned in the fire, and many more. These scrolls circulated throughout Jerusalem. Soon they were on everyone's lips. No king was mightier than God. All the soldiers in Judah could not stop the prophet from preaching God's word.

The Kingdom Falls

Jehoiakim's intrigues ended in disaster. After the Egyptians won a victory over the Babylonians, he switched his allegiance back to Egypt. Nebuchadnezzar, the king of Babylon, invaded Judah. His army besieged Jerusalem. Help from Egypt did not arrive.

Jerusalem surrendered. The king, the royal family, the nobles, the officers, all the skilled artisans and craftspeople in the land were marched off to exile in Babylon. Only the poorest and weakest were left behind. Nebuchadnezzar, the Babylonian king, stripped the royal palaces of their wealth. The gold and silver vessels of the Temple, along with every item of value, were carried off, too. Jerusalem survived, but with only a shadow of her former glory.

Nebuchadnezzar appointed Zedekiah, Jehoiakim's brother, to be king over Judah. He governed only with the consent of his masters, the Babylonians. Nebuchadnezzar was Judah's real ruler.

Egypt was subdued, but not conquered. Pharaoh sent messengers to Zedekiah, inviting him to join an alliance against the Babylonians. The people of Judah called for war, believing that God would surely fight on their side.

Jeremiah Bears the Yoke

Jeremiah knew that such hopes were foolish. The Babylonians were instruments of God's punishment. They could not be overcome. Judah could only hope to survive by humbling herself and submitting to God's will. This meant submitting to the Babylonians. To dramatize his belief, Jeremiah appeared before Zedekiah wearing a yoke around his neck. Only by accepting Nebuchadnezzar's yoke could Judah avoid disaster. The king refused to listen. As Jeremiah predicted, the

Babylonians were soon on the march. Once again Jerusalem found herself besieged.

Suddenly the siege lifted. The Babylonians had learned that an Egyptian army was on its way. They marched off to meet this threat from the south. Zedekiah sent for Jeremiah. He asked the prophet what God had to say about these events.

Jeremiah could not hold out false hopes. "These are the words of the God of Israel: Do not deceive yourself by expecting help from the Egyptians. They will not fight. Pharaoh's army is already on its way back to Egypt. The Babylonians will return. This time they will conquer the city and burn it to the ground."

Jeremiah in Prison

After leaving the palace, Jeremiah considered what to do. He saw no reason to remain in Jerusalem. No one listened to his words or heeded his counsel. The fall of Jerusalem was near, and he could do nothing to change the final outcome. For these reasons he decided to leave the city and go back to his home village of Anathoth. As he passed through the gate, the captain of the guard recognized him.

"Stop, traitor! You are going over to the Babylonians!"

Jeremiah denied he was going to the Babylonian camp, or that he had any sympathy at all for Judah's enemies. The captain of the guard refused to believe him. He ordered his soldiers to strip Jeremiah's robe from his back. They tied him to a post and whipped him savagely. Then they dragged the prophet to an abandoned house that served as a prison. They threw Jeremiah into a pit beneath the floor. Here he remained in darkness for several days.

Zedekiah soon learned of Jeremiah's imprisonment, but he dared not release him. Many of the king's officers regarded Jeremiah as a traitor. Instead of encouraging the people to resist the enemy, as Isaiah had done, Jeremiah preached that their cause was lost, that God had abandoned his people, and that their only hope was to surrender to Nebuchadnezzar.

Zedekiah feared his officers might kill Jeremiah or leave him to die in his underground prison. He ordered his soldiers to bring the prophet to the palace, where he would be safe. When Jeremiah arrived, Zedekiah asked if he had received any word from God.

Jeremiah spoke briefly, for he was so weak, he could not stand. "Yes," the prophet murmured. "You will be taken prisoner by the king of Babylon." He begged Zedekiah not to send him back to the underground cell, where he would surely die of hunger and neglect.

Zedekiah commanded his soldiers to lock Jeremiah in the palace guardhouse. They were to give him one loaf of bread to eat each day.

Jeremiah continued to preach in the guardhouse. He told anyone who would listen to flee Jerusalem. Those who remained within its walls would either die of hunger or disease, or else be killed by the Babylonians when they captured the city. Jerusalem was sure to fall. God Himself had said so.

Zedekiah's officers were outraged. "What is the use of fighting on the walls when this traitorous prophet tells our people to surrender!" They demanded that Jeremiah be put to death. Zedekiah, fearful of angering his commanders, said, "Do as you please."

The officers dragged Jeremiah from the guardhouse and lowered him into an abandoned cistern. Jeremiah sank to his waist in the mud at the bottom. The prophet tore his hair and wept. Had it all been in vain? Had he served God faithfully all his life, only to die a miserable death amid filth and darkness?

Jeremiah Is Rescued

But God had not abandoned Jeremiah. The prophet had a friend, a palace official named Ebed-Melech. He was an African from the land of Cush. Ebed-Melech knew that Jeremiah would die if he remained in the cistern. He went at once to Zedekiah and protested this cruel treatment. By now, Zedekiah also regretted allowing his officers to do as they pleased. He gave permission to remove Jeremiah from the cistern.

Ebed-Melech and three companions pulled Jeremiah out of the cistern and brought him back to the guardhouse. Several days later, after Jeremiah recovered his strength, Zedekiah had him brought to the Temple.

"I must ask you something," Zedekiah said. "Tell me the truth. Hold nothing back."

Jeremiah, still weak, answered, "What is the use? Why do you play these games with me? If I tell you the truth, you will put me to death. If I give you advice, you will not follow it."

Zedekiah promised not to punish Jeremiah for anything he said. The king apologized for delivering him to the officers. He promised not to do it again.

Jeremiah then spoke these words. "Hear the words of the God of Israel: If you surrender yourself to the king of Babylon, you and your family will live. If you do not, Jerusalem will be destroyed. You will not escape."

Zedekiah admitted he was afraid to surrender. He might be tortured in any number of terrible ways. Jeremiah reassured him.

"If you surrender and do as I tell you, as God commands, then you will live and not be harmed. But I say again, if you do not surrender, you will be taken prisoner by the king of Babylon, and Jerusalem will be burned to the ground."

Zedekiah concealed his intentions. He told Jeremiah, "You need not mention this discussion to anyone. If someone asks, say you came to beg me not to return you to that underground cell."

Jeremiah repeated this excuse to the officers at the guardhouse when he came back from the Temple. They did not question him further. He remained in their custody until the day Jerusalem fell.

The Fall of Jerusalem

Zedekiah did not follow Jeremiah's advice. He refused to surrender. He remained in the city until the end. Only after the Babylonians broke down the walls did he attempt to escape. He was captured and dragged before Nebuchadnezzar, as Jeremiah had foretold. Zedekiah was forced to watch as the Babylonians killed his sons and executed the nobles they captured with him. These terrible scenes were the last ones he ever witnessed. The Babylonians gouged out his eyes. Zedekiah, once king of Judah, was shackled with chains and driven along the road to Babylon; a blind, helpless slave stumbling into exile.

Jerusalem had become a Valley of Slaughter. Unburied bodies lay everywhere. The only living souls to be seen were a few crazed beggars, scavenging among the corpses in the ruins. God's holy Temple had been burned to ashes. Hardly one stone remained standing on another.

As for Jeremiah, the Babylonians treated him as an honored guest. Nebuchadnezzar's spies had told him how the prophet had always urged submission to Babylon. The Babylonian king ordered his soldiers to make sure Jeremiah came to no harm. His officers were to do whatever the prophet asked and see to all his needs.

Aftermath

Nebuchadnezzar left Judah, taking along his prisoners and the loot from the ruined city. At Jeremiah's urging, he appointed Gedaliah, son of Akim, to govern what remained of Judah.

Gedaliah spoke words that the prophet was glad to hear. He urged an end to war. He encouraged the people to rebuild towns, plant fields, orchards, and vineyards. There was no reason to fear the Babylonians as long as they submitted peacefully to Nebuchadnezzar's rule. This is what God wanted them to do. If they obeyed, the land would prosper once more.

Gedaliah's wise government did not endure. Judean rebels murdered him at a banquet. Then they fled to Egypt, taking Jeremiah and Baruch with them.

There Jeremiah died, far from the land he loved.

Jeremiah's Final Vision

Jeremiah spoke the truth throughout his life, but no one listened. He counseled peace, but saw endless war. He served God faithfully, but was rewarded with suffering. Yet he never gave up hope. He knew that God had not abandoned His people. Amid the despair of devastation and captivity, the prophet looked ahead to a Day of Redemption when God Himself would gather in the exiles of Judah and Israel from the four corners of the earth and bring them back to Jerusalem.

Hear the word of God, O Nations of the World!
Proclaim it on distant continents and islands!
God, Who scattered Israel, will bring them back again.
He guards His people like a shepherd guards his flock
And delivers them from the enemy's clutches.
They will come to Zion, shouting with joy,
Streaming toward God's bounty.
They will gather in the wheat, the wine, the newly pressed oil,
The young of flocks and herds.
They will become like a well-watered garden,
Never again to know hunger or thirst.
The maiden will dance with delight.
Young and old will rejoice.

"I will turn mourning into joy.
Gladness will overcome sorrow.
My priests will receive the fat of the land
And My people its abundance."

The Story of Ezekiel

The Babylonians were ruthless conquerors, but they were not cruel masters. The Judeans who survived the siege of Jerusalem and the long march into captivity found themselves treated with unexpected decency. Artists and craftspeople were allowed to resume their trades. Merchants were permitted to buy and sell in the markets of Babylon. Important members of the Judean royal family were kept under close guard, but they were lodged in palaces and treated with the respect due to princes. Even those people who had become slaves were allowed to buy their freedom or were ransomed by their countrymen within a few years.

The Babylonians did not insist that their Judean captives worship the gods of Babylon. As long as they submitted to King Nebuchadnezzar's rule, they could worship whatever god they chose. But which god should that be?

It was a time of confusion and despair for the exiles. They had survived the destruction of their country, but to what purpose? How could they continue to worship the God of Israel when they were no longer in Israel? How could they worship Him without a Temple, without priests to offer sacrifices? They composed a song to describe their sorrow.

> By the waters of Babylon we sat and wept when we remembered Zion.
> We hung our harps on the willows.
> Our new masters told us to sing, to play joyous music on our harps.
> "Sing for us one of your songs of Zion!"
> How can we sing God's song in an alien land?
> If I forget you, O Jerusalem, let my right hand be paralyzed.

Let my tongue stick to the roof of my mouth
If I fail to remember you,
If I fail to raise you above my greatest joy.

An even more difficult question lingered in their minds. Why should they continue worshiping a God who had abandoned them to their enemies?

Some answered by explaining that the people's sins had brought about their sufferings. But others protested that even if this were true, were the Babylonians less sinful? Why did Babylon rule the world while Judah and Israel no longer existed? Perhaps the God of Israel was not as powerful as He claimed to be. Perhaps it would be better for the exiles to forget the God of Moses and begin worshiping Bel and Marduk, the victorious gods of Babylon.

At this difficult time God chose another prophet to speak to His people. His name was Ezekiel. He lived in a small village called *Tel-Aviv,* or *Hill of Spring,* located near the city of Babylon on the banks of a canal called the River Chebar.

Ezekiel was a priest. He had served in the Temple during the days when Jeremiah had preached outside its gates. Because the exiles respected Ezekiel as a priest as well as a prophet, they turned to him for answers to their questions.

Ezekiel replied with a message of hope. "The God of Israel is not merely the god of one land," he told them. "He is the ruler of all Creation. He can be worshiped anywhere, in Babylon as well as Israel."

"If God is so great, why did Jerusalem fall?" a former nobleman asked. His hands and clothes were caked with dirt, for he now worked as a gardener's helper at Nebuchadnezzar's palace.

"Jerusalem fell because of the sins of her people," Ezekiel answered. "The great prophets Isaiah and Jeremiah prophesied what would happen over and over again. We refused to listen, so God delivered us into the hands of our enemies."

A washerwoman with a coarse, red face spoke up. Her husband and seven sons had all died of starvation in the siege of Jerusalem. "Some say the gods of Babylon are mightier than the God of Israel. Their gods Bel and Marduk have blessed them. That is why they have prospered."

"This is not true," Ezekiel told her. "Bel and Marduk do not exist. They are lifeless statues. There is only One God, the God of Israel. He Alone made heaven and earth. The Babylonians are his creations. He raised them up to carry out His judgment. In time, He will judge them in turn. As for us, if we would only obey His commandments and treat each other with justice, righteousness, and mercy, then surely He would restore the Temple and the whole land of Israel, bringing His scattered exiles back from the four corners of the earth with song and rejoicing."

Ezekiel was a seer as well as a teacher. God sent him astonishing visions, including one of God's throne and the image of God Himself. The prophet tried his best to describe what he saw, although no human language can ever encompass the reality of God.

One of Ezekiel's most startling visions was the one he had of a valley of dry bones.

The Valley of Dry Bones

"One day," the prophet told his listeners, "God's hand picked me up. It carried me to a desolate valley filled with human bones as far as I could see.

"God said to me, 'Son of Man, can these bones ever come to life?'

"I answered, 'God, only You know.'

"Then God said, 'Preach to these bones, Ezekiel. Say to them, 'O Dry Bones, listen to God's word. God says, 'I will breathe the breath of life into you and you will live again. I will fasten you together with fibers and tendons, nerves and muscles. I will cover you with skin and restore breath to your lungs, so that you will live once more. And you will know that I am God.'"

"I began to preach to the bones. As I spoke, I heard a great clatter and rattle as the jumbled bones fitted themselves together to form skeletons. Flesh covered them, then skin, until all the bodies were complete. But they lay on the ground like dead corpses because the breath of life was not yet in them.

"Then God spoke to me again, saying, 'Preach to the wind, O Son of Man. Say to it, Harken to God's word. Come, O Wind, from the four corners of the earth. Breathe into these corpses, so they might live.'

"As I spoke these words, the bodies began to breathe. They came to life, got up, and stood upon their feet, the whole vast multitude, filling the valley from end to end.

"God said to me, 'Son of Man, do you know whose bones these are? They belong to My people, the nation of Israel. Their hope is gone; their bones are dry; they are like unfinished fabric torn from a loom. Preach to them and say, 'O my people, hear the words of God. I will open your graves. I will lift you out of the earth. I will raise you up and bring you to the land of Israel. I will fill you with My Spirit, and you will live again. Then you will know that I am God.'"

The Story of Daniel

After the exiles from Judea arrived in Babylon, King Nebuchadnezzar ordered his officers to examine the captive boys and girls. They selected the most intelligent among them to be educated with the young nobles of Babylon. The king hoped that the best and brightest children of the captive nation might grow up to serve him as counselors and ministers.

Within a few years most of these children became Babylonians. They took new names. They forgot the Hebrew language. As the memory of their homeland faded, they joined their new friends in worshiping the gods of Babylon. And why not? The God of Israel hadn't saved them or their families, even on His own soil. Now they were in a foreign land where other gods ruled. So they prayed and sacrificed to Bel, Marduk, and Ishtar, and forgot the God of Israel.

Among these children were four boys who did not forget. Their Hebrew names were Hananiah, Mishael, Azariah, and Daniel. The Babylonians gave them new names. Hananiah became Shadrach; Mishael became Meshach; Azariah became Abednego; and they called Daniel Belteshazzar.

These boys remained faithful to the God of their ancestors. They declined to worship the gods of Babylon. They did not eat the food or drink the wine that the king provided, for it was not prepared according to the laws of Moses.

The king's steward was a kindly man. He feared the boys would fall ill if they did not eat. Since he was responsible for the boys' well-being, he worried that he would be punished for not taking better care of them. Daniel said to him, "Do as we ask for ten days. Give us only fruits, grains, and vegetables to eat and water to drink. After ten days, compare us to the other children. If we are not

stronger and healthier, you may do with us as you please."

The king's steward agreed to the experiment. He sent away the food from the royal kitchens and allowed the boys to prepare their own meals. At the end of ten days, they were healthier and stronger than any of the other children. From then on, the steward allowed them to eat as they preferred.

Because they remained faithful, God blessed these boys with knowledge and wisdom. They excelled in their studies, easily mastering whatever they set out to learn. God granted Daniel a special gift. He gave him the power to interpret dreams.

Nebuchadnezzar's Dream

One night King Nebuchadnezzar awoke from a disturbing dream. He sent for his astrologers and magicians, demanding that they tell him what his dream meant.

"O King, live forever. Tell us what you dreamed and we will interpret it for you," the astrologers and magicians replied.

The king became angry. "How can I know if you are speaking the truth? Tell me first what I dreamed. Then I will believe you. If you cannot, then I will know you are liars. I will have all of you chopped to pieces!"

Not one of the thousands of astrologers, seers, and magicians in Babylon could describe the king's dream, let alone interpret its meaning. Nebuchadnezzar, in a rage, ordered all the wise men in the kingdom put to death. His order included Daniel and his three companions.

Daniel stepped back in surprise when the captain of the guard came to arrest him.

"What have I done to deserve the king's wrath?" Daniel asked.

The officer explained the matter of Nebuchadnezzar's dream, and how all the wise men in Babylon had been condemned to die for failing to describe and interpret it. Daniel begged the officer for a little time to pray. Perhaps God would grant him the vision that had been denied to others.

Daniel and his three friends gathered together. They prayed to God to light up the darkness, to reveal the unknown.

Finally Daniel said to the captain, "Take me to the king."

When he arrived, Nebuchadnezzar asked him, "Can you describe my dream and tell me its meaning?"

Daniel answered, "The wisdom you seek is not given to wizards, seers, magicians, or astrologers. I myself have no greater understanding than ordinary people. God has revealed the secret to me so that you may know what will happen at the end of time."

Daniel continued. "First, I will tell you what you dreamed. You saw yourself standing before an enormous statue. The statue's head was gold; its arms and body were silver; its thighs and stomach were brass; its legs were iron, and its feet were iron mixed with clay. As you watched, a huge rough stone unmarked by human hands struck the statue, shattered it to pieces, and ground the fragments to dust. The wind blew the dust away so that not a trace remained. As for the stone, it grew and grew until it became a mountain that filled the world."

"That is exactly right! That is what I dreamed!" Nebuchadnezzar cried. "Now, tell me what it means."

"This is the explanation of your dream: God has made you ruler over all the earth. You are the statue's golden head. But your kingdom will not last forever. A second one, inferior to your own, will take its place. That is the meaning of the statue's silver arms and body. After that, a third kingdom, one of brass, will arise. It will be overthrown by a fourth, a nation as strong as iron. Like iron, it will crush everything in its path, breaking it to pieces. But the statue's legs are not completely made of iron. Its feet are iron mixed with clay. Just as iron and clay can never blend together to form one substance, so will this kingdom never become united. It will remain unstable, divided against itself, filling the world with strife and contention.

"At the end of days, when time comes to an end, God Himself will raise up another kingdom that will destroy the others, scattering them like dust blown by the wind. This is the stone unmarked by human hands that grew into a mountain filling the world. Thus will the Kingdom of God fill the whole world and last forever."

When Nebuchadnezzar heard these words, he fell to the ground before Daniel. "Surely your God must be the God of gods, the King of kings, to reveal this secret to you!"

Nebuchadnezzar canceled his decree. He spared the lives of the wise men of Babylon. At the same time he appointed Daniel to be their leader and named him governor over the whole province of Babylon. Hananiah, Mishael, and Azariah were made lieutenant governors and given great honors, too. But Daniel stood highest in the king's favor.

The Writing on the Wall

Nebuchadnezzar ruled Babylon for many years. When he died, his son Belshazzar succeeded him. Nebuchadnezzar had been a great king who honored the gods, especially the God of Israel. Belshazzar was a foolish young man who thought only of his own pleasure.

Belshazzar held a great banquet to celebrate his coronation. He ordered that the table be set with the golden cups, plates, and bowls taken from the Temple in Jerusalem. This was sacrilege. Mighty Nebuchadnezzar had burned the Temple to the ground, but he had never desecrated holy vessels.

Belshazzar's feast went on for hours. The wine flowed freely. As the servants entered the banquet hall with each new course, Belshazzar and his nobles raised their goblets in drunken toasts to the gods of Babylon. The golden goblets that once served the God of Israel were lifted in mocking praise of Bel, Marduk, and Ishtar.

Suddenly the room fell silent. A human hand appeared, floating in midair. As Belshazzar and his astonished guests watched, it extended one finger and began writing on the wall. The moving hand wrote four words in an unknown alphabet. Then it disappeared.

Belshazzar covered his face. He cried for someone to read these mysterious words and explain their meaning. The wisest magicians and astrologers in Babylon were summoned, but no one could read the writing on the wall, for it was written in an unknown tongue.

Then Belshazzar's queen said to him, "My lord, when your father Nebuchadnezzar lived, he often called on a Judean named Daniel to interpret dreams and strange events. Summon him. Perhaps he can tell you what these letters mean."

Belshazzar summoned Daniel to the palace. He said to him, "Read to me these letters on the wall. If you can tell me their meaning, I will give you a purple robe and a golden chain. You will rule with me as one of the mightiest men in Babylon."

Daniel answered, "O King, live forever! I desire neither wealth nor power. Give your gifts to someone else. I do not need them. But I will read these words to you. They are set down in the alphabet of the angels, in which the secrets of heaven are written. The words are MENE, MENE, TEKEL, UPHARSIN. Here is their meaning. MENE, MENE—God has numbered the days of your kingdom and will soon bring it to an end. TEKEL—you have been weighed in the Scales of Judgment and found wanting. UPHARSIN—your kingdom will be overthrown by your enemies, the Medes and Persians."

Babylon fell that night. Soldiers of Darius, the Persian king, scaled the walls under cover of darkness. They killed Belshazzar before he could put on his armor. His kingdom and all he possessed passed into the hands of the Persian king, as Daniel had foretold.

When Darius heard the story of Belshazzar's feast, he appointed Daniel to be one of the governors of his kingdom, honoring him above all others.

The Lions' Den

Daniel served Darius as faithfully as he once served Nebuchadnezzar. The Persian king rewarded his loyalty with increasing rank and power. Darius' nobles became jealous. "Have we not been the king's closest companions since boyhood? Why has he set this foreigner above us, that we should be forced to do him honor?" They urged Darius to dismiss Daniel, but the king could find no reason to do so. None of his governors served him better.

Daniel's enemies prepared a scheme to change the king's mind. They urged Darius to test the loyalty of his subjects. For the next thirty days, the king decreed, all prayers, petitions, and requests of any nature were to be directed to him alone. No one could ask anything of anyone else, neither god nor man, under penalty of death. Anyone found guilty of violating the decree would be thrown into a den of hungry lions.

Daniel ignored the decree. He continued praying to God three times a day, as he had done since he was a small boy. His enemies broke into his house. Finding Daniel at prayer, they arrested him for violating a royal command.

Daniel was put in chains and dragged before the king.

Darius was surprised to see Daniel chained like a common criminal. "Daniel is my faithful servant. What wrong has he done?" the king asked.

His nobles replied, "He disobeyed your decree. We caught him offering prayers to the God of Israel. He must be condemned to death."

Too late, Darius realized the error he had made. He never should have issued such a foolish decree. He looked for a way to save Daniel, but there was none. According to the ancient customs of the Medes and Persians, a royal decree was unchangeable. No one, not even the king himself, could alter it in any way.

Daniel was taken from the palace and thrown into a den of hungry lions. The king's guards rolled a stone over the mouth of the den to make sure no one could enter or leave. Darius himself sealed the stone with his own signet ring. Then he returned to his palace where he spent a long, sleepless night, grieving for his unfortunate servant Daniel.

Darius returned to the cave in the morning. "Daniel? Are you still alive?" he called out. "Has your God delivered you from the lions?"

To Darius' astonishment, he heard Daniel answer, "O King, live forever! God heard my prayer. He sent down angels to hold shut the lions' jaws. The lions have not harmed me."

Darius ordered his servants to unseal the cave door. He found Daniel sitting in the midst of the lions. The great beasts lay at his feet, purring like kittens, as Daniel scratched their powerful necks.

Darius released Daniel from the lions' den. The treacherous nobles who plotted against him were thrown to the lions themselves, along with their wives and children. The lions devoured them, every one, leaving nothing but gnawed bones.

Afterward, Darius issued another decree:

Know throughout my realm that the God of Daniel is revered.
He is the living God, for all eternity.
God's kingdom will last forever, even to the end of time.
God rescues His servants in times of trouble
By working wonders and miracles in heaven and on earth,
As He delivered Daniel from the savage lions.

Daniel rose even higher in the king's esteem. He prospered throughout the reign of Darius, and also through that of Cyrus, his successor.

Cyrus honored the Judeans for Daniel's sake. He gave them permission to return to their homeland. Led by their governor Nehemiah and the scribe Ezra, they rebuilt the land of Israel and raised a new Temple to God in Jerusalem.

EPILOGUE:

At the End of Time

The first part of the story of God and Israel now comes to an end. The rest will be written by other hands, in other books, in other languages.

Four thousand years have passed since God spoke to Abraham. The world has changed in many ways. Yet in others it remains the same. People still worship idols. These may no longer be statues of wood and stone, but they are false gods nonetheless. Some of their names are Wealth, Power, Greed, and Hatred. Sometimes Knowledge can become a false god, too, for it can be used for evil as well as for good.

Nations still go to war. More human beings have been killed in the wars of this century than in the wars of all previous centuries combined. The smallest nuclear weapon matches the force that annihilated Sodom and Gomorrah. Our daily newspapers are filled with pictures of cities burning, corpses lying in heaps, and thousands of people marching into exile, as in the days when Assyria and Babylon ruled the world.

Isaiah's words apply as much to modern cities as they did to the Jerusalem of his time. The rich live in palatial homes, while the poor scavenge in the streets. Slavery still exists. Kidnapped children are bought and sold, or forced to work long hours in filthy, dangerous factories, earning barely enough to keep themselves and their families alive. Justice, too, is for sale, as it was in the days of Amos and Jeremiah. The vast majority of people in prisons are poor. An alarming number can barely read or write. A poor person is much more likely to be arrested, and if convicted, to receive harsher punishment than a more affluent individual guilty of the same crime.

Yet there is hope. The words of the prophets still ring true, and thousands of people all over the world are listening. Together they join hands to bring an end to war and violence. They raise their voices against injustice and poverty. They work in their own communities, in schools, jails, courtrooms, libraries, youth centers, and shelters to help those in need and to provide the less fortunate with the knowledge and power to change their lives. Marching together, they have brought down tyrants and driven back the dark forces of hatred, greed, and ignorance with the shining light of Truth.

For the God of Israel is the God of all humanity. The redemption the prophets promised is not the triumph of one nation alone, but of all humankind.

It may not occur for a thousand years, or it may happen tomorrow. One day God's hope for Creation will be fulfilled. On that day the prophet Isaiah's vision of a world at peace will come true.

They will beat their swords into plowshares,
And their spears into pruning hooks.
Nation will not lift up sword against nation.
Never again will they study war.
The wolf will abide with the lamb.
The leopard will rest beside the kid.
The cow's calf and the lion's cub will walk together,
As a little child leads them.
The cow and the bear will graze side-by-side.
Their young will lie down with each other,
And the lion, like an ox, will eat hay.
An infant will play near an adder's hole,
And a toddler will reach into a viper's den.
The creatures of Creation will no longer harm each other,
For knowledge of God will fill the world
As water fills the oceans.

A NOTE ON SOURCES

Readers familiar with the biblical text have no doubt noticed that many of the stories included in this book are not to be found in the Bible. For instance, the Bible says nothing about Abraham smashing the idols in his father's shop or Pharaoh's testing the infant Moses with baskets of coals and jewels. Where do these stories come from?

They come from a parallel body of literature called the *Midrash. Midrashim* are stories and traditions, many as old as the Bible itself, that amplify and explain the terse and often challenging biblical text. One midrash reveals that the child whom Elijah brought back to life grew up to become the prophet Jonah. There is no evidence that this is true, but the idea does serve to link Jonah to the prophetic tradition and to explain why his peculiar book was included in the Bible.

Two outstanding collections of midrashim available in English are Louis Ginzberg's four-volume *The Legends of the Jews* (Jewish Publication Society of America, 1968) and the first volume of Micha Joseph bin Gorion's *Mimekor Yisrael: Classic Jewish Folktales* (Indiana University Press, 1976). Valuable sources for younger readers, which were among my favorite books as a child, are M.G. Glenn's *Jewish Tales and Legends* (Hebrew Publishing Company, 1929) and Hyman E. Goldin's three-volume *The Book of Legends* (Hebrew Publishing Company, 1929). Ellen Frankel's *The Classic Tales: 4000 Years of Jewish Lore* (Jason Aronson Inc., 1989) is another excellent source for midrashim and stories from all periods of Jewish history.

As for the Bible itself, my primary source was the original Hebrew text. I owe a great debt to my teachers at the East Midwood Jewish Center in Brooklyn, New York, for giving me the ability to read God's words as they were actually spoken. Anyone familiar with Hebrew realizes how "unbiblical" the language of the Bible is. The *"thees"* and *"thous"* commonly associated with biblical speech are actually derived from sixteenth-century English. Hebrew, far from being archaic and flowery, is a concise, direct language that compresses a great deal of meaning into a few simple words. The eighth commandment—"You shall not steal"—is only two words in Hebrew: *"Lo tignov."* I have attempted to preserve this precise, powerful language in retelling the stories, and especially when translating the actual text.

A number of books served as invaluable guides and models. Everett Fox's recently published *The Five Books of Moses* (Shocken Books, 1995) comes closer than any previous translation to capturing the impact of the original Hebrew in English. The Stone editions of the *Chumash* (Mesorah Publications, 1993) and the *Tanach* (Mesorah Publications, 1996), both edited by Rabbi Nosson Scherman, provide precise translations and classic commentaries formerly unavailable to English-speaking readers. M. J. Cohen's *Pathways Through the Bible* (Jewish Publication Society of America, 1956) is a stirring example of what a collection of Bible stories for young readers ought to be.

Finally, for background information about the different periods of biblical history, I relied heavily upon the *Encyclopedia Judaica* (Macmillan, 1971), the sections by A. Malamat and H. Tadmor in H. H. Ben-Sasson's *A History of the Jewish People* (Harvard University Press, 1976), Harry M. Orlinsky's *Ancient Israel* (Cornell University Press, 1954), Azaria Alon's *The Natural History of the Land of the Bible* (Paul Hamlyn, 1969), and Moshe Pearlman's *In the Footsteps of the Prophets* (Thomas Y. Crowell, 1975).

—Eric A. Kimmel

A NOTE FROM THE PUBLISHER: The first three maps in this book were extrapolated from numerous maps that can be found in *The Macmillan Bible Atlas* by Yohanan Aharoni and Michael Avi-Yonah (The Macmillan Company, 1968). We gratefully acknowledge this valuable resource.

The Middle East in the Years 2000 to 1500 B.C.E.
(Before the Common Era)

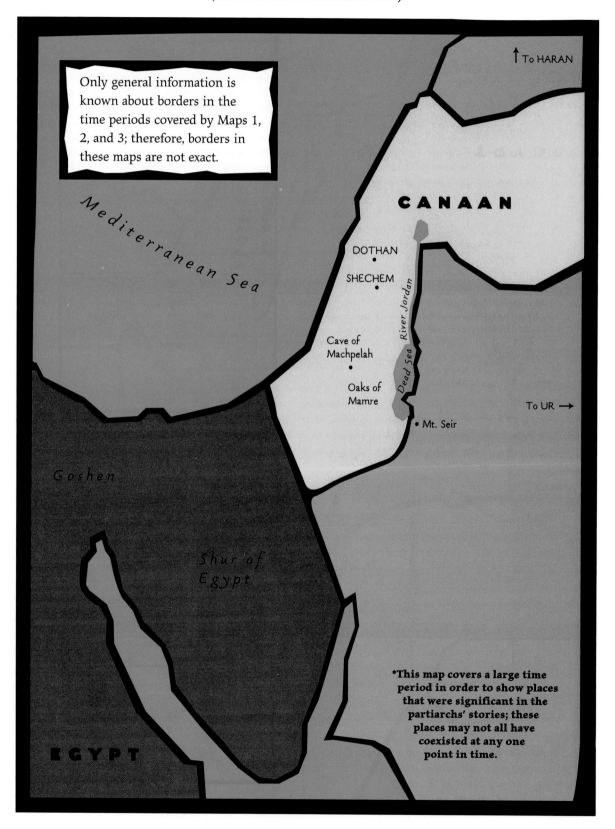

To HARAN

Only general information is known about borders in the time periods covered by Maps 1, 2, and 3; therefore, borders in these maps are not exact.

Mediterranean Sea

CANAAN

DOTHAN

SHECHEM

River Jordan

Cave of Machpelah

Dead Sea

Oaks of Mamre

To UR →

• Mt. Seir

Goshen

Shur of Egypt

*This map covers a large time period in order to show places that were significant in the partiarchs' stories; these places may not all have coexisted at any one point in time.

EGYPT

MAP 2

Moses' travels, early 13th Century B.C.E.,
and Joshua's Conquest of Canaan

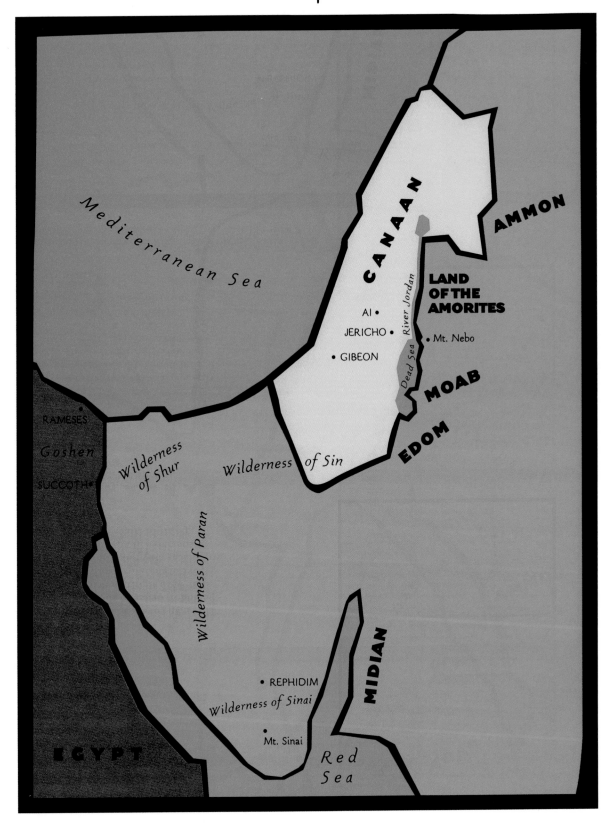

MAP 3

Judah and Israel in 928 B.C.E.

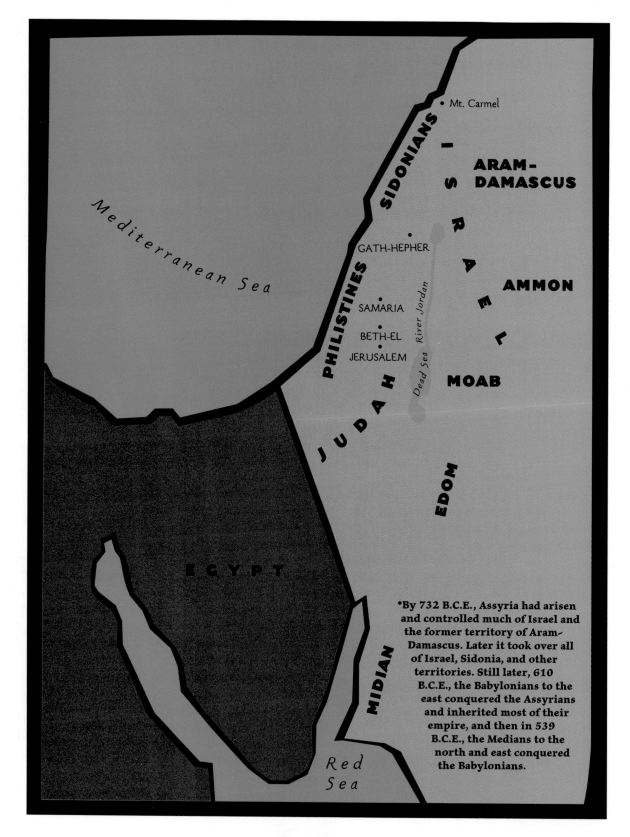

*By 732 B.C.E., Assyria had arisen and controlled much of Israel and the former territory of Aram-Damascus. Later it took over all of Israel, Sidonia, and other territories. Still later, 610 B.C.E., the Babylonians to the east conquered the Assyrians and inherited most of their empire, and then in 539 B.C.E., the Medians to the north and east conquered the Babylonians.

TIME LINE

The dates below are approximate and are all B. C. E. (Before the Common Era)

2000	First appearance of Hebrew/Hapiru people (Abraham, Isaac)
1720–1550	Descent into Egypt; Hebrews settle in Goshen (Jacob, Joseph)
1300	Exodus from Egypt (Moses)
1200–1000	Conquest of Canaan and Period of the Judges (Joshua, Deborah, Gideon, Samson, Samuel)
1020–1005	Reign of Saul
1004–965	Reign of David
965–928	Reign of Solomon
928	Nation splits into two kingdoms, Israel and Judah

ISRAEL

871–852	Reign of Ahab (Elijah)
852–783	Jonah, Elisha
783–739	Amos, Hosea
720	Fall of Samaria (Kingdom of Israel ends)

JUDAH

780–687	Isaiah
640–581	Jeremiah
586	Fall of Jerusalem (Kingdom of Judah ends)
592–540	Ezekiel, Daniel
400	Return to Judah (Ezra, Nehemiah)

Late 20th Century

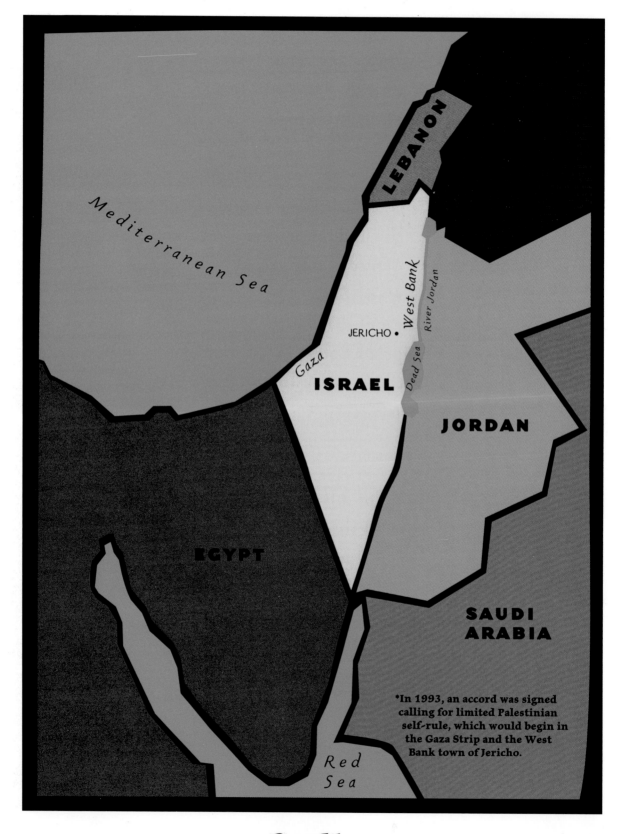

Mediterranean Sea

LEBANON

West Bank

River Jordan

JERICHO •

Gaza

Dead Sea

ISRAEL

JORDAN

EGYPT

SAUDI
ARABIA

*In 1993, an accord was signed
calling for limited Palestinian
self-rule, which would begin in
the Gaza Strip and the West
Bank town of Jericho.

Red
Sea